RAGE

ALSO BY LINDA CASTILLO

Sworn to Silence

Pray for Silence

Breaking Silence

Gone Missing

Her Last Breath

The Dead Will Tell

After the Storm

Among the Wicked

Down a Dark Road

A Gathering of Secrets

Shamed

Outsider

A Simple Murder
(A Kate Burkholder Short Story Collection)

Fallen

The Hidden One

An Evil Heart

The Burning

RAGE

A KATE BURKHOLDER NOVEL

Linda Castillo

MINOTAUR
BOOKS
NEW YORK

This is a work of fiction. All of the characters, organizations, and events portrayed in this novel are either products of the author's imagination or are used fictitiously.

First published in the United States by Minotaur Books, an imprint of St. Martin's Publishing Group

EU Representative: Macmillan Publishers Ireland Ltd, 1st Floor, The Liffey Trust Centre, 117–126 Sheriff Street Upper, Dublin 1, DO1 YC43

www.minotaurbooks.com

Designed by Omar Chapa

Library of Congress Cataloging-in-Publication Data

Names: Castillo, Linda, author.
Title: Rage / Linda Castillo.
Description: First edition. | New York : Minotaur Books, 2025. | Series: Kate Burkholder novel ; 17
Identifiers: LCCN 2025006488 | ISBN 9781250781147 (hardcover) | ISBN 9781250781154 (ebook)
Subjects: LCSH: Amish—Fiction. | LCGFT: Detective and mystery fiction. | Novels.
Classification: LCC PS3603.A8758 R34 2025 | DDC 813/.6223/eng/20250317—dcundefined
LC record available at https://lccn.loc.gov/2025006488

First Edition: 2025

10 9 8 7 6 5 4 3 2 1

This book is dedicated to my Texas Hill Country family. Bob and Doreen, Ed and Chris, Hilda and Randy, Heidi and Jim, Helen (and Dean, Alex, William, and Catherine), Sally and Rob, Liz and Perry, Don and Linda, Britney and Jordan (and the girls!), Cynthia and Ed, Patrice, Barbara K., Debbie and Bruce, Patty, and Barbara R. Through thick and thin. Love you guys!

Innocence is a priceless
commodity for which mankind suffers
an insatiable hunger.

—UNKNOWN

RAGE

PROLOGUE

Samuel Yutzy turned the horse and buggy in to the gravel lane and parked between the old barn and the stand of black walnut trees. For the span of several minutes, he sat on the bench seat, looking appreciatively at the rows of red maple, white oak, and shagbark hickory saplings. Most were a couple of years old and still in their plastic containers—fifteen, twenty, and thirty gallons. A few of the smaller trees' root balls were wrapped in burlap; some homeowners preferred that method because it was cheaper, which was fine by him.

Tying off the leather lines, he climbed down and breathed in deeply, liking the smells of freshly turned earth and growing things. He listened to the chip of the cardinal from atop the buckeye tree across the way, the morning song of the crickets as they wound down their nighttime antics, and the rising summer buzz of the cicadas.

Home, he thought, and for the first time in a long time, he was at peace. He'd built this nursery from the ground up, after all, opening the doors when he was just nineteen—two years ago—and turning a decent profit six months later. He'd done it with the sweat of his brow, the muscles in his back, and the last twenty bucks in his pocket. How in the name of God had he let himself stray so far?

But Samuel knew the answer and he wasn't proud of it. He wasn't proud of anything he'd done in the last year. The shame that followed was profound, reminding him of what his *dawdi* had told him about mistakes when he was a boy. *The worst kind a man can make are the ones he doesn't learn from.* Samuel figured he'd learned more in the last year than he had in the entirety of his life.

Most of what he'd done couldn't be fixed or undone. It was too late for that. But Samuel was an optimist and he knew some of his lapses *could* be remedied. Last night, as he'd lain awake praying to a God who'd become little more than a stranger in the last year, he swore he would make things right. He would change the things he could. Help those he'd harmed. He'd forgive the people who'd betrayed him. And try to forgive himself for the things he wasn't sure he deserved forgiveness for. It was a start. And if he was lucky, he might be able to live with himself, or God willing, save his soul.

This morning, however, work waited for him, and his old life welcomed him back. The summer had been hot and dry and the saplings needed watering. The shrubs demanded trimming. The manure pile required turning. If he had time, he might just start work on the old greenhouse and replace the panes that had been broken in the hailstorm last May.

Running his hand over the horse's rump, Samuel went to the rear of the buggy, pulled out the fifty-foot garden hose, and set it on the ground. He was threading the connector to the spigot when the crunch of tires on gravel drew his attention. He didn't have to look to know who'd come calling, but he did. He felt a tremor of dread when he recognized the vehicle. Sighing, he dropped the hose and walked out to meet them.

He stood in the gravel outside the driver's-side door, the hot sun beating down, and watched the driver speak into his cell phone without acknowledging him. He'd met the dark-haired man a dozen times in the last year. He'd drunk booze with him, taken meals with him, laughed with him, even fucked a girl with him once. Now, in excruciating hindsight, everything he had once admired about the man turned his stomach.

After a few minutes, the car door opened. Samuel stepped back as the man got out and brushed a speck of nonexistent lint from his shirt.

"You look like a goddamn pilgrim in those clothes," the man said.

Samuel held his gaze. "What do you want?"

"Ain't seen you around much."

Samuel looked past him, noticing the passenger, not liking it that the window tint was too dark for him to make out the man's features. "Been busy. Working. You should try it."

Squinting in the bright sunlight, the dark-haired man looked out across the nursery. "Nice place you got here."

"I think so." Samuel waited a beat. "Look, I got work to do, so if you got something to say, you should say it and go."

"I've got a message for you." The man's eyes slipped to the passenger.

Vaguely aware that the hairs at his nape were prickling, Samuel bent slightly for a closer look at the man in the passenger seat. He watched as the door opened and the man got out. Dark hair. Khaki pants. Untucked shirt—an ugly flowered thing. Sunglasses hid his eyes, but Samuel saw something unsettling in his expression, and the hairs on the back of his neck stood straight up.

"What message?" he asked.

"This one." The passenger lifted the hem of his shirt, reached into his waistband. Grasping something unseen. His arm coming up . . .

Samuel caught sight of the pistol an instant too late. A rush of adrenaline jolted his body like electricity. Raising his hands, he sidestepped. "Don't do it!"

The gunshot snapped through the air like a thunderclap. Something slammed into his left side below his ribs. A baseball bat affixed with a red-hot poker that sank in and went deep.

Pain doubled him over. Samuel's legs buckled. A sound tore from his throat as his knees hit the dirt. Heat streaked across his belly and went through all the way to his spine. He fell forward, broke his fall with his hands, his fingers digging into dirt.

The world around him spun and slowed to a crawl. He was aware of the passenger coming around the rear of the car. *Going to get off another shot,* he thought. *Finish it.* The man standing next to him stepped back. Getting out of the way.

Sons of bitches.

In that instant a thousand regrets rained down on him. He hadn't thought they would take it this far. It wasn't the first time he'd underestimated the savagery they were capable of.

Raising his head, Samuel looked up at the pistol. Semiauto. Sleek. Expensive. Of course it was. The passenger moved in slow motion. Eyes level and intent. Gun coming up. Finger inside the guard.

Sammy closed his fists, clutching handfuls of dirt, and flung them at the man's face. The gunman's stride faltered. Left hand going to his eyes. He spat. His pistol hand dropping down to his side.

"Fucking prick."

Samuel scrambled to his feet, lunged like a sprinter out of a block. Pain tore through his gut with every stride. Nausea rising. Bile boiling at the back of his throat. An invisible knife stabbing his rib cage every time his feet hit the ground.

Caught off guard, the gunman stumbled backward. Samuel ran for his life. Not sure where to go. There was no place to hide. He sped past the horse, entered the barn. A slash of pain gouged his belly, left to right and up to his chest. He glanced down, saw blood soaking through his shirt, spreading onto his trousers. He didn't know how badly he was hurt. Wasn't even sure where he was shot. He could feel the warm spread of blood soaking the front of his pants.

Midway through the barn his feet tangled. He went down hard. His face hit the ground. Nose breaking on impact. Dirt in his mouth. An explosion of pain in his belly. Turning his head, he spat, saw blood. No time to stop. He tried to get up, but his arms refused to support his weight. He groaned as he rolled onto his back. His legs flopped uselessly. The gunman reached him. Breathing hard. Eyes as blank as a taxidermist's glass. The pistol came up.

Samuel shifted his gaze up to the rafters. He wondered if he would be going to heaven. He thought about everything he'd done in the last year. The mistakes he'd made. The ones he hadn't had time to fix.

I'm not finished, he thought.

The blast was the last thing he heard.

CHAPTER 1

There was no way they were going to find her. Not here by the creek where the ground was soft and brush grew thick along the bank. The path leading to this part of the woods was narrow and overgrown with weeds. Last summer, her cousin had gotten poison ivy on her ankle and it spread all the way up to her behind. That wasn't to mention her little brother's fear of spiders. The eight-legged creepers were big as quarters. Last time they played here, one crawled onto his shirt and he ran screaming all the way home.

Remembering, Mandi Weaver giggled. She was the best of the best when it came to hide-and-seek. Even when her older brother cheated while counting to ten, he rarely found her. She could hear him counting now as she sprinted down the path. She was barefoot today and her feet smacked the damp ground like clapping hands. At the curve, she ducked beneath the branch of a gnarly oak tree, then made a beeline for the creek ten yards away.

"*Eight!*" he called out. "*Nine! Ten!*"

Mandi knew her brother was already barreling down the path. She didn't mind. She was a faster runner than her little brother; surely, he'd be found first. The little guy picked terrible hiding places. No, she thought with satisfaction, there was no way her older brother would find her down here.

"*Ready or not, here I come!*" came his voice from what seemed like a mile away.

Tongue sticking out in concentration, she ran past the big stump. The one with the mushrooms growing out the side. At the sound of the trickling water, she slowed, glanced behind her, and listened for footsteps. No one coming yet.

Breathless and giggling, she skidded down the incline on her heels. The creek was just ahead through the trees. At the big rock, she dodged left and hunkered down behind it. From a distance, she could hear her brother yelling.

"I'm going to find you!" he called out. "This time, you're going to be 'it' until next week!"

She was breathing hard, making too much noise, so she put her hand over her mouth, and tried not to laugh. The air was still and humid and Mandi was sweating like crazy beneath her dress. Her feet were filthy. There was mud on the hem of her dress. She was looking around, thinking she might put her feet in the creek to cool off, when she spotted the weird pile of dirt. It looked as if someone had been digging. She'd been here just a few days ago and the mound hadn't been there. No one ever came back this way. Their farm was the only one around for miles.

"You're the worst hider in the world!" came her older brother's voice.

"No fair!" her little brother squealed. "You cheated!"

"Did not!"

Mandi could hear them arguing, but her attention was on that strange mound of earth. Who would be digging back here and why? Buried treasure? A bag of money maybe? Curious, she left her hiding place and walked along the path, taking in a second pile. Too much dirt for a mole; the little vermin were always messing up Mamm's garden. Not quite right for a groundhog either.

She studied the piled-up earth. A few feet away a straw hat lay upside down in the weeds as if someone had tossed it aside. It was the kind of hat her *datt* wore. Had someone dropped it? She looked around, vaguely troubled, but there was no one there. It was so quiet she could hear the flies buzzing. A lot of them. Too many . . .

That's when she spotted the boot. It was a work boot, lying on its side a few feet from the hat. Why would someone leave their hat *and* a boot all the way down here? Craning her neck, Mandi sidled closer. Something sticking out of the boot. A stick? Some kind of cloth? It looked like the leg of the scarecrow her brother had put in the garden to keep out the crows. But why would anyone go to the trouble of burying a scarecrow down here by the creek?

Her feet took her closer before she even realized she was going to move. Though she was sweating like crazy beneath her *kapp* and dress, a chill quivered along her spine. Part of her didn't want to see any more. She could hear her heart pounding, feel the hard thump of blood in her head.

Mandi stopped and looked down. She was standing on a low mound of freshly turned earth. Next to her foot, she saw something pale that was partially buried. The sweat went cold on her skin. Kneeling, she brushed at the dirt. Her tummy flip-flopped when her fingertips touched something rubbery and cold.

She cocked her head. Stared hard at it, certain her eyes were deceiving her. It looked like a hand. The skin was sticky-looking and covered with mud. Everything inside her went still. A hundred flies buzzed and suddenly the sound was deafening.

This was no scarecrow, she realized, and suddenly she knew something bad had happened here. For the first time, she smelled the smell. The same smell she remembered from last year when they found that dead buck in the woods.

Horror sent her stumbling back so fast she fell in the weeds on her backside.

"Eli!"

She screamed her older brother's name as she scrambled to her feet. "*Eli!*"

Hide-and-seek forgotten, she spun and ran as fast as she could to the trail in search of her brother.

• • •

Visiting students at Painters Mill Elementary School is a tradition I've upheld annually since becoming chief of police almost nine years ago. For the last two years, my partner in crime, "Kip the Cow," has accompanied me. Kip is an expert on school safety, the kids love him, and they actually listen to what he has to say.

This morning, I'm standing next to the teacher's desk, trying not to imagine how profusely Officer Chuck "Skid" Skidmore is sweating beneath the "Kip the Cow" costume. The classroom smells of paper dust, industrial-strength pine cleaner, and two dozen sweaty second graders who spent their morning recess playing outside in the sweltering late-August heat.

It's the first week of school and the city pool is open one more week. I can tell by the way the students' eyes slide repeatedly to the window that every single one of them is wishing they were there instead of here.

"How many of you walk to school?" Skid's voice is muffled by the costume, but he's learned to speak loudly so that the kids can hear.

When no one responds, I raise my hand and look out at our audience. "Great question, Kip. Let's see a show of hands."

A smattering of students raises their hands. A typical number for a small-town community where most people live on farms or in a rural area and ride the bus.

"How many of you ride your bikes?" Kip the Cow asks.

A few hands drop and a couple of others go up.

I glance at Kip. "Do you have any safety tips for students who walk or ride their bikes to school?"

"I sure do!" he exclaims. "Did you know it's safer to walk or ride your bike if you're with a friend?"

"That's good to know," I say. "Do you have any other advice on how students can stay safe during the school year?"

"Kip the Cow always has good safety advice for kids, Chief Burkholder." Skid chuckles beneath the suit. "Here's an important one: If anyone bothers you while you're going to or from school, get away from that person as quickly as possible and tell your parents or your teacher."

"Great tip." My cell phone vibrates against my hip. I glance down, see a text from Lois, my first-shift dispatcher. The numbers 911 appear on the display, which is code for call immediately. Lois knows Skid and I are talking to students this morning, so I know it's important.

As unobtrusively as possible, I slip into the hall, and hit the speed dial for the station. "What's up?" I ask.

"Sorry to bother you, Chief," says Lois. "I just heard from Glock. He took a call out on Sweet Potato Ridge Road. Apparently, some Amish kids found a body."

"A body?" The muscles at the back of my neck tighten. "Are you sure?"

"Glock sounded pretty certain."

"Any idea who it is?"

"He didn't say."

"Call Doc Coblentz," I tell her, referring to the Holmes County coroner. "Tell him to stand by. The sheriff's office too."

"You got it."

"I'm on my way."

CHAPTER 2

Ten minutes later, Skid and I are in my city-issue Explorer. The engine hums as I blow the stoplight at Main Street and head out of town. Next to me, Skid has removed the Kip the Cow head and is in the process of escaping the costume bodice.

"Remind me to trade this cow gig with Mona next year," he mutters as he tosses the costume into the back seat. "She's the damn rookie. Gotta pay her dues like the rest of us."

"I don't know, Skid. You make a pretty good Kip." I glance over at him, see the sweat beaded on his forehead, and try not to smile. "Kids like you."

"The only reason those kids like Kip the Cow is because he's marginally more fun than a pop quiz." He sighs. "I'll take my chances with the dead body."

Sweet Potato Ridge Road is a two-mile stretch of pitted asphalt that cuts through river-bottom forest and runs parallel with Painters Creek. Not many people venture out this way. Because of its proximity to the waterway and its tendency to flood in the spring, there are just two farms and a tree nursery in the area. Unless a jogger was overcome by heat, I can't imagine how a dead body ended up here.

As I make the turn, massive trees on either side of the road close over the Explorer like knuckled fingers, casting us in shadow. Ahead, I see the flashing lights of Glock's cruiser. There's a horse and buggy parked on the shoulder. An Amish man and three children stand next to the buggy. The nursery and farms are another quarter mile down the road.

I park behind the cruiser, flick on my overhead lights, and get out. It's not yet noon and already the heat of the day presses down like a steaming-hot rag. The buzz of cicadas rises from the woods like a hundred mini chain saws.

I spot Glock emerging from the woods several yards ahead. He's in full uniform, his shirt wet with sweat beneath his arms and between his shoulder blades. Across the road, the Amish family huddles, watching us. I recognize the adult male; I've seen him around town, in the grocery or on the street, but I don't recall his name. Such is the nature of small-town Ohio.

"Chief."

Rupert "Glock" Maddox was the first officer I hired when I became chief. He's a former marine, coolheaded, and a law enforcement pro in every way. He's a father of four, a crack shot, a brown belt, and one of the nicest guys I know. Last I heard, he and his wife were considering a fifth child; somehow, he still finds time to coach Little League at the elementary school every Tuesday evening.

Skid and I greet him with handshakes. "What do you have?" I ask.

"According to Mr. Weaver, the kids were playing down by the creek and found a severed hand. Possibly a foot, too." Glock motions toward the barely visible trailhead from which he emerged. "They ran home, which is the farm a little way down the road. Told their dad. He hitched up and drove over to the Amish phone shanty, called 911, then came back out here to meet us."

Children discovering body parts in the woods is extremely unlikely in a town like Painters Mill. Usually, when a report like that comes in, it turns out to be a case of misidentification. A doll or discarded glove or boot, a practical joke, an honest mistake, or a ghost story run amok.

As if reading my skepticism, Glock grimaces. "The oldest boy led me down to the creek. Sure enough, there's a damn severed hand down there in those trees."

"Shit," Skid mutters. "I guess that eliminates the heatstroke theory."

"Anything else?" I ask.

Glock nods. "A foot. In a boot."

"Any idea who they belong to?" I ask.

He shakes his head. "Once I realized what we were dealing with, I got everyone out of there quick."

I glance at the Amish family standing next to the buggy. "You get statements?"

"Not yet," he says. "I've only been here fifteen minutes or so."

I bend my head to speak into my lapel mike. "Lois, get County out here," I say, referring to the Holmes County Sheriff's Office. "Find out where the coroner is. Tell him to expedite." I look at Skid. "Get this road blocked off to traffic. No one comes in or out unless they're LEO." Law enforcement officer. "Stay cognizant of evidence."

He gives me a mock salute. "You got it."

I look at Glock. "Hang tight for a sec."

"Yep."

I go to my Explorer and hit the fob for the rear door. Having been born Amish right here in Painters Mill, I'm mindful of the cultural divide between the Amish and English communities, especially when it comes to the police. As chief, I do everything in my power to bridge that divide, earn their trust—and respect. I dig into the small cooler I keep handy when it's hot, pull out four bottles of water, and approach the family.

"*Guder mariye,*" I say. Good morning. I pass out the water bottles. I can tell by the kids' body language that they're shaken from their find and nervous about talking to me.

"Is everyone okay?" I ask.

The Amish man nods. "We're fine," he says. "Sure gave us a start, though."

I show him my badge. "What are your names?"

"Ivan Weaver," the man tells me.

I look at him a little more closely. "I've seen you at the grain elevator."

"*Ja.* I work there." Beginning to relax, he sets a hand on the older son's shoulder. "This is Eli." He motions to the girl and younger boy. "Mandi and Joe."

I nod at the kids. "My officer and I are going to take a look at what you found," I tell them. "I'd like you to stay here so we can get your statements. Can you do that?"

"Of course," says the man.

We're standing in the sun and the day is warming up fast, so I motion to a shady area several yards away. "If you'd like, you can park over there in the shade. Let your horse cool off a little. I'll be back as soon as I can."

The Amish man nods, then says to the older boy, "*Rawsa da dach-waegli.*" Move the buggy.

I walk back to Glock. Two hundred yards away, I see Skid placing traffic cones on the road to keep any curious motorists from pulling in for a look.

"It's odd that the only things found were a hand and a foot," I say.

He gives me a grim look. "Sure doesn't bode well for the victim."

I'm sweating profusely beneath my uniform as we enter the trailhead.

Even in the shade, I suspect the temperature is on its way to ninety degrees. Combined with the humidity, it's sweltering.

"Keep your eyes open for footprints or anything out of place," I say.

"You got it," says Glock.

The trail is narrow, the ground damp beneath my boots. "How far?" I ask.

"Another fifty yards."

I scan our surroundings as we move more deeply into the woods. I take note of bare footprints in the dirt, likely from the children, all of whom were barefoot.

The trail narrows and twists left and right. Spindly fingers of raspberry and bramble scrape at my shirt as I pass. We step over a fallen log as thick as a man's waist. I'm aware of the buzz of insects, mosquitoes and flies, and the incessant whine of the cicadas all around.

"Here we go." Glock points. "Just past that rock."

Ten yards ahead, a rock the size of a recliner demarks another curve in the trail. Farther, I see several areas of disturbed earth.

"You smell that?" he asks.

I glance over at him and nod. Rotting flesh. It's faint, but present nonetheless. "Something dead."

We continue past the rock and Glock stops. "Girl's footprints are there in the dirt." He motions. "Just beyond is the hand. There's a straw hat over there."

I follow his point, spot the hat on the ground next to another mound of disturbed earth. "The hat is Amish," I tell him.

"Thought so."

"Glock, did you touch anything?"

"No, ma'am. Got pretty close to the hand, though. The footprint next to it is mine."

"Let's spread out, take a look around," I tell him. "Watch your step."

"You got it."

Keenly aware that if this turns out to be a crime scene we run the risk of contaminating evidence, I proceed to the pale object sticking out of the dirt. There are no other footprints aside from Glock's and the girl's. No broken branches or crushed weeds. Nothing out of place except for the hat and the odd piles of freshly turned dirt.

I stop a couple of feet away from the object and get my first up-close look. It definitely *looks* like a human hand. The fingers are slightly curled. The palm mottled and pale.

"How the hell did a hand get out here?" I mutter.

A few feet away from me, Glock makes a sound of incredulity. "Hospital or mortuary? Maybe an amputation that wasn't disposed of properly? Maybe a dog got ahold of it and dragged it out here."

"Maybe." But I see the doubt on his face; I feel that same doubt echoing inside me.

I study the surrounding area and for the first time I notice several additional areas of disturbed ground. Ten feet away from where I stand, I see the boot. And flies. Thousands of them. "Someone's been digging," I say.

"That's not good," he says. "Strange that there are no footprints."

"It rained a little last night." I lean closer to study the hand. It's topside down and partially buried. There's dirt beneath the nails. Some type of abrasion on the palm near the thumb. "Looks . . . Caucasian," I say. "No rings or visible tats."

Tugging nitrile gloves from my equipment belt, I slip them on. The last thing I want to do is risk contaminating the scene, but before I call out my law enforcement counterparts, I need to be certain this isn't the result of some prankster playing a joke. I reach down and brush some of the dirt away from the hand.

Grasping the index finger, I tug gently, but the hand doesn't come free. I grip the digit more securely and increase the force with steady pressure. Dirt falls away as the wrist comes into view. When the stump is free, I've no doubt what it is. I can see the red-black smear of blood that's gone brown and sticky at the edges. Dark hair on the wrist. The rust-white jut of bone. Flies swarming all around.

Shit.

"Chief."

I set the hand back where I found it and turn.

Glock is twenty feet away, looking down at a low rise of disturbed earth. "I've got part of . . . looks like a leg over here. Partly buried."

Something inside me sinks, an anvil plummeting into the dark depths of a pit. Until now, I'd been holding on to the hope that this is some innocuous mishandling of hospital biohazard.

I get to my feet and cross to him. I'm not squeamish, but the sight of a severed human leg puts an uncomfortable quiver in my gut. The foot is still attached, bare, and in a fixed position. The knee is bent at a forty-five-degree angle. The top of the thigh is little more than a jagged piece of red-black meat.

"Damn," I mutter.

Glock kneels next to the body part and indicates the torn flesh of the stub. "It looks like there's been scavenger activity," he says.

As much as I don't want to think about an animal chewing on or consuming human flesh, a closer look tells me he's right. "Teeth marks on the bone," I hear myself say.

"Looks that way."

Because that macabre length of human flesh is so difficult to look at, I find my eyes moving to the torn-up ground just beyond where he's standing. That's when I spot the paw print.

"Some kind of animal prints there." I go to it and kneel. "Dog or coyote."

Glock comes up beside me. "Coyote," he says.

I shoot him a questioning look.

"Coyote prints are narrower with more defined claws." He shrugs. "Went hunting with my dad last fall."

I nod, as troubled as I am uneasy. The back of my neck prickles and I find my eyes skimming the trees and brush around us.

"It looks like multiple holes have been dug," Glock says.

I force my attention back to our macabre find. "This was no hiker or hunter who collapsed from natural causes."

He nods. "It looks like these body parts were buried. Coyotes smelled them and dug them up."

I get to my feet and look around. "This is a pretty out-of-the-way place," I say. "Someone chose this place because they didn't want this found."

He grimaces. "I hate to say it, Chief, but I'm betting there are more body parts in the vicinity."

I nod, frowning because my mind has taken the exact same route. "We don't have the resources to investigate this on our own," I say.

A smile touches his mouth. "I hear you know a guy at BCI."

I smile back, but the exchange does little to loosen the knot of dread tightening in my gut. "Let's clear out," I say. "Get the area taped off."

CHAPTER 3

I hit the speed dial for John Tomasetti as I make my way toward the Explorer. He's an agent with the Ohio Bureau of Criminal Investigation and my significant other—not necessarily in that order.

He picks up on the second ring. "My favorite chief of police," he says. "I was just thinking about you."

"I may not be your favorite chief after I tell you why I'm calling." I tell him about the grisly discovery.

"No one said being married to you was going to be easy." But his voice has gone serious.

"In more ways than one," I say. "How's your caseload?"

"Manageable," he tells me.

"I think I'm going to need some help on this one."

"I know a forensic guy over in Bowling Green. I've used him several times over the years. He's good."

"How fast can he get here?"

"Let me make some calls." He pauses. "And Kate?"

"Yeah?"

"You're still my favorite."

• • •

At this early point in the investigation, I have no idea if the deceased was murdered and the killer dismembered and buried the body to hide his deed, or if the deceased died from natural causes—a drug overdose or accident—and for whatever reason, someone went to a great deal of difficulty to conceal the body.

A dozen questions play in my head as I watch the Holmes County coroner, Dr. Ludwig Coblentz, climb down from his Escalade and, medical bag in hand, start toward me.

"I understand you've got a dead body on your hands," he says.

"Parts of one, anyway." I cross to him; our gazes lock as we shake hands. "So far."

His eyes move to the woods behind me. "Just when you think you've used up your quota of bizarre calls, this one comes in."

"Someone keeps moving the bar."

The hint of a smile passes over his expression, and then he looks around. "Pretty out-of-the-way location. Any idea what we're dealing with?"

"The only thing I know for certain at this point is I've got a hand, along with part of a leg and a foot. Looks like the body parts were buried initially and unearthed by coyotes."

The doc stares at me for a moment, as if expecting me to raise my hands and tell him I'm joking. Of course, he knows me better than that.

"Bar moved, indeed," he says.

I've known Doc Coblentz since I became chief; we've worked several difficult cases over the years. A pediatrician first and part-time coroner second, he's a consummate professional and very good at what he does. Despite his close association with the dead, he maintains a prudent emotional distance. Even in the face of unspeakable horror, he sees the dead through the lens of the scientist he is and focuses on the puzzle that must be solved. We're not close on a personal level, but we work well together. In terms of my position as chief, he's one of my favorite counterparts.

We start toward the crime scene. Glock and Skid have utilized the abundance of trees to tape off an area that's roughly sixty feet in diameter. When we reach the tape, Doc sets his medical bag on the ground and digs inside.

"You know the drill." He passes me wrapped shoe covers, gloves, and a zippered Tyvek coverall.

Neither of us speaks as we suit up. Though the disposable paper coverall is whisper thin, and we forgo the hood and face mask, I start sweating again beneath my uniform.

When we're fully covered, I duck beneath the tape and raise it for the doc to follow. "Everything we found so far is marked with cones," I tell him.

He slips beneath the tape. "Have you IDed the deceased?"

I shake my head. "We haven't found an ID. Or clothing for that matter. We haven't located the head."

The doc arches a brow and I see his doctor's brain begin to grind. "What about decomp? Are we dealing with bones? Something else?"

"I don't think the remains have been here very long," I tell him. "A day or two. The heat may have sped up the decomposition process. I don't know."

"You mentioned scavenger activity."

I nod. "Glock says it looked like coyotes."

"Well, that's going to make our jobs a little more challenging."

We stop a few feet from the first cone. Next to it lies the pale length of the human hand. Despite the sweat dripping down my back, I motion toward the leg that Glock discovered. "Leg is there."

"May I?" the doc asks.

"This is your scene."

Eyes sharp, watching his step, he brushes past me. Upon reaching the dismembered hand, he sets the medical bag on the ground, goes to one knee, and rummages in the bag. I watch as he removes a sterile sheet, snaps it open, and spreads it over the leaves and weeds. He then grasps the member with gloved hands and lifts, studies it for a moment, and sets it atop the sheet.

"I can confirm the scavenger activity," he says. "Teeth marks on that small jut of bone there. Canine, probably."

Rising, eyes watchful for anything unexpected on the ground, he walks to where the leg lies among the leaves and dirt and he kneels. He spreads out a second sterile sheet and smooths it over the ground. He digs into the medical case and removes a lighted magnifier. The appendage is heavier, so he gently lifts one end—the thigh end—from which an ivory and red-black-colored length of bone protrudes. Setting his eye to the magnifier lens, he leans close to the bone and doesn't move for the span of a full minute.

"Depending on how much we find here, I'm going to need a forensic pathologist," he says. "Though there's still tissue present, we might have a forensic anthropologist on standby."

"The pathologist is en route," I tell him. "I'll get with Tomasetti about the anthropologist."

He continues to study the limb, concentrating on the protrusion of bone. "Scavenger activity here, too, Kate."

"Will that interfere with forensics?"

"It could." He shrugs. "For example, if there was some type of cutting instrument used, damage from a scavenger could make it more difficult to match tooling marks."

Being careful not to disturb anything on the ground, I close the distance between us. "Doc, I know you don't have much to work with here, but if there's anything you can tell me that might help us ID this victim, I'd like to hear it."

He places the leg on the sheet. "I think we both know I'm not going to be able to tell you much until after the autopsy." Tugging a sterile container from his bag, he places the magnifier inside and snaps the lid closed. "That said, I can share a few observations."

"I'll take it."

"I believe this victim is an adult white male. Likely not elderly. There are no visible tattoos. No jewelry." He looks at me over his shoulder. "I can tell you with a reasonable level of confidence that your observation about the decedent being dismembered is correct. The appendages were not chewed off by some scavenger." He indicates the protruding bone. "The bone was severed with some type of instrument or tool. The cut line is precise."

"Any idea what kind of tool?"

"If I were to guess, I'd say some type of saw."

"Handsaw?" I say. "Chain saw?"

"Handsaw more than likely. Perhaps a serrated knife. There's no crushing or breaking of the bone. I'll know more once I get these remains to the morgue and on the table."

I don't want to look too closely at the pieces of what was once a human being. I don't want to think about what it took to get the job done. But for the first time since I arrived, I'm studying the remains with the eye of a cop and in terms of what they can tell me.

"Can you give me a ballpark time of death?" I ask.

"Taking into consideration the heat and humidity, both of which are factors in the rate of decomp, and the possibility that these remains were buried at some point . . ." He shrugs. "Forty-eight hours. Don't quote me."

"What about cause of death?" I ask. "Manner of death?" I know even as I ask the questions, he's not going to give me an answer.

"No and no." He offers a small smile. "Good try, though."

I try to return the smile, but my mouth is so dry my lips stick to my teeth.

• • •

I've just finished taking statements from the Amish children who discovered the remains when I hear a vehicle pull up. I glance toward the road to see Tomasetti's Tahoe ease onto the gravel shoulder.

As I start toward him, I'm vaguely aware of the Holmes County sheriff's cruiser stopped on the roadway where Skid set up traffic cones. A uniformed deputy is standing in the shade of an oak tree, talking on his phone. To my left, I see Glock walking the perimeter just outside the crime scene tape, looking for anything we missed first go-round.

I set my sights on Tomasetti as he slides out of the Tahoe. "Any word from your forensic guy?" I ask.

"He's an hour out. Driving in from Bowling Green." He strides toward me, his eyes on Doc Coblentz's Escalade a few yards away. "Doc able to shed any light?"

"Confirmed what we already knew," I say. "Not enough."

We meet on the shoulder and, despite the fact that we're married, we opt for a handshake. Our gazes lock. He holds on to my hand a beat too long. Then he releases me and his eyes shift to the departing buggy.

"Kids able to tell you anything?" he asks.

I recap the story of their finding the remains.

"Hell of a way to end a game of hide-and-seek," he says. "Any neighbors around?"

"Farms are pretty spread out here. Pickles is talking to the farmer who lives down the road. Closest neighbor is actually a business. Tree nursery half a mile down the road. We haven't talked to them yet."

"Be nice if someone saw or heard something." He thinks about that a moment. "Isn't that the nursery where we bought those two dogwood trees?"

"I'm about to head that way," I say. "Want to come?"

"I've been thinking about putting a cherry tree in the side yard."

I roll my eyes. "I'll drive."

Yutzy's Tree Nursery is a scant half mile down Sweet Potato Ridge Road. As I pull into the gravel parking area, I spot the horse and buggy in front of the old bank barn.

"Looks like someone's here," Tomasetti says.

I park beneath the shade of an ancient buckeye tree near the barn the owner uses as an office and to store equipment, and we get out. The big sliding door stands open about four feet. Heat hammers down from a cloudless blue sky.

"He's got some nice-looking saplings," Tomasetti comments as we start toward the barn.

"We could use a shade tree out by the firepit, too," I say absently, our boots crunching in the gravel and dirt.

"Another dogwood in the back."

Remembering our last tree-planting endeavor, we smile at each other as we enter the barn. "Hello?" I call out. "Mr. Yutzy?"

We stand there for a moment, glad to be out of the sun, listening for a response, taking in our surroundings. The only sounds that come back to us are the coo of a pigeon from the rafters above and the squeak of the wind vane mounted on the cupola overhead.

"Hello!" I call out again. "It's Chief Burkholder with the police department! Anyone here?"

No reply.

Tomasetti looks at me and shrugs. "Maybe he's out watering the trees?"

"Maybe."

A beat-up wooden desk abuts the wall to my right. Next to it, a folding table holds a small cash register. A bulletin board covers the rustic plank wall. A calendar mounted above the desk tells us the date is three days ago.

"Let's check outside," I say.

"Hopefully, he didn't have a damn heatstroke," Tomasetti mutters.

We go through the door and back into the burning-hot sun. Tomasetti walks to the Explorer and hits the horn three times. I'm standing in the doorway of the barn, thinking about how to best locate him in the dozen or so rows of trees, when the buggy horse whinnies. I glance over, only giving the animal half of my attention. I notice immediately something isn't right. There's a large pile of manure on the ground below the horse's tail. The gelding's head is low. Flies crowd around the animal's eyes and nose. Its flanks are deeply sunken. The flesh along its topline and neck is pimpled with hundreds of mosquito bites. At first glance, I'd assumed this horse was older, fifteen or twenty years of age. Now that I'm paying attention, I recognize the star on its forehead, and I realize this is the same horse the owner, Amishman Samuel Yutzy, was using last time Tomasetti and I were here, a five-year-old Standardbred he'd purchased off the track.

I'm aware of Tomasetti making his way toward the far side of the barn, where a coiled garden hose has been tossed on the ground. I go to the animal, slowly, my hand out. "Whoa," I say. "Easy."

The gelding barely acknowledges me. I set my hand on the animal's withers, move closer, shoo the flies from its eyes. I look at his flanks, realize the horse is in distress.

"Tomasetti?" I call out.

He's kneeling next to the hose and raises his gaze to mine.

"This animal has been without water for some time. His flanks are sunken. Eyes, too." Even as I say the words, I pinch the horse's skin above his withers between my thumb and forefinger. When I release the flesh, it doesn't snap back into place quickly, which is a sure sign of dehydration.

Tomasetti cocks his head, wondering why I'm concerned about a thirsty horse when I have the much bigger problem of human remains on my hands. "Heat related?" he says.

"I'm guessing this animal hasn't been fed or watered in over twenty-four hours."

I grew up around horses; I know when something isn't right. Though Tomasetti was raised in the city, he knows that with as-of-yet-unidentified human remains discovered half a mile down the road, an abandoned horse and buggy isn't a good development.

I go to the leather lines and loosen them, so the horse can move its head freely. "Samuel Yutzy isn't the kind of guy to neglect a horse," I say. "Gotta be something else."

Rising, Tomasetti crosses to me. "So where the hell is he?"

I go to the buggy, look inside. A copy of the newspaper *The Budget* is folded on the bench seat. A plastic coffee cup lies on its side on the floorboard. A quart bottle of fly spray. Nothing out of place.

Tomasetti strides to the Explorer and lays on the horn, his eyes probing the dozen or so rows of trees. I go to the barn, spot the five-gallon bucket just inside the door, and take it to the faucet at the side of the barn. I fill it halfway with water and carry it to the horse. The animal eagerly lowers its head, slurping and gulping as it drinks.

"Easy," I say. "Not too fast. Easy does it."

"I'm going to take a look around." Tomasetti approaches me, but his attention is on the trees. "Does Yutzy keep money in that register?"

I set down the bucket. "I'll take a look and meet you out there."

"Eyes open."

"Yep."

The temperature drops ten degrees when I enter the shade of the barn. I go directly to the folding table and look down at the register. It's a small, inexpensive model, the kind a new business owner might buy at Sam's Club or Office Depot. A single key dangles from the cash drawer. I reach down, twist the key, pull open the drawer. An array of bills and a mishmash of change stare up at me, telling me that he does, indeed, keep cash on hand and that it's undisturbed.

I'm on my way to the door to join Tomasetti when he calls out, "Kate!"

I leave the barn and break into a jog, cross the gravel. I pass by several rows of trees before spotting him twenty yards down the final row. He's kneeling, studying something on the ground. I start toward him, a bad feeling spreading through my midsection. I've nearly reached him when I notice the circular area of discolored earth. It's about two feet in diameter. As if something has been spilled, soaked into the ground, and dried.

Tomasetti sighs. "Looks like blood."

I reach him and kneel, the hairs at my nape standing up. "Shit." I look over at him. "There was an Amish hat on the ground back at the scene." I can tell by the way he's looking back at me that we're thinking the same thing.

"I've got Hemastix in the Explorer." I get to my feet. Hemastix is an inexpensive field test all of my officers carry in their vehicles. It indicates whether a stain that's presumably blood actually contains hemoglobin.

"Good place to start," he murmurs.

I jog to the Explorer, hit the fob for the rear door. Terrible possibilities churn in my brain as I dig into my equipment box. I grab the bottle and trot back to where Tomasetti is standing.

"Been a while since I used this," I say as I kneel. "Hope I remember how to do it."

Quickly, I pull on nitrile gloves. I twist the lid off the Hemastix container and pluck out a single plastic strip. I'm not sure there's enough moisture left in the stain to react, but I press the colored end of the strip against the stain anyway. The knot that's taken up residence in my gut tightens another notch when the tip turns green.

"Definitely blood," Tomasetti says.

I pull out my cell phone and hit the speed dial for Dispatch.

Lois picks up on the first ring. "Hey, Chief."

"Tell Pickles I need him to run out to Samuel Yutzy's residence for a welfare check. Tell him do not enter the premises. No one comes in or out of the property. Tell him I'll be there as soon as I can."

"You got it."

"Run Yutzy through LEADS," I tell her, referring to the Law Enforcement Automated Data System. "Check for warrants. I need a background. Last known address. Next of kin."

"Okay."

"I need you to write up an affidavit and get it over to Judge Siebenthaler. I need a search warrant for Yutzy's tree nursery and his residence. Tell the judge I need it yesterday. Send me the doc electronically as soon as you have it."

A pause and then, "Chief, isn't Yutzy that nice kid who owns the nursery out there on Sweet Potato Ridge Road?"

"We're here now, trying to locate him."

A beat of silence. "Oh, no."

"We haven't IDed the remains yet, so we don't know anything at this point," I tell her. "Don't use the radio."

"Roger that."

I disconnect and look down at the stained ground. "That's a lot of blood," I murmur.

Tomasetti motions. "More there."

"What the hell happened here?"

He shakes his head. "We need to find Yutzy."

"If we haven't already."

CHAPTER 4

The general rule of thumb for a homicide that involves the dismemberment of a human body is that there are probably *two* crime scenes. The death scene, where the victim was murdered and/or dismembered, and the location where the body parts were disposed of and found.

After Tomasetti and I confirmed the presence of blood at the tree nursery, we marked everything we could find, and with assistance from a Holmes County deputy we secured the scene. The buggy horse was unharnessed and hauled to the barn of a local horse breeder to be cared for until we can figure out exactly what's going on. I wasn't surprised when Pickles called with word that there was no one at the Yutzy residence. At that point, Tomasetti and I headed back to the original location where the body parts were discovered.

It's after three P.M. now and I'm standing outside the crime scene tape, sweating like a sieve beneath my Tyvek suit, and watch as the remains are painstakingly recovered. Twenty feet away, a forensic pathologist from BCI kneels on a blue tarp and uses a hand shovel to unearth what appears to be another piece of human flesh. Next to him, a second forensic scientist has laid out a black zippered bag, upon which he has placed several scraps of fabric. Clothing, I realize. I've been watching them for some time as each fragment was meticulously unearthed, photographed, placed on the tarp, and bagged. Each bag was then sealed, marked, and taken to the coroner's van.

"Chief Burkholder!" The forensic pathologist I was introduced to earlier motions me over. "I think you're going to want to see this."

We've limited the number of people permitted entry inside the scene. As is always the case with a crime scene, especially a large and complex outdoor scene, the retrieval of evidence—and, in this case, the retrieval of the body itself—works against the preservation of evidence. With numerous body parts, multiple shallow graves, scavenger activity, and the sheer scale of the area, there's no way around the need for manpower.

I duck under the tape. As I cross to him, I see that he's excavated a hole that's about a foot deep, piling the excess dirt onto the mound next to it.

The pathologist looks up as I approach. "We just uncovered a head. It's intact. Is there anyone around who might be able to ID the victim?"

I've only met Samuel Yutzy once or twice. I don't know him and I'm well aware that violent death can change the appearance of an individual's facial features. That said, it's critical to the investigation to ID this victim as quickly as possible.

"I might be able to do it," I say.

There's something unbearably grotesque about the dismemberment of a human body. I don't want that image in my head. But there's no one else.

"Let's see if I can get the facial features uncovered for you." Reaching into the hole, the forensic pathologist uses a hand shovel to carefully remove loose dirt and plant debris.

I look down into the hole. The hair and forehead come into view as he painstakingly scrapes away dirt with the shovel. I brace as some of the details become visible. I mentally catalog the attributes that will help me ID the victim. Caucasian. Medium-brown hair. No gray. The forehead is flecked with dirt that sticks to the flesh. The pathologist runs the shovel close to the skin, pulling away the dirt. Next, using what looks like a paintbrush, he sweeps away the small bits that stick. He uncovers the temple and cheek. An ear becomes visible. No piercing there. A sideburn.

"Victim is male," I hear myself say.

"I think so," the FP says, but he's laser focused on his task, leaning close and brushing at specks of grass and leaves.

"I've got another area of disturbed earth over here!"

The sound of Tomasetti's voice reaches me, and I look over my shoulder to see him standing about thirty feet away. Yet another shallow grave at his feet.

"The head is here," I tell him.

We hold gazes for the span of several heartbeats. He nods and starts toward us.

I'm standing a few feet away from where the head is being uncovered. Around me, I hear the incessant buzz of flies. The buzz saw chorus of cicadas. Vaguely, I'm aware of the snap and whirr of a camera to my left. Sweat dripping down the center of my back. My stomach reminding me that it isn't made of steel.

"Let's see what we've got." Using a smaller brush the size of a makeup applicator, the FP sweeps away the last of the debris.

I take a step closer and squat. I can see the jawline now. Mouth partially open. A tongue the color of a plum sticking out and caked with dirt.

Dear God . . .

"Haircut looks Amish." Tomasetti comes up behind me.

"No beard," I say, the significance of that not lost on either of us. An unmarried Amish man is clean-shaven; Samuel Yutzy was not married.

When the head is free of dirt, a dozen photos are taken from different angles. The FP unfolds a sterile sheet, smooths it over the trampled grass. Next to the sheet, he lays out a bag, which is unzipped. Gently, he reaches into the hole, sets his hands just below the ears, and lifts.

"Here we go," he says quietly.

The jaw shifts as the head is placed on the bag faceup. I'm reminded that just a short time ago, this individual was alive and breathing and talking to loved ones. Not much of the neck is attached. I can just make out a flap of loose flesh. A pink nub of what looks like bone. A finger-size tail of tissue that's wet and caked with dirt.

"Jesus Christ," Tomasetti mutters.

Spit pools in my mouth. Nowhere to spit because we're in a crime scene. I swallow hard, force it down, hope my stomach settles.

The FP uses yet another brush to remove the dirt and specks of debris—grass and leaves and tiny roots—from the severed neck.

The image burning into my brain doesn't look real; the skin is waxy and gray-white. One of the eyes is closed; the other eyelid is halfway up, revealing an eyeball that's coated with dirt. Despite all of it, recognition kicks me square in the chest.

"It's Samuel Yutzy," I hear myself say.

"It's him," Tomasetti says roughly.

I look at the pathologist. "Any idea how long this victim has been dead?"

The young man grimaces. "Ballpark?"

"We'll take whatever you can give us," Tomasetti says.

The FP looks down at the head and squints. "Thirty-six to forty-eight hours is my best estimate." Reaching out, he shifts the head slightly, so that the severed neck comes into view.

The urge to look away is strong, but I don't and my brain can barely process the horror of what I'm seeing.

The FP continues. "Thyroid cartilage is visible and has been incised." He indicates a purple-red length of what looks like a garden hose. "Trachea is visible. Cleanly incised."

"Any idea what kind of cutting tool was used?" Tomasetti asks.

He looks up, squinting. "You know anything I tell you at this point is a guess and subject to change once the autopsy is performed, right?"

Tomasetti frowns at him. "Yeah, we get that."

The FP shrugs. "I'd say this was done by some type of blade. Sharp and heavy enough to cut through bone." He indicates the flesh at the base of the neck. "Initially, however, it looks as if the killer may have done some hacking. You can see the stylohyoid ligament there. Incised. Cervical spine is visible to C3."

"Any gunshot wounds?" I ask.

Using a gloved hand, the pathologist checks the scalp, rolling the skull as necessary, taking his time, using his fingers to separate the hair in multiple areas. "Difficult to say at this point, Chief Burkholder. There's too much dirt and blood and debris. But, just taking a cursory look at this victim's scalp, I don't see any kind of penetrating wound. Doc Coblentz will want to verify with a CT scan or X-ray."

The urge to push for more information is strong, but it's never wise to pressure someone for answers when they've already made it clear they don't have them.

I mutter a thank-you as I stand. Without looking at Tomasetti or the technician, I turn and get the hell out of there.

• • •

If there was ever a moment when I wanted to smoke a cigarette—lung cancer be damned—this is it. I'm shaking when I duck beneath the crime scene tape. For the first time since I laid eyes on that severed head, I feel like I can breathe. The world around me snaps back into focus as I peel off my gloves and unzip the Tyvek suit and booties. The back of my shirt is soaked with sweat and sticks to my skin. I'm wondering if I could throw up without anyone noticing when I see Tomasetti approaching.

I can tell by his expression that he's cognizant of my frame of mind. He stops a few feet away. Giving me a moment to collect myself, he removes his own protective clothing, adds it to mine, and wads all of it into a ball.

"Do you know the family?" he asks as he shoves it into a biohazard bag.

I shake my head. "I've met his parents a couple of times over the years," I say. "But only to say hello. They own a cheese shop a few miles out of town."

"What do you know about Yutzy?"

"Not much." I take a breath, fall back into cop mode. "I've seen him around town. He's young. Unmarried. No children. He seemed like a decent kid. Owned the tree nursery. I've got Lois digging up everything she can find on him."

"Odd that a straitlaced Amish kid would end up in pieces and buried in a shallow grave."

"Not to mention the killer leaving a register full of cash." I sigh. "What are you thinking?"

"Dismembering a body is extreme to say the least." He lifts a shoulder, lets it drop. "This has something of a big-city feel."

"The same thought crossed my mind," I say. "Whoever buried him wasn't anticipating coyotes."

"Seems like a local would have considered scavengers."

"I think so, too," I say. "Doesn't feel local."

Tomasetti's expression turns grim. "You going to talk to the parents?"

"Right now," I tell him. "The discovery of human remains is going to be big news. The Amish may not use phones, but that doesn't slow down the grapevine." I sigh. "I don't want them to hear it from someone else."

"You want some company?"

Seeing the concern in his expression, and appreciating it, I reach out and touch his hand. "Thank you," I say. "But with their being Amish, I think I should go alone."

"You sure?"

"If they have something to tell me about their son, I think they'll be more likely to open up if it's just me."

• • •

Orlah and Leona Yutzy live on a well-kept dairy farm six miles west of Painters Mill. A sign welcomes me to YUTZY FARM CHEESE SHOP as I make the turn in to the gravel lane. The house is a hundred-year-old frame farmhouse with dual brick chimneys and a wraparound front porch. The couple has transformed the front of their home into a shop and showroom for the cheeses they make on-site. I've bought my fair share over the years. Cheddar and bleu and goat. It's authentic, delicious, and popular with locals as well as tourists.

I park in the circular driveway and take the sidewalk to the porch where a second sign reads: WILKOMEN! KUMMA INSEID. Welcome! Come inside.

The front door stands open and I go through. "Hello?" I call out. "Mr. and Mrs. Yutzy?"

The first things I notice are the display cases and counter, and the not-quite-pleasant smell of curdled milk. There's an olive-green sofa against the wall. A dormant cast-iron stove in the corner. A coffee table piled high with Amish country tourist pamphlets.

Heavy footsteps sound, and then a large woman wearing a light blue dress, a kitchen towel slung over her shoulder, comes through an interior door and smiles at me. "Well, if it isn't my favorite ex-Amish chief of police! You must be here for some more of that bleu cheese you and that husband of yours like."

"Hi, Leona." I don't smile back as I show her my badge. "I'm afraid this is an official visit."

"Well, what in the world?"

I can tell by the way she's looking at me that she knows I've come bearing bad news. I look past her, expecting her husband to come through the swinging door of the kitchen. "Is Orlah here with you?" I ask. "I need to speak to both of you."

"He's in the kitchen." She steps back as if suddenly realizing it may not be safe to get too close. "What's this all about? Is everything all right?"

Her husband pushes open the door and comes through, a sandwich in hand. He's a large man. Six feet tall and three hundred pounds. He's wearing dark trousers with suspenders and a blue work shirt.

"Is there a problem?" he asks, his eyes going from his wife to me.

"Mr. and Mrs. Yutzy, I'm afraid I have some terrible news. Your son, Samuel, has been killed. I'm sorry."

Leona cocks her head, looking at me the way the condemned might look at their executioner. "Well, that can't hardly be true," she huffs. "Samuel's too young. Just twenty-one years old." She looks at her husband and forces a sound that doesn't quite sound like a laugh. "You got him mixed up with someone else is all."

"I'm sorry," I say, hating those words because at a time like this they feel like the most unhelpful words in the English language.

The sandwich drops to the floor. Orlah stands there, unmoving, looking down at it as if he doesn't know how it got on the floor and has no idea what to do about it. He tries to speak, but his lips quiver and the only sound that comes out is a squeak of his son's name. "Samuel? Dead?"

Feeling helpless and shitty, I look from husband to wife. "I know this is a terrible shock, but I need to ask both of you some questions about your son."

"What happened to him?" Orlah asks.

"We're waiting for the coroner to tell us," I say, hedging. "We found him at the nursery this morning, deceased."

Without warning, the Amish woman collapses. Her knees hit the floor with a *thump!* Both Orlah and I rush forward, reach for her upper arms just in time to keep her from pitching forward.

"*Ach du lieva,*" Orlah whispers. Oh my goodness.

"Let's get her over to the sofa," I say.

The woman's head lolls. For the span of several seconds, she's deadweight. She's also heavy, and it's not easy to keep her upright. I'm thinking about laying her out on the floor when she appears to come to and raises her head.

"I'm okay," she says, and struggles to her feet. "Just a shock, is all. My goodness, God doesn't usually take them so young."

"Let's sit you down." I glance at her husband, motioning to the sofa with my eyes.

He nods.

Leona makes a halfhearted attempt to dislodge our hands from her biceps. I stay with her and we settle her onto the sofa.

The Amish woman sags, puts her hands to her face, and begins to cry softly. "I can't believe he's gone."

Setting my hand on her shoulder, I squeeze, make eye contact with her husband. He stares back at me, a child waiting for a slap from a ruthless parent.

"What happened to him?" he asks.

"I don't know the cause of death," I say honestly. "All I can tell you is that his body was found in the woods near the nursery."

"In the *woods*?" As if not quite trusting his legs to support him, Orlah sinks onto the sofa beside his wife. "*Mein Gott.*" My God.

"Mr. and Mrs. Yutzy, when's the last time you saw Samuel?" I ask.

"He went to worship with us last Sunday over to the Hochstetler place," Orlah tells me.

"How did he seem?" I ask. "Was he worried about anything? Anyone? Was he having any problems?"

"Seemed fine," the Amish man says. "Talking about the nursery mostly. Said business was picking back up. He was going to get that old greenhouse repaired."

"He'd been away for a time, you know," Leona adds.

I think about the tree Tomasetti and I had purchased. Samuel had seemed to enjoy running the nursery. He'd been proud of it and was good at what he did. The place had been immaculate.

"He'd been away?" I ask.

Orlah frowns at his wife. "Samuel was on *rumspringa*, you know. Like a lot of Amish boys, he got to going out and running around. The way them English youngsters do. Drinking and whatnot."

Rumspringa refers to a period of time in a young Amish person's life before they become baptized. A time when they have the freedom to do as they please without the constraints of all those Amish rules.

"A little too much frolicking if you ask me," Leona mutters.

He frowns at her again.

This time, she frowns back. "Go on, Orly," she says, "tell her."

The Amish man's gaze hits the floor.

"Tell me what?" I press.

"There was a girl." Wiping her eyes, Leona makes a sound that's part sob, part exasperation. "Samuel got tangled up with her. She was a bad egg, that one. Knew it the first time I saw her. *Druvvel-machah.*" Troublemaker.

My cop's radar perks up. "What's her name?"

"Cass or some such," Leona says. "Don't know if that's even her real name."

"What can you tell me about her?" I ask.

"Not much. She wasn't real big on conversation." Leona tightens her lips. "But he was spending a lot of time with her." She shakes her head. "My goodness, she had that painted-up face and all those tattoos. Woman parts hanging out all over the place. Smoking cigarettes out by the barn and thinking we couldn't smell it."

"We just couldn't have her here," Orlah adds. "Not with the kids gawking at her the way they did."

I pull my notebook from my pocket, flip it open. "Is she Amish or English?"

The couple look at each other, their expressions puzzled.

"Neither one of them said," Orlah replies.

"She *looked* English," Leona tells me. "Sounded Amish, though."

"Didn't look like any Amish girl I ever seen," Orlah mutters. "Whatever the case, she's headed down the wrong road."

"Is she from Painters Mill?" I ask.

Leona shakes her head. "I think she lives down to the New Philly area."

"Address?"

"Don't know."

"Can you tell me what she looked like?" I ask.

"Oh, she's a pretty thing," Leona adds. "Bluest eyes I ever seen. Almost as tall as Samuel. Kind of thin. Hair dyed black and ugly as a rag."

Orlah heaves a sigh. "She got her hooks into Sammy quick."

"Does she have a family?" I ask. "Parents or siblings? Or a best friend? Is there anyone I can talk to about her?"

Orlah shakes his head. "We don't know."

"Does this young woman work?" I ask.

An odd silence ensues. I look from Orlah to Leona and a tiny red flag begins to flap. The sense that this heartbroken couple aren't being forthright sits in my stomach like a rock. Being formerly Amish myself, I understand the need to keep certain things private. When a young Amish person makes a mistake or takes a wrong turn, you don't talk about it. Not to a non-Amish person. And never to a cop.

"She never really said," Orlah replies.

Something there, I think, so I keep pushing. "How many times did you meet her?"

"Just that one time."

"Once was enough," Leona puts in. "He brought her over for dinner." The corners of her mouth turn down. "It wasn't a very nice evening."

"Do you have any idea how I might find this woman?" I ask.

"I just don't know," Leona says.

But Orlah's brows furrow. "Samuel's been running with some English fellow. Some fancy guy from out of town."

"What's his name?"

The Amish man shakes his head. "I didn't ask and he didn't say."

"How do you know Samuel was running around with him?" I ask.

"Well, the English fellow was there at the nursery when I picked up some of them red maple trees I planted out front here."

"What did he look like?"

He turns thoughtful. "Only thing I recall is the fancy clothes. I thought it was odd that he was wearing them shiny shoes to the kind of place where you usually get your feet muddy."

Frustration begins a slow boil in my gut. "Who else did Samuel spend time with?"

"Aaron Shetler's his best friend." Leona uses a wadded-up tissue to blot her nose. "They've been friends since their school days."

"Doyle and Ellen's boy?" I ask.

"He's their youngest," she tells me.

The Shetlers are a solid Amish family, well thought of. If memory serves me, Aaron Shetler works in the tire center of the local farm store.

I lower the notebook and pen. "Mr. and Mrs. Yutzy," I begin, "is there anything else you'd like to tell me about your son?" When neither of them speaks up, I add, "I'm just trying to find out what happened to him. That's all."

After a moment, Orlah reaches over and sets his hand over his wife's, then turns his attention to me. "You've been gone from the Amish for a long time, Kate Burkholder. I don't know if you can understand."

"Try me," I say.

As if frustrated with himself, with the situation, Orlah shakes his head. "Samuel started his *rumspringa* when he was seventeen. The truth of the matter is, he got kind of wild for a time. He strayed. A little too far. Ran around with some shifty types. We didn't approve of any of it."

"Some of his Amish friends didn't approve, either," Leona adds. "Most of them stopped coming around. I think they just didn't want anything to do with those sorts of things."

"What sorts of things?" I ask.

"All the drinking," Orlah says. "The loose English women. Staying out all night." He shakes his head. "Most of these good Amish boys he grew up with wanted no part of it."

"What about Aaron?"

"He's the only one stuck with him," he says.

I add the information to my notes.

"It's important that you know, Chief Burkholder," Leona says. "Samuel had come back to us in the last few months. He left all that other stuff behind. He started going to worship again. Went back to wearing the plain clothes. Even sold that car of his."

"He planned to be baptized in the fall," Orlah adds. "He asked me to talk to Bishop Troyer, which I did. He was going to start *die Gemee nooch geh* next month."

Translated, *die Gemee nooch geh* means "to follow the church" and consists of nine or so instruction classes for those who are planning to be baptized.

"Mr. and Mrs. Yutzy, did your son have any enemies?" I ask. "Did he have any disagreements with anyone? Money problems? Anything like that?"

Orlah's eyes narrow on mine. In their depths I see a flash of wariness. "Why are you asking all these questions about him?"

"Do you know of anyone who might've wanted to harm your son," I say.

The couple exchange another look, this one rife not only with grief, but with horror and disbelief. "Are you telling us someone . . . took his life?" Orlah asks. "Murdered him?"

"I believe so."

Leona chokes out a sob, puts her hand over her mouth as if to keep an even larger cry from escaping. "He was such a good boy," she whispers. "Who would do such a thing?"

"That's what I'm trying to find out," I tell her. "Please, if Samuel was having any problems. With his work. In his life. His relationships. I need to know."

After a too-long moment, Leona places her hand on her husband's forearm. "What about that big contract that got all messed up?"

The Amish man's brows pull together. "I don't know too much about it. I thought he got that all smoothed out."

"What contract?" I cut in.

"Samuel got a nice-size job with some big-bug up to Millersburg a while back," Orlah says. "Big-bug" is an Amish term for "rich person." "He signed on to landscape his house."

"Sammy was excited," Leona puts in. "That boy liked to work. Liked to get his hands dirty. It was a huge job. Good money. Said he was going to ask Aaron to help."

"What happened?" I ask.

"I'm not real clear on the details," Orlah says, "but the job required some grading. Samuel borrowed one of them Bobcat skid-steers from a guy down in Coshocton." He sighs. "I don't know all the ins and outs, but the job got messed up."

"Were there hard feelings between Samuel and the client?" I ask.

"The guy wasn't happy with the work," Orlah says. "And he was causing problems for Samuel."

"Threatened to sue if I recall," Leona huffs. "You know how people are these days."

"What's the customer's name?" I ask.

"Don't think he ever said," Orlah replies.

"You can count on this, though, Chief Burkholder," Leona says. "Sammy did good work. And he was honest. The man didn't have a leg to stand on."

I don't recall seeing a computer or file cabinet at the nursery, but I hadn't been specifically looking, so I make a mental note to look again. "Do you have any idea where Samuel kept his business files or paperwork?"

"Reckon it's at his house," Orlah tells me.

"Do you happen to have a key I could use?" I ask. "To take a look?"

The two exchange a look and shake their heads. "Never gave us one," Orlah says.

"He kept that old file cabinet in the extra bedroom," Leona adds.

"Had plans to add an office at the nursery, but he hadn't gotten around to it."

I fish my business card out of my pocket, jot my cell phone number on the back, and hand it to Orlah. "If you think of anything else, will you call me?"

The Amish man takes the card and nods.

"Chief Burkholder." Raising her head, Leona wipes tears from her cheeks. "Can you tell us when we'll get him back? I mean, from the funeral home?"

The question takes me aback. Generally, when there's a death, most Amish have the body embalmed. There's a viewing. The funeral is usually held on the third day following the death. None of that's going to happen for this family. I should have been prepared for the question, but I'm not. What can you say when someone's child was murdered, his body cut into pieces?

"Samuel's body will be taken to Pomerene Hospital," I tell her. "The coroner will be conducting an autopsy. I'm not sure about the timing of everything, but I'll find out and let you know."

I leave them sitting in the living room, their heads bowed, their lives shattered.

CHAPTER 5

Back in the Explorer, I start the engine, twist the AC on full blast, and let the cool air wash over my face. I feel like hell, a toxic mix of anger, frustration, and helplessness. Of all the things a cop has to do, notifying a family that a loved one will never be coming home is the most difficult.

Rapping my palm against the steering wheel, I put the Explorer in gear and start down the lane. As I make the turn onto the township road, I hail Dispatch. Only when my second-shift dispatcher, Jodie Metcalf, answers do I realize the day has somehow blown past.

"I need you to run Aaron Shetler through LEADS," I tell her. "Check for warrants. See if he's got a record. Get me the names of known associates. I need his most recent address. See if you can dig up a photo of him, too."

"Yes, ma'am."

"I'm on my way to Samuel Yutzy's residence." A look at the clock on my dash tells me it's now after five P.M. "Warrant come through?"

"Sending it now."

"Dig up everything you can find on Yutzy's Tree Nursery. Owned by Samuel Yutzy. Check to see if there's anyone else who invested in it or owns part of the business."

"Yep."

"See if there were any disputes. Lawsuits. Complaints. Legal problems. Burglaries."

"Sure."

"Jodie, is Lois still there?" I ask.

"She's getting ready to leave."

"If she can spare a few minutes, tell her I need her to contact everyone in the department and set up a quick briefing for seven P.M. I want everyone there. County, too. Check with Rasmussen to see if he's game for a presser at eight. I'll let Tomasetti know."

"Got it, Chief."

I start to hang up, think better of it. "Jodie?"

"Yeah?"

I can practically hear her bracing for more. "Thanks," I say, and rack the mike.

• • •

Samuel Yutzy lived in a modest frame house that's a couple of decades past its prime. It sits a short distance off the township road next to a small cinder-block building with a single bay portico. Half a dozen newly planted saplings adorn an otherwise bare front yard; the trees are staked, the base of each mounded with mulch. A vehicle I don't recognize is parked in front of the house, so I pull up behind it and get out. I'm midway to the car when I see Pickles slide out and start my way.

"Afternoon, Chief."

Roland "Pickles" Shumaker is just north of eighty years old. He's been a cop longer than my other officers have been alive. He semiretired a few years ago to become my only part-timer. He's slowed down some since I've been chief and now spends most of his workdays at the elementary school crosswalk.

While Pickles may look like your favorite grouchy-but-lovable grandpa, only an unwise person would underestimate him. He's a cop through and through and a sheepdog of the first order. Back in the eighties he single-handedly brought down one of the biggest drug rings in the state of Ohio. When the wolf growls at the door, you can bet your ass this man will stand at the ready to protect you.

"Nice set of wheels." I side-eye the vintage muscle car behind him.

"Picked her up in Dover a couple weeks ago." He slaps his hand against mine and we share a hearty shake. "Nineteen seventy-two Dodge Charger. Three eighty. V-8."

"I didn't know you restored cars."

"Jury's still out on that, but I'm going to give it a shot." His eyes narrow on mine. "What's up with Yutzy?"

I tell him what little we know so far. "You ever hear anything about him?"

"I've seen him around town some. Never any trouble. In fact, I bought some trees from him last summer. Seemed like a nice kid."

"So everyone says." I turn my attention to the house. "Since we basically don't know shit at this point, I thought it might be a good idea to take a look around."

I motion toward the cinder-block building. "Check the workshop. I'll start in the house. Be cognizant of evidence. Use gloves. Watch your step."

"You got it, Chief."

I go to the front of the house and ascend the concrete steps. The screen door opens, but the main door is locked. I trot down the steps and go around the side to the back. I take the steps to a newish-looking wood deck. Relief flits through me when I find the back door unlocked.

I step into a small kitchen. The first thing I notice is the heat; it's unbearably stuffy inside, so I leave the door open behind me. There are dark wood cabinets. Linoleum floor. Tile countertops. To my right, a white stove that's scabbed with rust hulks against the wall. Next to it, a robin's-egg-blue refrigerator wheezes. Through the wide doorway ahead, I see a living room with paneled walls and secondhand-shop furniture. To my left, a small table has been shoved against the wall, a stack of mail on its surface.

I'm not exactly sure what I'm looking for. Any legal correspondence regarding the landscaping dispute. A cell phone or laptop. Tugging gloves from my equipment belt, I go to the table, page through the mail. Bills mostly. Cable TV. Electricity. Gas. An advertisement with coupons from the local grocery.

I enter the living room. Green carpet circa 1970 covers the floor. There's a TV tray set up in front of the couch. A decent-size TV. A window-unit air conditioner. Seeing nothing of interest, I take the hall to the rear of the house. I pass by a small bathroom, flip on the light. The smell of mildew tickles my nose when I step inside. A towel lies tangled on the floor. I check the medicine cabinet, find a bottle of Advil. Aftershave. A razor and shave cream. Cough syrup.

I back out and continue down the hall. There are two bedrooms. The first is barely large enough to accommodate a bed and is being used as an office. A high-end e-bike with a rear wire basket is propped against the wall. While the e-bike technology isn't accepted by all Amish in Holmes County, there are no rules against using them and they've become quite popular in the last year or so. Next to the bike, a bookcase is stacked with paperbacks and magazines. There's a steel vertical file cabinet in the corner. I start there.

The top drawer contains hanging files jammed with folders. I page through. Credit card statements. Bank statements. *Northeast Ohio Natural Gas Corp. Holmes-Wayne Electric Co-op. Holmes County Bank and Trust.* Two wider hanging files contain manila folders. One is marked CLOSED. The other is marked CURRENT. I go to the CURRENT file and page through. Each folder is labeled with the last name of a client, and the folders are in alphabetical order. Abbott. Denninger. Hightower. Smith. Most contain simple work orders for landscaping jobs. There are invoices in various stages of payment. I'm midway through when I spot the overstuffed folder in the back. The frayed tab is marked BROOKS, CARTER—CONTRACT and highlighted in yellow.

I pull out the folder and open it, page through. I find a dozen or so invoices. A few check stubs indicating payment from Carter Brooks with a Millersburg address. I find a Landscaping Services Agreement for a job from March of this year. The description includes labor and material costs for a pavestone walkway, two dozen shrubs, six shade trees, and a walkway with grading. There are handwritten notes, a sketch of the landscaping design, and a few printed copies of emails. At the back of the file, I find an Intent to File a Lawsuit letter from Carter Brooks and skim the legalese.

I hired Samuel Yutzy, owner of Yutzy's Tree Nursery, to landscape my home located at 1923 Marigold Road in Millersburg. The contract called for a hedge, six shade trees, two ornamental trees, and a pavestone walkway. I paid $10,569 on May 19. A storm came through in May and flooded the window wells of my house, sending water into the basement and damaging the floor, walls, insulation, and my home office equipment. I consulted an engineer who told me my landscaper

(Yutzy) caused water to be trapped against the house with the pave-stone walkway because he did not install a drain. Another landscaping company reshot the grade and determined that the original landscaper (Yutzy) was at fault. The repair cost an additional $4,892 (invoice attached). Damage to the building/structure and electronics came in at $10,921 (estimate attached).

Because of Yutzy's shoddy workmanship, I had to pay a contractor to repair the damage in my basement (first water damage mitigation then replace carpets, drywall, etc.). I'm currently working with an attorney who says next step is a lawsuit. Yutzy has stopped taking my calls and no longer responds to my emails. Please remit $15,813 within thirty days or I will have no recourse but to sue.

"Hello," I mutter. Tugging out my cell phone, I snap a photo of the Intent to File letter.

Back in the hall, I call Jodie.

"Hey, Chief," she says, her voice breathless.

"You sound busy."

She snorts.

"Put Lois on," I say.

I wait a beat, and then my first-shift dispatcher greets me with "You know it's a madhouse here, right?"

"I'm assuming that's an understatement."

She blows out a raucous laugh.

"Are you game for some OT?" I ask.

"I *do* need that new car." But there's a smile in her voice. "Bring it."

"Did anything of interest come back on Yutzy or Shetler?"

"No warrants. No record. Shetler is twenty-one. Red hair. Six feet. One sixty. I found a few photos on social media."

"Print copies of everything you have and have them ready for the briefing."

"'Kay."

"Dig up everything you can find on Carter Brooks in Millersburg. Check for warrants. See if he's got a record. I need the names of known associates, including his lawyer if he has one. Go through all our regular channels and social media, too."

"Will do. The briefing is a go, by the way. Rasmussen will do the presser."

"Thanks for staying late."

"Wouldn't miss it."

Tucking my cell back into its case on my belt, I go to the larger bedroom and turn on the light. I know immediately this is the one Samuel used. A full-size bed is draped with a tatty Amish quilt. A dark blanket covers the single window, probably to block the light. I go to the night table next to the bed and pull open the top drawer. A copy of *Es Nei Teshtament un Pennsylvania Deitsh un English* stares up at me. In stark contrast, a pack of Marlboro Reds and a lighter are nestled against the Bible. The second drawer contains a single unwrapped condom. A deck of cards. A pad of grid paper, likely for sketching landscaping plans.

I go to the third drawer. Samuel was Amish, so I likely won't find anything as easy as a cell phone or laptop. Still, I look. There's a box of tissues. A book of checks. A couple of magazines. Nothing even remotely helpful.

I pick up the grid paper pad to look beneath it when something slips out and flutters to the floor. I pick it up, do a double take upon spotting the photo. A woman. She's beautiful despite the heavy makeup. Scantily clad in a tiny sequin bolero held together by a gold link, the tops of her breasts barely covered. Her arms are raised, as if she's dancing. Part of a tattoo peeks out at me from beneath the neckline of her shirt. Her head is thrown back in laughter and she's beaming a one-thousand-watt smile at whoever took the photo. A head full of black hair spills over her shoulders.

I think of the woman Leona Yutzy referred to as *druvvel-machah.* The photo certainly meets the description. "Well, if it isn't our friendly neighborhood troublemaker," I whisper.

I flip the photo over, hoping for a name, but there's nothing written on the back. Pulling out my cell, I snap a shot, replace it, and head toward the door.

• • •

I arrive at the police station six minutes late for my briefing. I'm not a big fan of meetings and do my best to keep them at a minimum. But with a major case bearing down, it's vital for me to keep everyone on the same page and delegate everything I can.

As I pull nose-in to my space, I take note of the dozen or so vehicles parked on the street, and I remind myself I shouldn't be surprised that news of the murder has spread like wildfire. Grabbing my laptop case off the back seat, I get out and head toward the entrance.

"Chief Burkholder!"

I glance left to see a woman in a stylish orange suit rush toward me, eyes on fire, microphone in hand. "What can you tell us about the murder?"

"Press conference at eight." I sidle away to reach the door before she can block me.

The woman isn't deterred and thrusts the mike inches from my face. "Can you confirm that the victim was decapitated? Do you have a suspect?"

"No comment," I tell her.

A hissed curse follows me as I go through the door. The reception area is jammed with people—concerned citizens, local business owners, and cops from several jurisdictions—and I realize that's why the journalist outside didn't follow me inside. To my right, I see Glock talking to a couple of Holmes County deputies. Farther in, the owner of the Butterhorn Bakery gestures animatedly as he talks to Auggie Brock, the mayor. I can only imagine the whoppers being traded.

"Chief!"

I turn to see my floater dispatcher, Margaret, get to her feet. I start toward her. She's got the headset clamped over her cropped silver-brown hair and she's waving her hands at me like a drowning woman reaching for a life vest.

"The mayor's looking for you," she tells me.

I reach her, pluck messages from my slot. "I see him."

"Sheriff Rasmussen, too."

"I'll find him." Head down, I start for my office, brush past a town councilman and the principal of the high school.

"Any chance I could have a moment with the chief?"

I glance left and see Tomasetti standing in the hall, looking at me.

"You're a sight for sore eyes," I say on a sigh.

"That's what all the female chiefs of police tell me," he says.

"So I've heard." I unlock my office and slip inside. I'd expected him to continue on to the "war room" for the briefing, but he slips in behind me and closes the door.

"You're not going to drop some atomic bomb of bad news on me, are you?" I ask.

"Not a chance." Eyes locked on mine, he crosses to me and presses a chaste kiss to my forehead. "You got this."

Despite the tension running like barbed wire across my shoulders, I smile. "See you in two minutes."

And then he's gone.

I go to my laptop first. My email box overflows with information from the queries I put in to Lois and Jodie. I skim the highlights as best I can and print the details I need for the briefing. Two minutes later, I walk into the war room to find it packed to the gills. Every officer in my department is there along with two of my dispatchers. I count three Holmes County deputies. A detective with the Ohio State Highway Patrol. Mayor Brock. Sheriff Rasmussen. And, of course, Tomasetti.

I nod at the sheriff as I stride past, letting him know I'll talk with him after the briefing. At the half podium, I give the mike a sharp tap.

"Since it's a hundred degrees in this room and every single one of us has our work cut out for us this evening, I'll make this briefing short and sweet."

The hum of conversation ceases.

"Here's what we have so far." I start with the victim's name and recap what little we know. I run through each of the bullet points I jotted down throughout the day. "According to the coroner, Samuel Yutzy was murdered thirty-six to forty-eight hours ago. No criminal record. No warrants." I recite his address.

"Do we have cause or manner of death?" Sheriff Mike Rasmussen asks.

"No and no," I tell him. "Doc Coblentz will be doing the autopsy, probably in the morning. I anticipate being able to answer at least one of those questions shortly thereafter."

I look out at the small ocean of faces. "Information is scarce at this point, but I'll give you what I have so far.

"Logistics." I turn to the map of Painters Mill secured to the wall behind me. Using a red marker, I draw an X where the body was uncovered. I circle the location of the tree nursery. "A large amount of blood was discovered at the tree nursery. Both scenes are still being processed by BCI." I turn to face the crowd. "In theory, I believe the murder and dismemberment happened at the nursery. The killer or killers may have then transported the remains roughly a quarter of a mile into the woods. There, they dug several shallow holes, and buried everything."

"What about motive?" one of the deputies asks.

"The Amish use cash," says another deputy. "Any chance it was a robbery gone wrong?"

I shake my head. "The register at the nursery contained cash." I look at Sheriff Rasmussen. "Do you know if there are any CCTV cameras or game cams in the vicinity?"

The sheriff stands. "We checked with a few of the property owners in the area, Kate, and we got nothing."

I point at Skid. "I want you to go back out there this evening and talk to every residence within a five-mile radius. Find out if anyone saw any strange vehicles or buggies in the area. Check to see if anyone has a game cam or CCTV that we overlooked."

He sends me a two-finger salute.

I look at Rasmussen. "Anything turn up on the grid search?"

The sheriff shakes his head. "I still got two deputies out there with a metal detector. We located a garbage bag. There was blood on it, but nothing inside. Everything was sent to the lab."

"So, conceivably, the killer or killers could have transported the remains in the bag?" I ask.

The sheriff nods. "That's what I'm thinking. The bag, by the way, is polyethylene, which is good news because that particular material may retain prints, so the lab will be looking for latents, too."

"Excellent." I point at T.J. "When we finish up here, I want you to check any and all trash containers or dumpsters in the area. Dismembering a body is a messy job. Whoever did it may have gotten rid of clothes or towels. He may have tossed tools."

"You got it," he says.

"Until we have a suspect, everyone who knew or had contact with Yutzy is a person of interest." I glance down at my notes. "According to Yutzy's parents, Aaron Shetler was his best friend. He's Amish. Local. Shetler also has a clean record. No warrants. He's employed at Quality Implement." I catch Glock's attention. "When we're finished here, find him, pick him up. Bring him in so we can talk to him."

"Yes, ma'am," he says.

I turn my attention to Mona Kurtz. She's the first female to grace the ranks of the department, a good cop, and one of my favorite officers. "I want you to cruise around on social media. Focus on Yutzy and Shetler. Personal lives. Girlfriends. Look for any disputes or arguments. See what you can find."

"On it," she says.

I look out at the group. "According to Yutzy's parents, Yutzy and a Millersburg man by the name of Carter Brooks were involved in some kind of contractual dispute. I did a cursory search of Yutzy's residence and sure enough, I found some docs that confirm as much." I turn my attention to Lois. "Anything interesting on Brooks?"

Dispatchers generally don't get too involved with investigations, particularly of the homicide variety. But because my department is invariably short-staffed, I'm never shy about asking them to step in. They're well versed on using the police databases we have access to and mining information from various sites on the internet when that's all we've got.

Lois straightens her shoulders. "Thirty-nine years old. Divorced. No kids. Millersburg residence. He's part owner, manager, and stakeholder of a microbrewery in Millersburg. Blue Lake Tap and Brewery. No active warrants. However . . ." She looks down at the paper in her hand to skim her notes. "Brooks was arrested last year. Initially, he was stopped for speeding. Eighty-two miles an hour in a thirty-five. An open container led to a search of the vehicle, at which time a loaded weapon was found. Brooks was not a licensed concealed-carry permit holder in Ohio, so an arrest was made. Blood test cleared him of the OVI. He took a plea deal on the weapon charge, and got it knocked down to a misdemeanor."

"Lucky guy," someone mutters.

"Must have a good lawyer."

I soak in the information greedily. "According to Yutzy's parents, Brooks and Yutzy were involved in a serious dispute over a landscaping job and presumably money."

"What kind of money are we talking about?" Rasmussen asks.

"Brooks was asking for over fifteen thousand dollars," I tell him.

One of the deputies whistles. "That'll ruin your day."

"People have been killed for less," someone else throws out.

I look at Lois. "Send me everything you have on Brooks."

"Yes, ma'am."

I go to the next topic. "We also have a female person of interest." I hold up the enlarged image of the mystery woman whose photo I found in Yutzy's bedroom. "I found this when I searched Yutzy's home. I've not been able to positively identify her. The only name we have to go on is Cass or some variation thereof. Based on my conversation with Yutzy's parents, I believe he may have been romantically involved with her."

"Lot of skin," mutters one of the deputies.

"Not to mention tats," someone else says.

"Gotta be Amish," comes another voice.

A round of chuckles ensues, but I ignore it and make eye contact with T.J. "If we don't get her IDed by end of day, I want you to take the photo to Steve Ressler over at *The Advocate* first thing in the morning," I say, referring to the weekly newspaper. "Ask him to run it on the website with a request for assistance to the community at large."

"You bet," he says.

Tomasetti pipes up. "If you supply me with a high-res, I'll plug it into a database and see if I can come up with a match. Long shot, but we might get lucky."

"Will do."

I'm about to move on to my next point when Skid clears his throat. "Uh . . . Chief, can I have a closer look at that photo for a sec?"

Curious, I move around the head of the table. He rises and meets me halfway. "You recognize her?" I ask.

"Well, not *her,*" he says. "I think I recognize the location where the photo was taken."

Something off about his demeanor, I think. He looks uncomfortable. Skid is *not* an uncomfortable kind of guy; he's not shy—not by any stretch. In fact, he'll be the first to crack an inappropriate joke or take a topic into unseemly territory.

"Where?" I ask.

"Uh . . . well, looks like the gentleman's club over in New Philly. The Cheetah Lounge."

Someone in the crowd cuts loose with a laugh, covers it with a cough.

I blink, glance over at the photo, tap it with my index finger. "You've seen her there?"

"No, but I recognize that backdrop. That riser behind her. The curtain." He clears his throat. "And that uh . . . pole there in the background."

A round of snickers erupts, but I don't look away from Skid. He stares at the photo, a splotch of color climbing up his neck. I turn my attention back to the photo. Sure enough, there's a stagelike riser behind the woman. A curtainlike shimmering skirt. A chrome dancing pole. I've frequented my share of bars, but I can honestly say I've never ventured into a gentleman's club. Of course, it doesn't take much of an imagination to make the connection.

"How long ago were you there?" I ask.

"Couple of weeks."

"He's a regular," someone mutters.

"Goes with his mom."

I ignore them, look at Skid. "Get me the address."

"Ah . . . sure."

I turn to the deputies sitting at the back of the room. "The rest of you shut up."

• • •

"Kate!"

I'm pushing through the ocean of bodies, on my way to my office, when Tomasetti calls out my name.

I turn to see him working his way toward me. We meet in the hall outside my office.

"We're going to have to stop meeting like this," I mutter beneath my breath.

"And ruin all this fun?" But his smile is grim, telling me he has news. "Crime scene tech called a few minutes ago. They found a chain saw. It tested positive for blood. And bleach."

"Where?"

"The nursery," he says. "It was hanging on the wall with some other tools. A sharp-eyed CSI happened to spot a fleck of what looked like blood on the chain."

"Prints?"

"Checking now." He grimaces. "I thought I'd head out there."

"I wish I could tag along, but I'm going to talk to Mr. Brooks."

"You taking someone with you?" he asks casually.

It's not a casual question, but I let it go. "I thought I'd take Mona."

"I'll meet you at the farm later." He lays an exaggerated frown on me. "Before midnight?"

"I'll see what I can do." Looking past him, I lower my voice. "You're not smitten with me, are you?"

"To put it mildly."

We're both pressed for time. Too busy to linger. Too stressed to indulge in silly banter. I savor the moment anyway.

"See you later," he says, and then he's gone.

CHAPTER 6

Blue Lake Tap and Brewery is located on Washington Street just south of downtown in Millersburg. The two-story brick building has been capably transformed from 1950s ugly to twenty-first-century shabby chic. As I pull into the lot at the rear, the clock on my dash tells me it's 8:02 P.M. I think of the presser that began two minutes ago and remind myself that Mike Rasmussen is a hell of a lot better at public relations than me.

The parking lot is jammed with cars and SUVs. Most are newer models. No junkers here at the Blue Lake Tap and Brewery.

"That's his vehicle there." Next to me, Mona points. "Plate's a match."

The sporty BMW coupe looks as if it was just driven off the showroom floor and is parked nose-in nearest the back door. A sign artfully painted onto the weathered brick proclaims the spot belongs to the HEAD BREWMASTER.

I pull around to the side lot, which is also full, and end up parking in the gravel just off the alley. "Parking is certainly at a premium."

"This place has some of the best beer in the state of Ohio."

I shoot her a sideways glance. "Good to know I have the resident expert to keep me up to speed."

She grins and we take the alley around to the front of the building. The double doors are refurbished antiques of carved wood and beveled glass. We go through and are met with a funky Black Keys number, the enticing aroma of bar food, the din of conversation, and the clinking of dishes. To my right, the bar is jammed with early-evening revelers, mostly thirty-something men, watching the Guardians trounce the Royals. Behind the bar, three huge copper fermentation vats gleam beneath the lights, adding a hip microbrewery vibe. To my left, a dozen bistro tables are packed with patrons, couples and families alike. The tabletops are crowded with plates of food, beer mugs, and sweating glasses.

A young female server takes an order at one of the tables. Another balances a tray the size of a tire as she dances through the throng. The two bartenders behind the bar are in motion, too, but not as frenetic, so I head that way.

"Smells good," Mona mutters.

"Food any good?" I ask.

"Fair to middling, but they've got a dynamite IPA."

I reach the bar and sidle over to the nearest bartender, who's chatting with a couple sampling a flight of beer. I show the bartender my badge.

Grinning, he grips his chest as if in the throes of a heart attack. "Patrons tell me our beer is so good it should be illegal. I thought they were kidding!"

I laugh, give him a moment to enjoy his joke. "I'm looking for Carter Brooks. Is he here?"

"Yeah, he's around. Back in the office, I think." Curiosity flickers in his eyes as he snaps up a glass and fills it from the tap. "Want me to call him for you?"

"Sure."

Nodding, he slides an iPhone from his pocket and thumbs in a speed dial. "A couple of cops are out here asking to see you." His face remains impassive; then he laughs. "I'll let her know."

He drops the cell into his pocket and smiles at me. "He'll be out in a sec."

The bartender serves us two ice waters with a wedge of lime. I've just taken my first sip when the double doors leading to the kitchen swing open. I recognize Brooks immediately. He's six four. Two hundred pounds. Attractive with dark brown hair, a full beard, and puppy-dog eyes.

"Ron says you're looking for me?" he says as he approaches, mouthing a thank-you to his bartender.

I show him my badge and extend my hand for a shake. "If you've got a few minutes, I'd like to ask you some questions about Samuel Yutzy."

His expression goes sober. "Jeez. I just saw on the news that he was killed. That's crazy." His eyes flick to Mona and back to me. "You guys catch the guy who did it?"

"We're working on it."

"Well, I've got a few minutes. Is my office okay?"

"Perfect," I tell him.

He turns and we follow. He takes us through the crowd, greeting patrons, slapping backs, unbothered by the curious looks of people wondering why the police are following him to his office. We go through the swinging doors, past a high-tech kitchen of stainless steel and butcherblock, and two cooks clad in white aprons. He takes us down a short hall past a private restroom. His office is as sleek and shabby-chic as the rest of the place.

"Come on in." He motions to a couple of sled chairs, then settles into a high-back leather chair at the desk.

The wall behind him is antique brick and holds a dozen or so plaques, framed certificates, and periodical cuttings that proclaim Blue Lake Tap and Brewery to be one of OHIO'S MOST LOVED MICROBREWERIES, the BEST IPA OF 2022, and BEST CRAFT BEER OF 2023.

"Nice place you've got here." I eye the plaques. "You've won a lot of awards."

His chest visibly swells. "Thanks. It's been a tough haul. Didn't turn a profit for over a year. So I'm pretty proud." Smiling, he pats his stomach. "I'm a lover of craft beer so it's a labor of love." His demeanor turns pensive. "But then you're not here to talk about beer."

"How well did you know Samuel?" I begin.

"I met him about six months ago, I guess. He did some work for me. Two-week job."

"How did you meet?"

"I'm a member of the country club over in Painters Mill."

"The Club at Paint Creek?" I ask.

He nods. "I was there one afternoon for a round of golf. I was admiring the landscaping, mainly because I was looking for someone to landscape my house. I asked the manager about it and he gave me the number for Samuel's company." He shrugs. "I called him, met with him, liked him, and hired him on the spot. The guy did great work. Worked his ass off. Finished the job in record time."

Hefting a sigh, he leans back in the chair. "Then we got that big storm and my basement flooded. I guess that's why you're here."

"How serious was the dispute between you and Mr. Yutzy?" I say.

His eyes widen. "You don't think I had anything to do with . . ." He laughs, but it's a forced, uncomfortable sound. "Look, I was just an unhappy customer. All I wanted was a refund for some of the work he did."

"Fifteen thousand dollars is a lot of money."

He frowns at me. "Do I need a lawyer?" His eyes flick from me to Mona and back to me. "Am I a suspect or something?"

"Hiring a lawyer is certainly your prerogative," I say easily. "We're talking to everyone who was close to or did business with Mr. Yutzy. Your name came up because of the dispute, so we're here to get your side of the story."

"My side of the story, huh?" He leans back in the chair and folds his arms across his chest. "Or maybe you're here because I screwed up and got myself arrested on some dumb charge last year."

Mona smiles. "Eighty-two in a thirty-five?"

Her comment seems to break the ice. He offers her a self-deprecating smile. "I know. Dumb. But in my defense, it was a new vehicle and boy was she nice. I wanted to see how she performed."

"Lucky for you the weapon charge was dropped," I say.

He shakes his head. "You probably already know this, but there's been a spate of robberies in the area in the last few months. I leave alone, late at night, and sometimes I carry large amounts of cash. I'd been planning on getting my concealed-carry license for some time. I just hadn't gotten around to it."

"Understood." I glance down at my notes. "Can you run me through the dispute?"

"I hired him in April. Samuel finished the work in about two weeks and, believe me, it looked great. He planted a bunch of trees. Some shrubs. Added the walkway with pavers. I paid him and we parted ways. Everyone was happy." He grimaces. "Until we got that big rain a month later. To make a long story short, the walkway trapped all that water against the house. It poured in through the window wells and flooded my basement. I had a ton of damage. Not just structural stuff, but my office equipment."

He shakes his head as if the memory pains him. "At that point, I had a landscaping engineer come out and he told me a drain should have been installed between the walkway and the house. I contacted Samuel and told him I wanted my money back and compensation for the damage.

Turns out, he didn't have insurance and balked. Shortly thereafter, he stopped returning my calls and the situation went downhill from there."

"Do you think Samuel misrepresented his abilities?" I ask.

"Not really. He had a good reputation. I'd checked his references. He showed me photos of his work. I figured if he could handle a job as large as the country club, he could damn well handle my humble abode." He thinks about that a moment. "He screwed up, but in his defense I think Samuel was an honest guy. I think he just got in over his head with the grading. He didn't realize he needed to install the drain." He shrugs. "To tell you the truth, I'd have settled for less than the fifteen. It was sort of an ask-for-a-lot-get-a-little strategy."

I jot the highlights in my notebook. "Did you argue with Mr. Yutzy?"

"A few times," he admits. "Over the phone mostly. I mean, it was a mess."

"Were there any threats made?" I ask. "Anything like that?"

"I threatened to sue him." He huffs. "Guess that's not going to work out."

"When's the last time you saw Samuel?" I ask.

"Probably been a month or so," he says.

"Where were you Thursday morning?"

"Got up around seven A.M. Had a cup of coffee. And came directly here."

"What about Wednesday evening?"

Impatience flares in his eyes, but he quashes it quickly. "I was here, at the brewery. Last man out the door. Like always."

"Can anyone substantiate that?"

A flash of anger this time, as if he's chafed because I've used up my quota of time and questions. He looks away, purses his lips. "The bartender left at two A.M. I left around two thirty."

"Where did you go after you left here?"

"I was beat. Went home."

"Is there someone who can vouch for that?"

"My cat, but he's not much of a conversationalist."

I don't smile. "Mr. Brooks, do you know if Samuel Yutzy was having any problems with anyone else?"

He shakes his head. "I never heard anything negative about him. Sure, we had that dispute. It happens. People screw up; they make mistakes. It was unpleasant." He turns pensive. "To tell you the truth, Chief Burkholder, Samuel was a stand-up guy. He had that Amish way about him, you know? He was quiet. Quick to smile. Didn't cuss or act like a fool. I still can't believe someone murdered a guy like that. Craziest damn thing I ever heard."

• • •

"What do you think?"

I glance over at Mona as I back out of my parking space. "I think Mr. Brooks is under the impression that his charm supersedes any suspicions a female LEO might have about his relationship with Samuel Yutzy."

"You think he's lying about something?"

"Probably not, but for my own peace of mind, I'd like to keep him simmering on a front burner for now."

I call Skid as I pull onto the highway. "Where you at?"

"Just talked to the neighbor on the south side of the tree nursery."

"Anything?"

"Nothing."

"Mona and I are on our way back to the station," I tell him. "Meet me there in twenty minutes and we'll make a run down to The Cheetah Lounge."

An extra beat of silence and then, "Roger that."

CHAPTER 7

The Cheetah Lounge is located in a derelict industrial area on the south side of New Philadelphia. There's an auto body shop to the south and what looks like some sort of vacant warehouse on the north side.

"Parking's in the rear," Skid says helpfully.

I glance over at him, wondering if he realizes that knowing the best place to park at a topless club is nothing to write home about. "Looks like a full house."

"Yeah, Fridays are busy." He clears his throat. "So I'm told."

"Parking lot" is a loose term for half an acre of dirt that's been pounded to dust and coated with a scant sprinkling of crushed limestone. I shouldn't be surprised by the number of vehicles, but I am. There's no place to park in the lot, so I opt for the grass.

"Judging from the clothes our mystery woman was wearing, do you think it's safe to assume she works here?" I ask as I reach for the door handle.

We get out and he looks at me over the hood of the Explorer. "I don't recall seeing her." His expression becomes pinched; it takes me a second to realize he's uncomfortable. "But that uh . . . top she was wearing seems about right."

In the back of my mind, I remind myself that even if we find her here tonight, she may not be able to help us. Quite possibly Samuel Yutzy simply snapped a photo of one of the dancers and that was the end of it.

"Well, we're here," I say as I start toward the club. "May as well ask around. Maybe she's here or someone might know who she is."

Skid falls into step beside me. "Chief?"

I glance over at him.

"Look, I just want you to know . . . I don't come here . . . regularly. I mean, it was just a few times with a friend of mine. He was going through a tough time. A divorce. And I've never come in uniform."

"I appreciate that," I say. "And just so you know . . . what you do on your off time isn't my business."

"I wanted to clear the air." He offers a cockeyed grin. "Defend my reputation."

"Put it this way, Skid. If we come away with some good information tonight, your reputation is officially salvaged."

I take in our surroundings as we cross the lot. Behind us, just off the parking area, an RV is hitched to a Ford dually. The windows glow with light and I wonder why it's there and who's inside. Beyond the RV, a dark wall of trees offers a false sense of seclusion. At the edge of the lot, a metal building is surrounded by a six-foot-tall chain-link fence topped with triple strands of barbed wire. The club is housed in a low-slung building with barn-red siding. We round the side and take the sidewalk toward the front entrance. Two windows face the street; the glass has been painted black, presumably for privacy or to block the light or both. An overhang shelters the sidewalk to protect patrons from inclement weather when there's a line.

String lights blink in a cacophony of purple and red. A lighted letter sign proclaims that PINK PANTY PUNCH IS ONLY $4 ON FRIDAY NITE! The front door swings open and bangs against the wall. A denim-clad man, his arm draped over the shoulders of a pretty brunette, stumbles down the steps. I make eye contact with the man as they pass.

I hear a muttered, "Fuckin' cops."

Skid and I exchange a smile of solidarity and go through the door.

The thunderous drum of some chainsaw-rock number I don't recognize boxes my ears when we enter. I'm not exactly sure what I was expecting. A dive teeming with drunken men and scantily clad women, the smells of spilled beer and drugstore cologne hovering above sweaty bodies. The sight that accosts me is anything but. While the exterior of The Cheetah Lounge conjures a bad-side-of-town vibe, the interior speaks of uptown panache. A performance hall–like stage with a lighted floor, spotlights dangling from above, and shimmering curtains signify the front of the room. There's a forestage area and a mirrored backdrop. Despite the pomp of the stage, the dancer making use of it is the star of the show. She's about twenty-five years old and clad in a shimmering thong. Purple light rains down on flawless skin slicked with oil, dark tattoos contrasting against pale flesh, the whole of her wrapped around a gleaming chrome dance pole.

I'm aware of Skid's head turned in her direction, and I actually feel his brain cells scatter to the wind.

The place is crowded, mostly with men, but there are a few couples. Half a dozen sleek booths line the wall to my right. A smattering of tables and chairs are situated just off the stage. To my left, an antique-looking bar of carved wood and black marble lines the length of the wall. Beveled-glass shelves hold dozens of bottles of liquor, including the top-shelf stuff. The bartender's back is to us. White shirt. Black slacks. A bow tie. I see him looking at me in the mirror, and he frowns.

Tilting my head toward Skid, I start toward the bar. "Do you know the bartender?"

"No, ma'am." Skid falls into step beside me, his eyes on the man in question. "Doesn't look like the friendly type."

I'm aware of curious eyes taking in our uniforms as we weave through the crowd. A female server wearing a sequin bikini strides toward us, a tray expertly hoisted over her shoulder. She beams a grin and blows both of us a kiss as she passes.

Every barstool is occupied, so I sidle to the end of the bar where the barkeep finger-punches something into a vintage cash register. I guess him to be about forty years old. In-vogue stubble. Expensive haircut. Physically fit. Good at what he does.

"Hi." I hold up my shield. "Do you have a minute?"

He is in constant motion and side-eyes me as he glides over to one of his customers. I wait while he pours Patrón into frozen glasses. He moves with the grace of a dancer as he tops off another glass and then sidles back to Skid and me. "Is it okay if we talk while I work?"

"If I can keep up," I say.

That earns me a grin. Swiping two frozen mugs from a shelf beneath the bar, he thrusts them beneath the keg, and carries both to a man at the other end of the bar.

He comes back to the cash register, so I pull the photo of the mystery woman from my pocket and show it to him. "Have you ever seen this woman?"

His eyes flick to the photo as he punches keys on the cash register. I watch for some sign of recognition, but he gives me nothing. "Never seen her before." He eyes his customers at the bar as he speaks.

"Are you sure?" I offer the photo again. "I was told she works here."

"I'm only here three nights a week." He shrugs. "Maybe check with the other bartender?"

I have the photo of Samuel Yutzy at the ready. "What about him?"

The bartender's eyes widen at the sight and for the first time he gives me his undivided attention. "He's the dude got beheaded over in Painters Mill?"

I nod. "How did you hear about that?"

"Are you kidding? Everyone and their grandma's talking about it. Been all over the news this evening."

"Did he ever come in here?" Skid speaks up for the first time.

"Not that I recall." His eyes narrow as he studies the photo. "I don't know. He's familiar, but I can't tell you if I ever seen him here." He looks at Skid and laughs. "Seen you a time or two, though."

Skid stares back at him, deadpan.

Unaffected, the bartender swivels his head, spots two patrons waiting for drinks at the end of the bar. "Look, I gotta get back to work."

"Is the manager here?" I ask.

"He's around here somewhere." He turns his back, waving us off. "Make yourselves at home."

I look at Skid. "So much for fruitful."

"Mr. Information in the flesh."

"Might be smarter to cut to the chase if we can." Tugging out my cell, I dial Dispatch. "See if you can dig up the name of the person who owns The Cheetah Lounge Gentleman's Club in New Philly."

"I'll get right on it."

"While you're at it, cruise out to their social media accounts and dig around. See if anything interesting pops."

"Are you looking for something in particular?"

"A mention or photo of the mystery woman for starters. Any mention or photo of Samuel Yutzy or Aaron Shetler. Contact info for management."

"You got it."

I drop my phone back in my pocket. Skid is standing at the bar, using the mirror to watch the dancer onstage. "Any idea where the office is?" I ask.

He shakes his head. "You want me to take a look around?"

"Let's split up and circle around," I tell him. "Meet you back here in ten minutes."

He gives me a salute and starts toward the front of the room. I go in the opposite direction, toward the rear. I'm keenly aware of my surroundings, the people I pass, and the vague air of standoffishness that comes back at me.

Over the years I've learned there are two types of bars. First is the kind in which the patrons—their tongues loosened by alcohol—flock over to talk to you, mainly because they're bored or nosy and want to be part of the excitement. The second kind of bar is the one where no patron will be caught dead talking to a cop. The patrons who do only do so to mislead. The few who are left hit the exits as if the place is on fire. The Cheetah Lounge falls into the latter category.

A lighted RESTROOMS sign leads me to a hall in the back of the main room. At the end of the hall, I see an exterior door with a push bar and lighted red EXIT sign. On my right, two interior doors are marked WOMEN and MEN. A third door, to my left, is marked OFFICE. A steady flow of patrons come and go from the restrooms. I wait for a lull, sidle over to the OFFICE door, and knock. I wait a few beats and try the knob. Locked.

I turn and nearly run into a chest the size of a tank. "Can I help you?"

The man with the tanklike chest is standing a scant foot away, looking down at me. I guess him to be about six four, two hundred and fifty pounds. He's wearing a black T-shirt with the logo of the club emblazoned front and center. Bouncer, I realize. Forty years old. Silver-black hair combed straight back, a stylish goatee, gold earring, and a mouth pulled into an I-caught-you smile.

Though I'm wearing my uniform, I pull out my shield. "I'm looking for the manager."

Eyes the color of a winter sky flick down the front of me. "You putting in an application?"

"You're a funny guy, aren't you?"

"Usually." His mouth twists into a smile. "Jokes are falling flat tonight, I guess. No pun."

I don't smile. "Where's the manager?"

"I believe he left to grab a bite to eat."

"What's his name?"

"I think I'll let him tell you that."

I nod, take a moment to look around. "Who owns this place?"

"No idea."

"Do you work here?"

"Sometimes," he says.

Knowing he's not going to be any help, I pull the photo of the mystery woman from my pocket. "I'm looking for her," I say. "Do you know who she is? Have you seen her around?"

He keeps his eyes level on mine, not bothering to look at the photo. "Nope."

I show him the photo of Samuel Yutzy. "What about this guy?"

Before he can answer, I catch sight of Skid approaching, his expression taut with annoyance. The man behind him is the size of a sumo wrestler, dressed similarly to the man I'm speaking to, and I wonder if we're about to get bounced out.

"If you're not going to order something to eat or drink," Sumo Guy says, "I'm going to have to ask you to leave. Nothing personal, but those are the house rules."

"We're looking for the manager," I say.

"Can't help you," Sumo tells me.

"Who's in charge?" Skid asks.

"My wife, usually." One side of his mouth hikes, snarl or smile, I can't discern.

I look at Skid. "I didn't realize this place was a comedy club."

"I hear they're not that funny," Skid says.

Sumo loses his smile. "Maybe you and Barney Fife will have better luck if you call in the morning and make an appointment."

"One more quick question." I show him the photo of Samuel Yutzy. "Have you seen him here at the club?" I ask. "Do you recognize him?"

Both men look at the photo, but neither of them responds. They move closer to me, crowding me. I don't give up any space.

Taking my time, I tuck the photo into my pocket. "Appreciate the help," I say, and we start toward the door.

• • •

"Well, that went south pretty quick," Skid mutters.

I've just put the Explorer in gear when I catch sight of a figure coming toward us. Female. Long hair. Skinny pants. High heels. High-neck halter top. "Two o'clock," I say to Skid.

He glances right. "Yep."

I put the Explorer in park, watch as she crosses in front of my vehicle, and I roll down my window. "Can I help you?"

The woman is young. Barely into her twenties. Dark hair. Pretty. A tattoo of a crown on her left shoulder. "I hear you're asking about Cassidy." She whispers the words as if not wanting anyone to overhear what she's telling us.

"Do you know her?" I fish the photo out of my pocket and show it to her.

"I seen her around."

"What's her last name?"

"No one uses their last name around here."

"She works here?" I ask. "As a dancer?"

She nods. "Quit a few days ago. Didn't say a word to anyone."

I don't miss the way she keeps looking over her shoulder toward the club, as if she doesn't want to be seen talking to us. Because she's on the clock? Or something else?

"Do you know where I can find her?" I ask.

"No clue." She bites her lip. "But I'm worried about her."

"Why are you worried?"

She hesitates, considers not answering, and then says, "She wouldn't have left without telling me."

"What do you think happened?"

"I don't know."

I have the photo of Samuel Yutzy at the ready. "You ever seen him?"

She takes a quick glance at the photo, looks toward the club again. "He used to come here. He was . . . nice. Tipped good."

"Did you ever see them together?" I ask.

"I think they were an item for a while."

My interest surges. "They were involved?"

Her head swivels for another look over her shoulder. No one there and she seems to relax. "Cassidy was crazy about him." She laughs as if the memory amuses her. "We called them the odd couple. I mean, she's this beautiful wild child and he was like this wholesome Amish dude that just fell off the turnip truck."

"Do you have any idea where I can find her?"

"No."

"Do you know why she quit?"

"She never said a word to any of us." Grimacing, she shakes her head. "Just . . . left. Didn't even say goodbye."

"Was that unusual?"

"We worked together for almost three months. I thought we were friends." She shrugs. "I tried texting her a couple times, but she didn't respond. Figured she just moved on."

Skid leans forward from his place in the passenger seat to make eye contact with her. "Did Yutzy ever have any problems with anyone here that you know of?"

"I didn't really know him that well." But she seems to consider the question. "The only thing I know for certain about him is that he was good to her and it was about damn time someone treated her well."

"Angelica!"

She does a half turn and gasps. "Shit."

I follow her stare to see Sumo Guy standing next to the door, scowling at us, his arms crossed at his chest.

"I gotta go," she hisses.

Covertly, I pass her my card. "We're looking for Cassidy. If you think of anything else, call me. Day or night."

"Whatever." She takes the card without looking at it and then she's gone.

CHAPTER 8

When you're a cop and working on a case, especially a homicide, information is the name of the game. It is the be-all and end-all. The alpha and omega. Without it, you will flounder, your case will go cold, and, in the end, you won't solve a damn thing.

If information is king, time is queen. During the crucial first hours of a case, there are hundreds of things that must be done concurrently. There are witnesses to interview. There is evidence to be protected, gathered, analyzed, and interpreted. There's grunt work galore. And no matter how driven an investigator, there's never enough time to get everything done or enough manpower with which to do it.

It's ten P.M. when I drop Skid at the police station with instructions to dig up everything he can find on Cassidy, our mystery woman. I'm sitting in the Explorer checking text messages when I notice the missed call and follow-up text from Glock.

Unable to locate Shetler.

I hit the speed dial for him as I pull out of my parking space. "Tell me about Shetler."

"His employer hasn't seen him for two days," Glock tells me. "According to his boss, the guy has never missed a day of work. Shetler didn't call in."

"You checked his residence?"

"First thing. No one there. Place is secure. Neighbor says he hasn't seen Shetler in a couple days."

A low-grade alarm begins to trill in the back of my brain. "It would be nice to take a look inside his residence." I look at the clock and sigh. "Too late to get a warrant tonight."

"I hear Judge Siebenthaler is an early riser," he says. "Do you want me to write up an affidavit?"

"Hand-deliver first thing in the morning?"

"You got it."

• • •

I'm not sure what to think about Aaron Shetler being momentarily missing in action. According to Samuel Yutzy's parents, the two young men were friends. Despite Yutzy engaging in some practices contrary to his Amish upbringing, Shetler had remained loyal. With Samuel Yutzy dead and his best friend unaccounted for, should I be concerned about Shetler's well-being? Or should I be looking for him in earnest because he may have done something horrific and gone on the run?

It's too late to rouse Aaron Shetler's parents from their beds with questions about their son. As I make the turn onto the township road, I know that's exactly what I'm going to do. In light of the circumstances, an after-hours visit is warranted.

"Winning hearts and minds one sleepless night at a time," I mutter as I head out of town.

The Shetler chicken farm is in a remote area six miles east of Painters Mill. Without streetlamps or porch lights, this part of the county is ink black. My headlights bore through thick darkness as I pull into a lane that's more dirt than gravel. I catch a glimpse of a low-slung white building to my right. A dusting of feathers covers the ground outside the massive fan at the side door. A small frame house appears dead ahead. I park in the gravel area nearest the front door and take the sidewalk to the porch.

Using the heel of my hand, I knock. Twice. Several minutes pass before I hear footsteps on the other side of the door.

"Who's there?"

The door swings open and Ellen Shetler, dressed in a plain white nightgown, thrusts a lantern at me, squinting. "My goodness, what's all the racket about this time of night?"

"Mrs. Shetler." I hold out my badge to let her know this is an official visit. "I'm sorry to bother you so late."

"What's going on?" She looks past me, her expression more worried than curious. "Is everything okay?"

"I'd like to talk to you about your son Aaron." I extend my hand to her and we exchange a quick shake. "Is he here?"

"Of course he's not here." She cocks her head. "Is he in some kind of trouble?"

"Do you know where he is?" I ask. "Where I might find him?"

"Home, I reckon." I can tell by the way she's looking at me that she knows I've already checked.

"When's the last time you talked to him?"

"Been two or three weeks, I guess."

"Seems like a long time," I say. "Is that unusual?"

"Well, a little, I guess. But he works a lot, you know. Keeps busy."

The sound of footfalls on the steps draws my attention. I look past her and see her husband coming down the stairs, fully dressed, lantern in hand, his eyes on me. "*Was der schinner is letz?*" he snaps. What in the world is wrong?

"I'm sorry to bother you so late, Mr. Shetler," I say.

Looking from me to his wife, he strides toward us. "Is there a problem?"

"I'd like to talk to you about your son," I say. "Can I come in?"

The couple exchange a look. In the instant their eyes connect, I get the impression that they're not completely surprised and that this moment is something they've expected—and dreaded—for some time.

"*Ich zayl macha kaffi,*" Ellen says, and starts toward the kitchen. I'll make coffee.

A few minutes later we're seated at the kitchen table. A propane floor lamp hisses from its place in the corner and throws off a generous amount of light. The window is open, but the house is stuffy and warm and I can smell the ammonia stench of the chicken operation outside.

"Is Aaron in trouble?" Doyle asks.

"No, but I'm concerned. No one has been able to locate him."

Tightening his mouth, he looks down at the coffee in front of him and shakes his head. "Like she just told you, we ain't seen him for a time."

"Two weeks ago?" I ask.

He looks at his wife, then back to me.

"Three weeks," Ellen amends.

They fall silent, neither of them making eye contact with me. *Something not quite right,* a little voice whispers in my ear, so I keep going.

"He hasn't been at work for two days," I say. "He didn't call in."

The couple share another look. They didn't know, I realize, and for the first time since I arrived, they look alarmed.

"Are you sure?" Ellen asks.

"Aaron's never missed a day of work," Doyle says.

"Mr. and Mrs. Shetler, Samuel Yutzy was found dead this morning," I tell them. "I don't have the official ruling yet from the coroner, but I believe he was murdered."

"We heard." Doyle looks down at the tabletop. *"Mein Gott."*

"Most awful thing anyone can imagine." Ellen shakes her head. "Poor Leona."

"I'm told Aaron and Samuel were close," I say.

The woman's face contorts as if she's grappling with some acute physical pain. "Those two boys have been best friends since they were little."

"Aaron's been helping Samuel with that tree-planting business of his," Doyle tells me.

"Aaron was working for Samuel?" I ask.

"On and off," Doyle says. "Aaron puts in a full week at the farm store, you know. Helps Samuel when he can. On his days off mostly."

"Have there been any problems between the two of them?" I ask. "Any disagreements? Over money? The business? A woman? Anything you can think of?"

"Not those two," Doyle says adamantly. "They got along like brothers. Never seen them argue about anything. Not once in all the years they've been friends."

"Do either of you have any idea where I might find Aaron? Is there someone he visits? A place where he goes for leisure? Fishing or hunting?"

Doyle's eyes skate away from mine. "I don't know where he is." He concentrates a little too hard on picking up his coffee cup and sipping. "Hard telling these days." Ellen sets her hand on her husband's arm as if to shush him, but he shakes it off. "Chief Burkholder, we had a falling-out with Aaron a few weeks back," she says. "He hasn't come around since."

"What was the falling-out about?" I ask.

The man's eyes hit the floor. I wait a beat, but no one responds, so I turn my attention to his wife. "Mrs. Shetler?"

She presses her hand to her mouth, looks at me over the tops of fingers, her face anguished. "I can't."

Impatience flares, but I curb it, turn my attention to her husband. "In light of what happened to Samuel, I think we may have reason to be concerned about Aaron. I need to find him and make sure he's okay."

Doyle raises his gaze to mine, holds it. "I told him not to come around anymore."

"Why?" I ask.

Ellen drops her hand away from her face. "We thought he was a bad influence on the children. They're younger, you know. Innocent."

"How was he a bad influence?" I ask.

The couple look at each other again. It's obvious that whatever problem they're having with their son, they don't want to discuss it.

After a moment, Doyle sighs. "There have been some changes in the boy over the last few months," he says. "We don't know what got into him."

"What kind of changes?" I ask.

"He's a good boy," Ellen puts in.

Doyle waves her off. "Wearing all them fancy clothes. Driving that car of his. Hanging out with all them slick *Englischers.*"

"What *Englischers*?" I sit up straighter. "Give me a name."

"Don't know their names," he snaps. "Don't care to know."

I see anger, guilt, and shame on his face. A too-long moment of silence ensues. I'm about to give them another push when Ellen puts her hand on her husband's shoulder, then turns her attention to me. "We've had some . . . tax problems last couple of years," she says. "You know, with the farm. We owed, but we didn't have the money to pay."

"Ain't nothing we can't handle on our own," Doyle grumbles.

She grimaces at her husband. "We're managing, but . . . last time Aaron was here, he tried giving us a big bundle of cash money. He said we should take it, use it to pay off the taxes, and be thankful for it."

"Don't know where he came into that kind of cash," Doyle adds. "Don't know what he had to do to get it. The boy works at the farm store and he don't make that much. I wanted no part of that kind of handout."

The Amish woman sighs her husband's name. "We didn't take the money."

Doyle shakes his head. "When he argued with me, I told him to leave. You know what he had the gall to do?" The muscles in his jaw tighten as if he's grinding his teeth. "He gave a stack of twenty-dollar bills to William, our sixteen-year-old."

"How much money are we talking about?" I ask.

Doyle shakes his head fervidly. "Didn't count it. Didn't need to know how much. I know what dirty money looks like so I took it out to the trash pit and burned it."

"Did Aaron say where he got the money?" I ask.

"No," the Amish man replies. "And we didn't ask."

"Mr. and Mrs. Shetler, did Aaron have any problems or disagreements with anyone that you know of? Friends or coworkers? Amish or English?"

Ellen shakes her head. "Never heard of such a thing."

"Does he have a girlfriend?"

"Not that we know of."

"Is there anyone else Aaron is close to? Someone I can talk to about him?"

"He ran around with the Stoltzfoos boy for a time," Ellen says. "Haven't seen him around in a while, though."

"First name?"

"Joseph," Doyle tells me. "Good kid. Good family. Hard worker. He was friendly with Samuel, too."

I write down the name. "You said Joseph hasn't come around for a while," I say. "Was there some kind of falling-out?"

"They just sort of drifted apart, I think," Ellen says.

I pull out the photo of Cassidy and show it to them. "Have you ever seen this woman?" I ask. "With Aaron or Samuel? Around town?"

Both heads shake in unison.

"Is there anything at all you can tell me about any of the English people Aaron was hanging out with?" I ask.

"Never asked about them," Doyle says. "Aaron never volunteered any information."

The Amish man sighs tiredly. "To tell you the truth, Chief Burkholder, we really didn't want to know."

• • •

I'm twenty minutes from home, pondering my conversation with the Shetlers, when the call comes in. **HOLMES COUNTY CORONER** pops up on the screen and I hit answer. "Hey, Doc."

"I know it's late," Doc Coblentz begins. "In light of the circumstances, I figured you'd still be working."

"It's a scary thing when the coroner knows you so well."

He chuckles. "I'm here at the morgue with the forensic pathologist, Kate. The autopsy is scheduled for first thing in the morning. We've gotten the evidence couriered and the victim cleaned up. There's not much information to glean at this point, but we may be able to answer a few topical questions if you'd like to come by before we call it a day."

The morgue is the last place I want to be, especially when it's late and I want nothing more than a shower, a meal, and a couple of hours of uninterrupted sleep. Of course, those trivial human essentials will have to wait. I'm going to subject myself to seeing what's left of a young Amish man whose life ended long before it should have. My brain will ponder how in the name of God someone could do such a thing to another human being. I'm going to take that first step toward knowing Samuel Yutzy. I'll know firsthand the violence he endured. The degradations done to him after he was killed. All in the hope that I'll walk away with some smidgen of information that will set me on track to finding the person responsible.

"I'll be there in ten minutes," I tell the doc, and disconnect.

CHAPTER 9

I don't think about my destination during the drive to Pomerene Hospital. I call Dispatch on the way and schedule a briefing for tomorrow, requesting a representative from the Ohio State Police attend as well as someone from the Holmes County Sheriff's Office since we'll likely be forming a task force. I also put out a BOLO for Aaron Shetler.

The morgue is located in the basement of the hospital. My mood darkens as I take the elevator down. Usually, Doc Coblentz's assistant, Carmen, is there to greet me, but it's after hours and reception is deserted. I go through the door to the administrative section, and I'm greeted by an old Neil Young rocker that's turned up a tad too loud. Doc Coblentz—an improbable lover of classic rock and roll—is standing in his office doorway, looking at me. He's dressed in blue scrubs with a matching blue head covering and his iconic tie-dyed Crocs. Across from him, a middle-aged woman clad in Scooby-Doo scrubs and sneakers scrolls through her cell phone.

"You have good timing," Doc says by way of greeting.

"That's the first time anyone has ever said that to this chronically late chief of police."

The woman looks up from her cell phone and laughs good-naturedly. She's got watchful eyes, close-cropped gray hair, and black caterpillar brows.

Doc extends his hand when I reach them and we shake. "This is Dr. Matrone from Franklin County."

I turn my attention to the woman and introduce myself.

"Frederika," she says. "Everyone calls me Ricky."

"She just got in from Columbus a little while ago," Doc says. "Hence my comment about timing."

"We're glad you're here," I tell her.

"Ricky won't claim the title," Doc says, "but she's one of the best forensic pathologists in the country."

"Phooey." The woman waves away the statement, giving me a thoughtful once-over. "So, you're the woman brave enough to marry John Tomasetti."

I can't help it; I grin. "Guilty as charged."

She grins back. "He sure as hell won't claim the title, and there are probably a few people out there who might argue the point, but he's a good man."

Despite the reason for my being here, the statement warms me. "He is."

"Tomasetti's the one who called me, by the way." Ricky sobers. "I do quite a bit of work for BCI. Doc was just filling me in on the case."

I look at the coroner. "Anything new you can share?"

"Some." He grimaces. "Suit up and we'll take a look."

Though the morgue is kept at a cool sixty-two degrees, I'm sweating beneath my uniform as I slip a paper gown on over my shirt. Next come the head covering, mask, and shoe covers. I emerge from the alcove to find Dr. Matrone and Doc Coblentz waiting outside the double doors that will take us to the medical side of the facility.

I'm glad for the mask as I stride toward them; tension knots the muscles at the back of my neck and I'm sure my face shows it. The *swish-swish* of paper seems unduly loud in the silence of the corridor as we go through the doors. We pass a yellow-and-black biohazard sign and a plaque that reads MORGUE AUTHORIZED PERSONNEL. Doc pushes open one of the doors to the autopsy suite and the three of us enter.

The smells of formalin, antiseptic, and the darker undertones of death offend my olfactory nerves. The room is encased in floor-to-ceiling subway tile. I'm aware of my heart beating too fast, the slow boil of adrenaline in my gut, as we approach the stainless-steel gurney. Doc Coblentz's technical assistant is standing at the counter. He glances at us over his shoulder, and raises his hand in greeting.

"Hey, Chief Burkholder."

I don't trust my voice so I settle for a nod. My attention is already riveted to the gurney. Even from a distance, I can plainly see that the remains we're about to view aren't in the form of a human body, but arranged in mounds beneath a sterile paper sheet that's dotted with watery pink spots of fluid that have leaked through.

"The clothing was sent to the BCI lab in London, Ohio, for processing," Doc Coblentz begins. "We've X-rayed the torso and various appendages and taken a CT scan of the skull. Blood and urine samples were taken for DNA and toxicology, and of course fingerprints, which have been sent to AFIS. We've got dental imprints, too. We took anal swabs to check for sexual assault."

"The entire body was recovered?" I ask.

"I believe we got everything." Doc looks over his shoulder at his assistant. "Jared, what time was the last piece logged in?"

The young man picks up an electronic pad and scrolls. "Seventeen oh two," he replies.

"We've organized the remains in anatomical form and cleaned up what we could for visual examination. First thing in the morning, Dr. Matrone and I will perform the Y-incision examination and take a look at the thoracic and abdominal cavities. We'll also perform the coronal incision to open and examine the cranial cavity."

Doc reaches the gurney first and goes around to the other side. "This is what we've found so far."

Carefully, he peels down the sheet. I thought I was prepared to see what's left of Samuel Yutzy. I'm not. No one can ever be ready to see the dismembered parts of a human body. Each piece has been painstakingly labeled and then placed on the gurney in the approximate location of where it would have been had the body been intact. Head at the top. Shoulders. Upper arms. Forearms. The abdomen is the color of wax, the flesh covered with a layer of thin black hair. Same with the genitals. The thighs and calves.

Dear God in heaven . . .

"There are eleven excised body parts . . ." Doc Coblentz's voice fades to babel as my brain is besieged by the dreadful sight. The flesh is waxy and shockingly pale. The cuts are primitive and jagged and brownish-red in color. I see tissue I can't readily identify. The pink protrusion of bones and muscle and tendons. A face that's barely recognizable. I'm aware of the smell of death all around. Saliva pools in my mouth. I swallow carefully, hoping my stomach holds.

"Chief?"

I snap my gaze to Doc's. His eyes are sharp on mine above his mask and through the goggles he's wearing. I'm not sure what he said or how many times he said it.

"I'm fine," I say, my voice sounding snappish. "Keep going."

He eyes me a moment longer, then returns his attention to the body. “As you can see,” he says, “the decedent was dismembered. The dismemberment was performed postmortem. The cutting was primitive. We’ll know more after the autopsy.”

A hundred questions badgered me during the drive here. As I stare down at the pieces of Samuel Yutzy, every cogent thought rushes from my brain.

“Do you have any idea of the time of death?” I manage.

“Preliminarily, thirty-six hours, give or take,” Doc replies. “As you know, we can usually calculate a TOD estimate by using the body temp.” Doc looks at his assistant. “Jared, what was the liver temp?”

The young man swipes through several pages of his iPad. “Seventy-four point seven.”

The doc nods. “In this case, the body had reached ambient temperature, which is the soil temp. Warmer than average due to the heat wave. But the body temperature and the postmortem loss of heat also depend on the size of the body mass. In this case, because the body was dismembered, cooling likely happened more quickly, skewing any typical TOD estimate. Still, there are other ways to calculate an estimated TOD. For example”—he touches the knee joint of the right leg, which is still intact—“rigor sets in at about two hours, usually in the face area first, and is released after about thirty-six hours. When I examined the joints—namely the larger knee joints—there was a small degree of rigor present.

“Additionally,” the doc continues, “there was very little insect activity, mainly because the body was buried and protected from fly larvae. There was little in the way of decomp. The odor that was detectable at the scene was likely from blood that had spilled onto the soil and baked in the sun, and, of course, there were bodily excretions.”

I nod, anxious for him to move on. “Do you have any idea what kind of cutting tool was used?”

Dr. Matrone takes it from there. "I examined several of the bones that were cut and/or severed, Chief Burkholder. One of the largest bones I looked at was the anatomical right femur shaft." She indicates one of the thighs. "The initial cut through the bone was nearer the proximal end of the shaft. It was a primitive cut that was undertaken with a crude tool. Under magnification, evidence of serration or possibly sawteeth is visible."

"So the killer may have used a large serrated knife? Or a saw?"

She grimaces. "In addition to a chain saw. One cut was made by a chain saw. There were at least three distinctive tools used."

"So there could have been more than one individual doing the cutting?"

It's an impossible question to answer at this point, but Dr. Matrone is game. "That would be my guess. I'll take a closer look during autopsy. It's a long shot, but we may be able to pinpoint some minute difference in the cutting technique that may tell us how many individuals participated in the dismemberment."

I think about what the act of dismembering a human body entails and feel a rush of gooseflesh, the sweat on my back going cold. "Do you think the perpetrator had any kind of medical training?" I ask. "Veterinary training? Anything like that?"

"In my estimation, the person who dismembered this victim had no measurable skill set. The cuts were made in odd areas. For example, in an area where the bone was thickest, which would make for a more difficult or laborious cut. I would also venture to say that the person who did the cutting had no idea where the joints were located or how to cut through them."

"What about cause of death?" I'm looking at Doc Coblentz when I ask the question. I see the answer in his eyes even before he speaks.

"Upon examination of the abdomen and skull, we were able to identify two penetrating wounds."

He goes to the head first, which has been placed on a headblock in a supine position. Using a swab, he indicates a small, red-black hole at the hairline just behind the left ear.

"Looks like a gunshot wound," I say.

"That is my opinion."

"We missed it at the scene."

"Not surprising," he says. "The projectile entered at the mastoid process of the temporal bone. You missed it because it's within the hairline and bleeding was minimal."

"Is there an exit wound?" I ask.

"There is." Using both hands, Doc shifts the head so that the other side is visible. "The missile penetrated the skull and exited through the squamous part of the temporal bone."

The detached head is such a horror to behold, it's difficult to see it from a scientific perspective. I do my best. "So the bullet basically went through and through."

Doc nods. "We'll know more, of course, when we get a look inside the cranium. But the CT scan revealed lanes of opaque bone and missile fragments through the cerebral parenchyma all along the course of the missile, which basically allowed us to see the track."

I think about that a moment. "So there are likely fragments still at the scene where the murder took place."

"That would be my guess."

I make a mental note to get another metal detector out there. "You mentioned two gunshot wounds."

I'm relieved when he covers the head with the sheet. He sidles back to the abdomen and, using a fresh swab, indicates a small hole. "Single penetrating wound to the upper left quadrant."

"Entrance wound?" I say.

"It is."

"So they shot him in the front," I say, thinking aloud.

He saw it coming . . .

Doc nods, then looks over his shoulder at his assistant. "Jared?"

The younger man approaches. Though he's fresh out of college and relatively new here at the morgue, he's completely unfazed standing in the presence of a human body that has been cut into eleven pieces.

"Let's turn him over so we can get a visual of the exit wound," Doc says.

I look away as they gently lift and roll the torso to a prone position. I try not to listen to the sound of moist flesh being released from the stainless-steel surface.

"As you can see, there's quite a bit more damage involved with the exit wound," Doc says. "Which is typical."

The wound is an inch in diameter. The edges are jagged. A single drop of clear red-tinted fluid makes its way to the stainless-steel surface.

Doc Coblentz continues. "The X-ray revealed a fracture of the tenth rib. The transverse colon was damaged. Of course, we'll know more once we complete the autopsy."

"Do you have any idea what caliber bullet was used?"

"Larger caliber," he says. "Likely not a twenty-two. When we go in, we may be able to pick up some fragments. That's about all I can do on my end."

I look down at what's left of a twenty-one-year-old Amish man. I feel a shudder in my shoulders. The bitter taste of bile at the back of my throat. Outrage pulsing in my chest. "Yutzy was alive when he was shot?"

Doc Coblentz nods. "There is evidence of bleeding, particularly with regard to the abdominal gunshot wound. So, yes, his heart was beating when he sustained the gunshot wounds."

"Were the gunshot wounds fatal?" I ask.

Doc makes a growling sound in his throat. "The gunshot wound to the head was fatal," he tells me. "If I find anything to the contrary when we take a look inside the cranium, I'll let you know."

• • •

It's nearly one A.M. when I pull into the lane of the farm I share with Tomasetti. The lights are on inside, telling me he's already here. That he waited up for me.

One of the things I try not to do is bring my responsibilities as chief home with me. A homicide case in particular makes for very bad company. Of course, I rarely succeed. When you're a cop, a homicide investigation hijacks every facet of your life; it's all-encompassing, and despite your best efforts you live it 24/7. Tonight, the best I can hope for is some quiet time with my husband, some food, a shower, and sleep. All with the knowledge that both of us will be back at it before dawn.

Despite the late hour and my troubled state of mind, a sense of peace settles over me as I go through the back door. Tomasetti sits at the kitchen table, his laptop open in front of him. He looks at me over his shoulder. "Now there's a sight for sore eyes."

"Says the man who looks good after putting in a twenty-hour day."

He smiles and another truckload of tension slips off my shoulders. I see a bottle of Pinot Noir breathing on the counter. A single glass next to it. The other on the table next to his laptop.

"You started without me," I say.

"I wasn't sure if you'd make it home tonight."

"Jury might still be out on that."

"In that case, let's make the best of what might turn out to be a limited amount of time." He rises and we meet between the door and his chair.

The unpleasantries of the day fall away when he puts his arms around me. A burst of something precious and sweet swells in my chest when he lowers his mouth to mine. It's a chaste kiss. One that speaks of affection and comfort. It's a stolen moment and I soak it in greedily because I know it's fleeting.

Easing away from me, he goes to the counter and pours. "How did it go with the coroner?"

And just like that we're cops again. The darkness of our profession has followed us to this place of reprieve. Everything else that means so much slides onto that blasted back burner. "The victim was shot twice," I tell him. "Once in the abdomen. Once in the head."

He hands me the wine glass. "Caliber? Fragments?"

"We don't know yet." I recite from memory everything I learned from Doc Coblentz. "He's going to do the autopsy early tomorrow. There may be fragments at the nursery location, so I'm going to get a metal detector out to the scene first thing in the morning."

"Probably won't get enough to be helpful."

"Gotta try."

I pull out a chair and he joins me at the table. For a moment, we sit there, staring at each other, our thoughts churning and troubled. His eyes are bloodshot. I see exhaustion on his face, in the slight sag of his shoulders, the hollows of his cheeks. I feel that same exhaustion and intensity weighing me down.

Welcome to homicide.

"His best friend is missing," I say. "Aaron Shetler. He's Amish. Same age."

"I saw the BOLO."

"Tomasetti, this homicide . . . it has an odd vibe to it," I say. "Don't ask me to qualify that statement."

"Definitely not typical, especially for this area."

I reach for details, hating it that I'm tired, that my brain is operating at about sixty percent. "You mentioned earlier today that it felt more like a big-city type of crime. The more I learn, the more strongly I agree."

"Let's run with it."

"This was not a crime of passion or jealousy." I think about that a moment. "With that sort of crime, there's usually a high level of emotion. Anger or jealousy or fear. There's a certain level of panic. Mistakes are made. I don't think that was the case here."

He takes it from there. "Dismembering a body takes resolve. A certain kind of mindset. It also takes privacy. Time. A relative certainty that you won't be interrupted."

"To a degree, this feels planned," I say. "The decision to murder Yutzy wasn't a spur-of-the-moment impulse."

"Whoever came into that nursery went in to kill him."

In my mind's eye, I see the way the body looked lying on the gurney. Eleven pieces of what had been a twenty-one-year-old Amish man. "They shot him in the abdomen first," I say. "The head shot was the fatal wound."

"Maybe that second shot came after he was down."

I nod. "And even though it was not a crime of passion, the killer or killers still made a number of mistakes."

"The body parts were buried too shallowly. The killer didn't anticipate scavengers."

"Coyotes are common to this area," I say. "A local would have known."

"Maybe." Tomasetti takes his glass to the counter, refills it, and returns to the table. "It's concerning that the best friend is missing."

I nod. "Is Shetler on the run because he did the murder? Or did something happen to him, too?"

"Did you get anything from either of the families?" he asks.

"The most interesting development is the woman Yutzy was seeing."

"The woman in the photo from the briefing?"

I nod. "According to Yutzy's parents, she had visible tattoos. Dyed black hair. She wore inappropriate clothes. Smoked cigarettes. One of the dancers at The Cheetah Lounge claims her name is Cassidy. No last name."

Tomasetti offers a wry smile. "I'm doing some loose profiling here, but she doesn't seem like the kind of woman a young Amish man would take home to his parents."

I smile back at him. "You know love is blind, though, right?"

Not for the first time I'm amazed that even as we mine the depths of such a dreadful topic, he reminds me that life—and people—are good.

"With regard to Aaron Shetler," I say, "his parents barred him from their farm. They believed he was a bad influence on the younger children."

"Sounds like both young men may have been heading down the same road."

"According to his parents, Shetler was throwing around a lot of cash."

"How much cash are we talking about?"

I shake my head. "Shetler works at a farm store."

"So he's not exactly rolling in cash."

I nod. "His boss hasn't seen him for two days."

Tomasetti considers a moment. "It's not too much of a stretch to imagine two young males falling in with a bad crowd. They're twenty-one years old. Amish and getting their first taste of freedom."

"Naïve," I put in.

"Maybe Yutzy met this Cassidy at The Cheetah Lounge. Maybe he talked too much and she assumed Yutzy had money. She charmed her way into his life. All the while, she was setting him up for some scam or con or robbery. Things went south and he ended up dead."

"Could be a realistic scenario," I say. "But it doesn't explain the five hundred dollars in the cash register at the nursery."

"What about drugs?"

"Maybe. I don't know."

"Other known associates?"

"Still looking."

He nods. "That takes us back to the business. You mentioned a contractual dispute earlier."

I tell him about Carter Brooks. "According to the parents, Aaron worked with Samuel on occasion."

"What do you think of Brooks?"

"I think he's a slick guy. Tough to read."

"Does he have an alibi?"

"Nope."

In the silence that follows, I can practically hear the whirr of our brains grinding through the possibilities.

After a moment, Tomasetti says, "I don't think we're going to solve this tonight." He glances at the clock. "It's after one A.M. Five rolls around fast."

"Maybe we ought to sleep on it. Hit it fresh in the morning."

"Great minds." Rising, he takes my hand and pulls me to my feet. "Anyone ever tell you that you're a good brainstormer?"

"Yeah, all the attractive and charming male BCI agents tell me that."

Groaning, he puts his arm around me and heads toward our bedroom.

CHAPTER 10

They'd named her Druvvel—which meant "Trouble" in English—and the heifer had been living up to her namesake since the day she was born. She'd been just an hour old when her mama rejected her. They moved her into the barn and bottle-fed her for nine weeks. Just when they thought their problems were over, she got a bad case of pink eye, which required a trip to the vet and cost them a pretty penny to boot. Then came the scours, another visit to the vet, and a final assault on Ivan Hershberger's wallet. Finally, when she was strong and healthy at eighteen months of age, they bred her to their prize bull. Now here she was, a new mama with a healthy newborn calf at her side, and both were stuck at the bottom of a ravine, unable to get out.

"*Ferwas bischt allfatt so schtarrkeppich?*" Why are you so stubborn?

Standing at the edge of the ravine, Ivan Hershberger shook his head as he watched Druvvel nurse her new baby. In the coming hours, Mama would need water. Getting the calf out was not going to be a problem. Getting Mama out was another story.

"Well, there's eighteen hundred pounds of trouble for you."

Ivan glanced over at his neighbor, Perry, and grinned. "Trouble is trouble, I reckon."

"Need a hand getting her out?"

"I don't know what a couple of fat old men are going to do with an eighteen-hundred-pound cow that doesn't have a lick of sense."

"I believe that's why God blessed us with teenaged sons."

The two men laughed.

Ivan figured it was a good thing he'd brought their Percheron gelding, the old hay wagon, and an extra harness with them. When he'd left the house twenty minutes ago, he hadn't been sure how he was going to get the cow out of the ravine. But a plan was starting to take shape.

"Druvvel's tame as a dog," he said. "Hand raised, you know. Maybe we could send the boys down there and rig up that harness on her. We'll tie it up to my gelding and pull her out."

"Horse looks up to the task," Perry said.

"Old Johnny's a good puller." Turning, Ivan brought his fingers to his mouth and whistled to the boys who were standing next to the wagon. "*Redd up!*" Ready up. "*Sis unvergleichlich hays.*" It's terribly hot. "Druvvel's been without water for a few hours now and has that nice-looking little bull to feed."

Grabbing the leather harness, Ivan's son walked to the edge of the ravine and tossed it to the base. Perry's son tied the rope to the wagon. Both boys used the rope to skitter down into the ravine. They carried the calf up first. Mama was none too happy about being separated from her newborn and landed a couple of well-placed kicks before the boys were able to get the harness on her. Topside, Ivan backed the gelding into place and tied the rope to the tug chains. The gelding hauled Druvvel out of the ravine as if she weighed nothing.

"Difficulty is a miracle at its first stage," Perry said.

"That is the truth." Ivan had just poured water into a bucket for the cow to drink when a yell emanated from down in the ravine.

"*Datt!* Someone dumped a barrel down here! Do you want us to bring it up?"

Ivan and Perry walked to the ravine's edge and looked down. Sure enough, among the tangle of raspberry and bramble, a blue plastic drum lay on its side.

"*Dumm-kobb,*" Ivan muttered. Dumb people. "Fools dumping trash again."

"Nice barrel, though," Perry said.

A few unsavory individuals had been sneaking in through the gate at the back of the property and using the ravine to dump trash. Garbage bags. Old tires. Ivan even found a mattress once. The ravine was easily accessed from the township road, and despite the KEEP OUT sign Ivan had hung on the gate, people came in anyway.

"Does look brand-new," Ivan said.

"Might be able to use it for feed or something," Perry said.

"Depends what's inside." But even chemicals could be cleaned out with some good old-fashioned elbow grease. "Let's check."

Ivan crossed to the wagon and reached into the back for the pry bar and sledgehammer. "You coming?" he asked.

Perry eyed the steep sides of the ravine and shook his head. "How about if I keep an eye on that cow for you?"

"Don't blame you," Ivan grumbled, but he was grinning as he tossed the tools into the ravine. Grabbing the rope, he skidded down the steep side to where the boys stood.

"Is the barrel empty?" he asked his son.

The boy shook his head. "Heavy," he said. "Full of something."

"Let's take a look."

His son picked up the pry bar and set the tip to the seal. Ivan lifted the sledgehammer and set to work. *Clang! Clang! Clang!* The fourth whack sent the lid flying. Ivan caught sight of what looked like fur inside. The stench hit an instant later with the force of bird shot. Something dead inside. *Slaughter renderings,* he thought.

Vaguely, Ivan was aware of his son stumbling back. Perry's son yelping and following suit. Dropping the sledgehammer, Ivan moved to the barrel, looked inside. He saw red hair caked with blood. The pale skin of a face. A person, he thought. Mouth open. Tongue sticking out. An arm twisted at a terrible angle.

"*Ach!*"

Ivan lurched back so fast, his feet tangled and he went down on his backside. Spooked, he scrambled to his feet, went to his son, and motioned to the rope. "Climb up," he said urgently. "Hurry. Both of you. Go!"

Neither boy hesitated.

"Run as fast as you can to Mr. McIntire's place. Call the police. Hurry." He looked back at the barrel and shuddered. "Tell them something very bad has happened."

• • •

It's not yet eight A.M. and the temperature displayed on my dashboard already registers eighty-two degrees. Before heading in to the station, I decided to swing by Aaron Shetler's residence on the outside chance he's there. There's no vehicle in the driveway. No lights on inside that I can see.

Sighing, I pick up my radio and hail Dispatch. "I'm ten-twenty-three," I say, letting them know I've arrived on scene.

"Roger that," comes Margaret's voice.

"Is Glock in?" I ask, wondering about the warrant.

"On his way."

"Tell him to meet me here. I'm going to take a quick look around."

The small bungalow is set on a generous-size lot. Across the gravel parking area is a small detached garage. I pull up between the house and garage and kill the engine. A few yards to my left, a loafing shed is filled with firewood. A chain-link fence encircles the backyard. The grass is uncut and yellowed from the heat.

I get out and take the narrow sidewalk around to the front door. I open the screen and knock. "Painters Mill Police Department!" I call out. "Aaron Shetler? Come on out and talk to me!"

I wait a full minute, listening for movement inside, but no one comes.

No one home, Kate.

I walk around to the rear of the house and knock, but no one answers.

"Where the hell are you?" I mutter.

I'm on my way back to the Explorer when on impulse I cross to the garage. Both overhead doors are closed. There are no windows; I can't tell if there's a vehicle inside. I take a beaten-down path to the man door at the side. I'm about to try the knob when I spot a smear of something dark on the jamb. Not oil or dirt. It looks like dried blood.

I step back, glance down at the ground, and notice droplets of more in the dirt, on the concrete, and on the threshold. Not fresh, but dark and dry with age. Pulling my duty gloves from my belt, I slip them on and try the knob. Locked.

"Shit."

Normally, in a situation like this I wouldn't be overly concerned. Aaron Shetler is a farm kid, after all. He works with his hands. A cut or injury isn't out of the ordinary. But in light of his best friend having been found murdered and dismembered, my mind takes me into the darker nooks and crannies. Is it possible something happened to Aaron Shetler, too? Or is this someone else's blood? Samuel Yutzy's? Has Shetler gone on the run because of something he did?

I don't have the warrant in hand yet. That said, blood qualifies as exigent circumstances. Those two things run through my mind as I study the door. It's an old thing with worn hinges and a cheap lock. The wood frame is warped and dry, the paint peeling away.

I try the door again, bump it with my shoulder. It doesn't budge. I back up a few steps and land a solid kick next to the knob. The door shudders, wood creaking.

"Painters Mill Police!" I call out.

I land another kick, the heel of my boot landing just above the knob. The door flies open, swings wide, and bangs against the wall. I pull out my .38 and step inside.

"Aaron Shetler! Police department! Show yourself!"

There's a vehicle inside. I hit the light switch with my left hand. I take in a dozen things at once. An air compressor against the wall. A rollaway toolbox. Workbench. I smell the blood before I see it. A sick copper smell that's gone rancid in the heat. Hairs on my back standing up, eyes everywhere, I stride to the overhead door, spot the side lock, kick it open. Bending, I lift the door. Light pours in. The pool of blood is the diameter of a car tire. Sticky and black against the concrete. Flies everywhere.

Keenly aware that I'm likely standing in a crime scene, I exit through the overhead door and back away. Only when I'm outside do I realize I'd been holding my breath.

I call Tomasetti first. "I've got blood at Aaron Shetler's place," I say without preamble. "A lot of it."

"You alone?"

"Glock's on his way."

He growls. "Keep your eyes open, Chief. I'll get a crime scene van out there ASAP."

• • •

I'm stretching crime scene tape from traffic cone to traffic cone between the house and garage when Glock pulls into the driveway, emergency lights flaring. His cruiser skids to a stop behind my Explorer and then he's out, striding over to me.

"You okay, Chief?"

"Fine." I motion to the garage. "Not so sure about Shetler. I've got blood in the garage. Crime scene unit is on the way."

"Might explain why we haven't been able to locate him." Shaking his head, he takes the roll of tape from my hand. "I got this."

I've just hit the number for Mike Rasmussen when my phone rings. Simultaneously, both Glock's and my own radio light up with a burst of traffic.

What now?

I answer with a curt utterance of my name.

"Chief." Margaret's usually unshakable voice comes at me too fast, too loud, and I know instantly something is afoot.

"I just took a call from Ivan Hershberger's son," she tells me. "He says they found a body."

The world around me goes silent. "Do they know who it is?" I ask.

"No, ma'am."

I think about the logistics of the Hershberger farm and the sheer size of the property. "Did he say where the body is?"

"At the back of the property. Down in some ravine that's just off the township road."

"I know it." I look at Glock, who's looking back at me over his shoulder. "I'm on my way."

• • •

I've known Ivan Hershberger since our school days. Back then he was a prankster known for talking too much and invariably getting into trouble for it. Today, he's well thought of with a big family and runs a few dozen head of cattle on his farm. I've been called to his address several times over the years, each time to investigate illegal dumping. The ravine at the back of his property is a favorite spot for people to dump the large trash items they don't want to take to the dump.

It takes me six minutes to reach the township road. Ivan's gate is standing wide open as if he's expecting me, so I pull onto the shoulder next to it and cut the engine. I spot the young Amish man walking toward me as I get out.

"What happened?" I ask as I stride to him.

"We found a dead person." Turning, he points with a shaking hand. "Down in that ravine."

I guess him to be in his late teens. Pole skinny with a bad case of acne and looking a little green around the gills.

"Show me."

Nodding, he turns and we go through the gate. Fifty yards ahead, I see a big gray draft horse harnessed to a wagon. Two Amish men standing near the back of the wagon, one of whom I recognize as Ivan. I spot a second teenage boy a few yards away, bent over, his hands on his knees, retching.

"*Guder mariye.*" Good morning. I approach the men. "I understand you found a body?"

Ivan makes eye contact with me and shakes his head. Usually, he's a jovial man. Quick with a joke and a laugh. This morning, he looks as if he's about to lose his breakfast.

"*Ach,* Katie, it's bad. The devil's workings, I tell you." He crosses to me. When we shake, I feel his hand shaking. "There's a dead man." He motions. "Been stuffed in that blue drum down there in the ravine."

The second man is standing next to the wagon, watching, smoke wafting up from his pipe, his elbows on the bed rail.

"Never seen anything like it in all of God's world," Ivan finishes. "Don't think I'll ever forget it, either."

"Do you have any idea who it is?" I ask.

The Amish man receives the question like a punch to his solar plexus. "All I seen about him was red hair." He lowers his voice. "I ain't saying it's Aaron Shetler, but that boy's got red hair. Just like I saw in that drum."

Dread twists in my chest. "Did you see anyone else down there?" I ask. "Anyone in the area? A car? Or buggy?"

"No, ma'am," he says.

"Tracks?"

"No."

"What were you doing down there?"

"Cow went missing. Didn't show up for feed this morning. Boys walked the pasture looking for her, and found her down in the ravine with her calf."

I go to the edge of the ravine and look down. The steep sides are torn up, probably by the cow as she was being pulled out. The bottom of the ravine is thick with bramble and blackberry and weeds as tall as a man's shoulders. Ten yards away, a blue plastic barrel lies on its side. I can't see inside it from where I'm standing, but I discern the stench of death.

Shit.

Tilting my head, I speak into my radio. "Margaret, get the coroner out here."

CHAPTER 11

I'm in relatively good physical condition—or so I like to tell myself. Getting to the bottom of the ravine is no easy task. The sides are steep, more crumbling dirt than rock, and inhabited by every thorny bush known to mankind. Ivan set me up with the rope he used to extract the cow and I utilize it to inexpertly rappel down, narrowly avoiding busting my ass.

Humidity presses down as I disentangle myself from the rope. The back of my shirt is already damp with sweat. From where I'm standing, I can just make out a patch of blue from the drum twenty feet away. A barely there path cuts through a tangle of raspberry, probably from the cow or the boys when they came down to retrieve her.

The incessant buzz of flies seems inordinately loud as I start toward the barrel. There's no way around the profusion of brush so I fight my way through, trying not to tear my shirt or get pricked by thorns. The smell of decaying flesh intensifies as I close in. The barrel is lying on its side, the open end facing away from me. Twice I stop to snap photos. Not for evidence—photos from cell phones aren't good enough quality—but for my own reference. All the while, I hope these men are wrong about what's inside the barrel. I'm holding on to the hope that someone disposed of a dead animal or butchering renderings. Those hopes are dashed when I get my first look inside.

I see the top of a head first. Red hair, matted and wet-looking. The shoulders are visible. The blue plaid of a shirt, horribly stained with what looks like blood. An arm and hand spilling over the side . . .

Son of a bitch.

My stomach does a quick seesaw, but I ignore it, swallow the spit at the back of my throat. I move closer, stop at about four feet away from the open end of the drum, and I snap six photos in quick succession. While my stomach threatens to rebel, my mind tries to process the horror of what I'm seeing. The body inside is that of a Caucasian male. Red hair. Blunt-cut bangs. Blue shirt. I look at the hand. No wedding ring. No visible tattoos.

Shaken, I take an involuntary step back, catch my breath, and I hail Dispatch. "Margaret, tell the coroner to expedite," I say. "Get the sheriff's office out here. I need both ends of the township road blocked ASAP. We're going to need the fire department, too."

"Roger that."

Cognizant that I'm standing in the midst of a crime scene, I back away from the drum and retrace my path back to the rope that will take me topside.

• • •

It's still early when Tomasetti's Tahoe rolls up behind my Explorer. I'm standing at the rear of the hay wagon, talking with Ivan and Perry, trying in vain not to sweat, when I see him get out and start toward us, three bottles of water in hand. He looks unduly fresh considering we didn't get much sleep last night and the thermometer is a hair away from ninety.

He hands me and the two Amish men water bottles. "Any idea who our vic is?"

"I couldn't see his face. Didn't want to search for an ID. But the victim has red hair."

His eyes sharpen on mine. "Shetler's a redhead."

I give him the details on what was found at Aaron Shetler's place. "His car's there, too. He's missing." I sigh. "I hope I'm wrong."

"If this is Shetler, I think it's safe to assume these two homicides are related."

"First a dismembered body and now a body in a barrel." I shake my head. "What the hell?"

"They were into something," he says.

"We've found no evidence of drugs." I find myself thinking about the mysterious Cassidy and her purported connection to Yutzy. The tales of Shetler's recklessness with cash. "Whatever it is, they made some bad decisions. Got in over their heads."

"Pissed off the wrong person."

"Or persons." I look past him, see the coroner's van pull up. "If it's drugs, we'll find them," I say. "There's always a trail."

"And contrary to popular belief, there's no honor among thieves," he says nastily. "You put a dealer in an interrogation room facing hard time and he'll sell out his mother for a deal."

• • •

I'm anxious to confirm the ID of the body. Of course, nothing ever happens quickly when it comes to the processing of a crime scene. It takes nearly an hour for the fire department's rescue team to equip Doc

Coblentz with a rappelling harness so that he can be safely lowered into the ravine. The gully isn't unduly deep—just twenty feet or so—but the sides are steep and crumbling, with copious overgrowth rife with stickers as prickly as cactus spines.

Despite his size and not-quite-up-to-par physical condition, Doc rappels into the ravine like a pro. A younger technician, armed with a medical bag and camera, uses a second rope to scale the wall behind him. The last thing I want to do is go back down there. I don't have a choice.

Doc and I wade through bramble. I hear the tech behind us, the snap and whirr of the camera as he documents the scene. All of us donned the usual biohazard protection—Tyvek suits, shoe covers, masks, and gloves. The thorns have nearly shredded our suits by the time we reach the barrel.

My stomach quivers as I sidle around to the open end of the drum and look inside. The top of the head and shoulders are covered with flies. The smell has worsened, probably due to the heat and lack of air circulation here at the base of the ravine.

Doc sighs. "Let's document as best we can," he says to the technician, and then turns his attention to me. "We're not going to remove this body from the barrel down here," he says.

I agree with the statement, but I don't like it.

"We need to ID him," I say. His expression turns dubious so I add, "Even if I can get a look at his face or take a photo for my own use, I may be able to identify him that way."

"I don't have to tell you facial constructs change with death. And with all this heat . . ." His mask flutters with another sigh. "Let's see what we can do."

Doc Coblentz makes eye contact with his technician. "You have photos of the victim and scene?"

"I do."

"We're going to move the head so that the face is visible," Doc says. "For identification purposes."

"Sure." Raising his hands to protect the camera and medical bag from the clutching thorns, the tech wades over to us.

"A lot of biohazard," Doc says. "Double up your gloves."

The tech opens the medical bag and pulls out three pair, passes two to us. I'm sweating profusely as I slip the second pair of gloves over the first. I can feel the sun beating down on my head and shoulders.

The doc moves to the barrel. I watch as the technician pushes through brush and goes to the opposite side.

"We may be dealing with rigor at this stage," Doc says.

The technician looks down at the body. Not with the horror of seeing a decaying human body packed into a drum, but with the cool curiosity of a science student faced with a baffling puzzle and nearly impossible challenge.

"Let's reach inside," Doc begins. "We might be able to get some leverage beneath the chin. Let's lift the head as much as we can and tilt the face upward so that it's visible."

"Retractor?" the technician asks.

"Let's start with the four-prong," Doc replies.

Digging into his medical equipment bag, the technician locates the tool he's looking for.

"Slide it beneath the chin and lift," Doc says. "See if we can get a look at this poor young man."

I'm keenly aware of bile climbing up the back of my throat as the technician maneuvers the retractor into place. A combination of the sight of the body, the heat, the mask I'm wearing, and the stench of death is nauseating and claustrophobic.

I watch as the head shifts slightly. I see the jaw loll. The mouth open.

"I got rigor," the technician says.

Nodding, Doc Coblentz digs into the bag and removes some type of curved, flat-ended probe. Gently, he sets the flat end against the victim's jaw and uses the edge of the barrel for leverage.

"If this doesn't work, we're out of options, Kate." He looks at me through the lenses of his protective goggles. "You'll have to wait for that ID."

The head shifts. The sickening sound of flesh peeling away from the side of the drum sounds. The back of the head tilts downward. The face comes into view. The mouth is open. I see broken teeth. Swollen lips the color of eggplant stretched taut. A tongue that's been bitten nearly in half. The eyes are partially open and so cloudy I can't discern the color of the irises. I recognize him at about the same time the horror of it seizes my brain and shakes. I take an involuntary step back. Too hot. Not enough air. I need to throw up, but the mask is in the way.

"It's Shetler," I hear myself say. "Shit."

Turning, I set my eyes on the rope that will take me out of the ravine. My head is swimming. No idea if I can make it up. One foot in front of the other. One step at a time.

I hear the doc and technician talking behind me. "Let's get this poor young man topside."

I reach for the rope and climb.

• • •

For a community that largely rejects the use of cell phones and social media, news—especially of the dreadful variety—travels at the speed of wildfire. I know the instant I pull into the lane of the Shetler farm that word is out about the death of their son. A buggy I don't recognize is parked at the side of the house. Three Amish women and two men stand next to it. I park behind the buggy and recognize Mr. Shetler as I get out. He's standing alone, head down, his arms crossed. He is the picture of anguish.

As I'm getting out of the Explorer, I see the back door of the house swing open. Mrs. Shetler rushes onto the porch. Her right hand is over her mouth. Left arm flailing as she takes the steps at a too fast rate of speed. Her eyes are riveted to me as she leaves the porch, but she doesn't seem to see me. She hits the sidewalk at a run.

Mr. Shetler tries to intercept her, but he's not fast enough. I hear her sobbing a second before she reaches me.

"Where's my son?" she cries. "Where's Aaron? We've heard terrible things. What's happened to him?"

"Mrs. Shetler." I reach out to take her hands, partly to comfort her, partly because she's not steady on her feet, but she jerks away and steps back.

"Why didn't you tell us he was in danger?" she cries. "We would've stepped in. Done something."

When it comes to high emotion—whether it's grief or happiness or fear—the Amish are generally more stoic than their English counterparts. But there is some pain that's so unbearable that it cannot be contained. The death of a child is a prime example.

"You were just here." She sways beneath my hands. "Why didn't you say something? Why didn't you warn us? Why didn't you save him?"

They're irrational questions and I hate it that I don't have an answer for her. Even if I did, I don't think she would hear me. Or even care what I said.

"Is it true?"

I look over my shoulder and see Doyle striding toward us. His expression is impassive, but his jaws are clamped tight and I see tears on his cheeks.

"Answer me," he says. "Is it true?"

I look at him, nod, and I feel a small piece of his pain pierce the center of me. "I'm sorry," I say.

The words fall excruciatingly short, even to my own ears. All of the sorry and regret in the world isn't going to bring back a young life that has been lost.

"Let's get her inside and talk," I say.

And we leave their Amish neighbors looking after us, their heads bowed, their hearts heavy.

• • •

Doyle leads his wife and me to the kitchen. He helps her into a chair and then lowers himself into the one next to her. "How did it happen?" he asks.

I take the chair across from them, the weight of the question, of their grief, pressing down with crushing force. "I don't know," I say honestly. "His body was discovered in a ravine off the township road. That's all I know at this point."

"How on earth did he get into a ravine?" he asks. "Was it a fall? A car wreck? What?"

The last thing I want to do is get into the details about their son's death. I don't know much; what little I do know is so unspeakable, it will do nothing but cause them even more grief and horror. The one thing I must do is tell them the truth.

"I think your son was murdered," I tell him.

Ellen gasps, her face crumpling. "Oh, dear Lord."

"*Murdered?*" Doyle chokes out a sound that's part exhale, part sob. "I don't understand. Someone *killed* our boy?"

"I believe so," I say.

"But . . . who?" Ellen asks. "Why would they do such a thing?"

"That's what I'm trying to figure out," I say. "All I can tell you at this point is that I'm going to do everything in my power to find the person responsible and bring them to justice. Right now, I need information. Anything you can tell me that might help me figure out who did this."

We spend twenty minutes going over many of the same points we've already covered or that I've learned elsewhere. I'm all too aware that questioning parents mere minutes after they've been notified of the death of their child is a far cry from an ideal circumstance. It's painful. Cruel even. I don't let that stop me because right or wrong, pain be damned, the responsibility to find the killer falls on my shoulders.

"The last time I talked to you," I say, "you mentioned that Aaron had tried to give you some cash. Is there anyone you can think of who might know where that cash came from? Or know where Aaron was getting it?"

"I don't know." Doyle shakes his head. "I wish to God I'd asked. Warned him away from whatever he was doing. I might've been able to stop this and we might still have our boy."

"This isn't your fault," I tell him.

No one responds.

We fall silent. The couple look exhausted and broken. As if their souls have been sucked from their bodies and there's nothing left but the shell.

I rise and set my hand first on Ellen's shoulder and then on Doyle's. "If you need anything or if you think of something I might need to know, please call me. Day or night."

"No offense, Chief Burkholder, but I think I could live the rest of my days quite happily never speaking to you again," Ellen says.

I set my card on the table and let myself out through the front door.

As I take the flagstone path to the Explorer, the remnants of their grief follow, a dark presence that's as heavy and menacing as death itself.

"Damn it." I hit the fob, slide behind the wheel. As I pull the door closed, I hear someone call out my name.

"Chief Burkholder!"

I glance left to see an Amish teenager jogging toward me from the barn. Sixteen or seventeen years old. Rail thin. His blue shirt is sweat stained. His work pants are dusty. I've never met him before, but his facial features tell me he's a Shetler.

I roll down the window. At first glance I can tell he's been crying. "Hi," I say.

"Is it true?" he asks. "Aaron's gone?"

I nod. "I'm sorry," I tell him.

"How did he die?"

"You should probably go inside and talk to your parents about that."

Blinking hard, he looks back at the barn as if wishing he were there instead of here, and I see him struggling to hold in emotions that are pushing at the gates to get out.

"Are you his brother?" I ask.

He nods. "William."

The sibling Aaron had tried to give the money to.

A cop has to be cautious when questioning or even talking to a minor child. Asking questions about a case that will likely go to court is not to be done without the express permission of a parent or legal guardian.

I go with a statement instead of a question and wait. "You're the one Aaron tried to give the money to."

His eyes meet mine and he looks at me, hard. My *mamm* used to call that kind of eye contact *deef awwa.* Deep eyes.

"Everyone was talking bad about him." Despite the strong façade, the boy's voice breaks. "He was a good guy. He got that money fair and square."

"How?" I ask.

"That landscape job he helped Samuel with. The one at that fancy *Englischer* club."

"What club?"

He gives me a confused look. "The fancy one here in Painters Mill."

"The Club at Paint Creek?"

He nods. "Aaron and Samuel are the ones put in all them trees. Thirty of them, I think. A hedge, too." He looks away, swipes covertly at his eyes. "I wanted to help, but Sammy said I wasn't old enough. He didn't talk much about the job because the guy paid in cash. You know, so they wouldn't have to pay taxes on it."

It takes a moment for me to make the connection. I recall my conversation with Carter Brooks.

I was there one afternoon for a round of golf.

. . . admiring the landscaping . . .

I asked the manager about it . . .

. . . gave me the number for Samuel's company.

. . . hired him on the spot.

"Do you know the name of the person at the club who Aaron and Samuel worked for?" I ask.

He shakes his head. "No idea."

"Did your brother say anything to you when he gave you the money?" I ask.

The boy purses his lips. "I didn't think too much about it at the time, but he said something like: Don't do what I did."

"Do you know what he meant by that?"

"No, ma'am."

"Anything else?" I ask.

He shakes his head. "I just wanted you to know. Aaron wasn't no thief. He never stole anything in his whole life. He earned that money planting all them trees and Sammy paid him well. That's all I got to say about it."

CHAPTER 12

Watching the boy walk away, I call Dispatch. "Get me everything you can find on The Club at Paint Creek."

"Come again?" Lois stutters, likely because she's as shocked as I am that the club has come up in connection to a police investigation.

"Find out who the manager is," I tell her. "Get me all pertinent contact info, including the name of the grounds manager, if there is one." Two Amish buggies wait to turn in to the Shetler lane as I pull onto the township road. I raise my hand and wave as I pass them. "Run their names through LEADS."

"You got it."

I thank her and call Tomasetti.

"How did the notification go?" he asks by way of greeting.

"If I'd had the option of bamboo slivers being shoved beneath my nails I would have taken it."

"Yeah." He sighs. "Anything new?"

I tell him about my conversation with the son, William. "It's the second time I've heard The Club at Paint Creek mentioned in relation to this case."

"Which links the club to Samuel Yutzy via the landscaping business," he says.

"Kind of a loose connection," I say.

"You never know where some random connection might lead," he says. "Might be worth a quick look-see."

"Meet me at the station?" I ask.

"See you in ten minutes."

• • •

The Club at Paint Creek is the premier country club in the entirety of Holmes County. It sits on two hundred acres of lush grassland and rolling hills interspersed with hundred-year-old elm and oak trees. It boasts an eighteen-hole golf course, an Olympic-size swimming pool, and a clubhouse that rivals any venue in the state. According to Lois, it's owned by a corporate conglomerate out of Cincinnati and managed by a local man by the name of Lance Wingate.

I'm in the Explorer with Tomasetti riding shotgun. "Wingate is forty-six years old," I tell him. "Never been arrested. No record. No lawsuits. Married. Two minor children."

"Any connection to Yutzy or Shetler?" he asks.

"Just the landscaping job," I say. "Based on the word of Shetler's younger brother."

"Did Wingate deal with Samuel directly?" he asks. "Or is there a groundskeeper?"

"Lois couldn't come up with the name of a grounds manager."

"Maybe Mr. Wingate will be able to fill in the blanks."

I make the turn onto a sleek asphalt driveway lined with stately elms. Beyond, the main building greets us with an austere façade of red brick, mullioned windows, and a grand portico with Ionic columns. The architecture is unusual for this part of Ohio, an aesthetically pleasing mix of Georgian colonial and Colorado rustic.

I park in the spacious lot at the side and we take a pavestone walkway around to the front. Entering The Club at Paint Creek is an assault on every pleasure center of the brain. From the intricately laid marble floors to the lush tropical greenery to the arched doorways and gleaming cypress woodwork, the club rivals any five-star hotel.

"Who says rural Ohio isn't fancy?" Tomasetti mutters.

"I think they're called farmers."

He gives me the side-eye. "Evidently."

I grin as we enter the lobby. A smattering of tables to my right offer a view of a sparkling pool. Poolside, I see patio tables with umbrellas emblazoned with the club logo. To my left, two leather-tufted sofas are poised for conversation; there's an antique coffee table in between. A massive river-rock fireplace takes up an entire corner. Wood beams as thick as a man's waist hover overhead. An attractive woman of about forty stands at a carved wood counter next to an areca palm, tapping something into a sleek laptop.

She smiles when we approach. "Welcome to The Club at Paint Creek," she says. "What can I do for you?"

Matching her smile, I show her my badge. "We'd like to speak with Lance Wingate."

"Oh." Frowning, she looks down at the laptop, taps a few keys. "Is this about the fundraiser for bodycams? I thought that was for the sheriff's office. I think he donated to that, didn't he? You know, if I'm not mistaken, he's in a meeting this afternoon. Can I have him call you?"

"Anita?"

At the sound of the deep male voice, I turn to see a smartly dressed man striding toward us, cell phone in hand, a stack of pamphlets in the other. He's sandy haired and tall with the build of a distance runner.

"Hi, Mr. Wingate." Her gaze flicks to me. "Chief Burkholder was just asking to speak with you."

"Hey, no problem." He sets the pamphlets on the counter. "These are good to go, by the way. Make sure the whole team gets a stack."

"Of course."

Wingate turns his attention to Tomasetti and me and offers his hand, his expression open and curious. "What can I do for you?"

"We'd like to ask you some questions about Samuel Yutzy if you have a few minutes," I say.

His expression falls. "I heard what happened to him and I'm absolutely stunned." He cocks his head. "Are you wondering about the landscaping job he did?"

"We're interested in anything you can share," I say.

"Sure." Wingate turns his attention to Tomasetti and sticks out his hand. "I'm not sure how I can help, but we can talk in my office. Come on."

We follow him down a paneled hall. The walls are packed with framed certificates, photos of the club, and several shots of visiting celebrities.

"Here we are." He opens a door and motions us inside.

I go through first. It's a spacious office, all dark wood and leather, a wall of books, and a picture-perfect view of the golf course. The desk is midcentury modern and stacked high with pamphlets. Dueling laptops are open and humming. In the corner, there's a round table at which two little girls sit, busy with crayons and coloring books.

"Ah . . . sorry." Wingate offers a self-deprecating smile. "Uh . . . this is the meeting Anita was referring to." He clears his throat. "Wife had to run down to Cincy. I got the girls today. Had some stuff to finish up, so I brought them with me."

"No problem." I smile, liking him.

"Probably the best meeting you'll have all week," Tomasetti says.

"Ain't that the truth." He strides to the desk and snatches up a land-line phone. "Anita, sorry to bother you, but can you come get the girls? Keep an eye on them for a bit?"

A few minutes later, Tomasetti and I are seated in the matching wing chairs opposite the desk. The girls and their coloring books are gone. The only sound comes from the quiet hiss of the laptops and the Hall and Oates tune pouring from sleek speakers on the credenza.

"Like I said, I was shocked to hear about Mr. Yutzy being murdered." Grimacing, Wingate looks from Tomasetti to me. "Couldn't believe it. He's . . . *was* a hell of a nice kid. And right here in Painters Mill." He shakes his head. "You guys find out who did it?"

"Working on it," Tomasetti says.

"Mr. Wingate," I begin, "how well did you know Samuel?"

"I only met him a few times." He makes a face. "When I hired him. And, a few times while he was here at the club, working on the landscaping."

"How did you meet him?" Tomasetti asks.

"If memory serves me, I was talking to one of our members. I was looking for someone to landscape the parking and pool areas. He recommended Yutzy and I cold-called him that afternoon."

"How long ago was that?" I ask.

"Six or seven months. We signed a simple contract. I can look it up and get the exact date if you'd like."

"That would be great." I think about that a moment. "Did Samuel work alone? Or did he have a crew?"

"Just one other dude. Young guy. Amish. About the same age as him. Name was Aaron, I think."

Tomasetti leans back in the chair. "Did you know Aaron?"

"Just to say hello. I'd stop by where they were working sometimes to see how things were going and we'd shoot the breeze." He turns thoughtful as if remembering. "I'd never dealt with the Amish before and it was always interesting to talk to them. I'd heard they're hardworking and honest. Let me tell you something, those guys worked their asses off. They were here by seven every morning. Stayed till dark. They got a damn big job done under budget and with time to spare."

"Did you hear about what happened to Aaron Shetler?" I purposefully keep the question open to interpretation.

"What do you mean?" Wingate's eyes sharpen on mine. "What happened to him?"

I wait a beat, watching him for any indication that he already knows. He holds my gaze, focused, his eyes demanding an answer.

"He was found dead this morning," I say.

"Holy cow. You've got to be kidding. I hadn't heard." He sets his hands on his desktop, looks down at them. "Are you telling me he was murdered?"

I nod. "Mr. Wingate, right now we're looking for information on both young men. Is there anything you can tell us about Samuel or Aaron that might help us find the person or persons responsible?"

"Wow, I'm still trying to process the murder part of it." Wingate shakes his head. "Hard to believe someone would murder two young Amish guys like that. Do you have any idea why?"

"We don't know much at this point," I respond, keeping my answer vague. "Did you happen to notice anything unusual when they were working for you?"

"Unusual like what?"

I shrug. "Were they having any problems that you know of? Were there any ongoing disputes? Did they argue with anyone? Have money problems? Anything like that?"

"All I can tell you about those two young men is that they were hard workers. I mean, they were kind of no-nonsense. Reliable. Quiet. Didn't cause any problems. They worked a full day and then they left."

"Did they interact with anyone while they were here at the club?" Tomasetti asks. "Any clients or employees?"

He thinks about that a moment. "Not that I saw, but like I said I only saw them a few times. Some days, I didn't see them at all."

"So there was never an indication that they had any problems with anyone?"

"Nothing that I saw."

"You were pleased with the job when it was complete?" I ask.

"Hey, they did great work. I paid them in full. Told them if they ever needed a reference I'd give it to them."

"Did anyone ever call or inquire about hiring them?" I ask.

He scratches his head. "No one ever did. If they had, I would have given a glowing review."

• • •

I'm sitting at my desk at the police station. I've gone through every photo, police report, interview, and my own scrawled notes on the Yutzy and Shetler cases too many times to count. Somehow another day has blown by and I have nothing more than a big fat zero to show for it in terms of progress.

I haven't seen or heard from Tomasetti since our trip to the country club earlier. I wonder if he's home, if he's gotten any rest. Or if he's stuck at a desk, same as me, torturing himself with these horrific photos and details of two murders brutal enough to give even seasoned detectives nightmares.

I've just reopened the media software on my laptop to rewatch one of the videos of the crime scene at the nursery when my cell vibrates. I brace, expecting to see the coroner's name pop up. Surprise ripples through me when I see **UNKNOWN CALLER**.

"Burkholder."

"If you want to talk to Cassidy, she's here to pick up her check," comes a harried female voice.

It takes me a few seconds to recognize who it belongs to. The woman at The Cheetah Lounge who came out to the parking lot to speak with me and Skid. "Hi, Angelica," I say easily. "Cassidy's there?"

"Hurry." She's whispering as if she doesn't want anyone to hear her. Talking too fast. "I think there's something going on."

"Like what?"

"I gotta go."

I get to my feet. "Angelica, wait—"

A resonant click ends the call.

"Crap." I drop the cell into my pocket and start toward reception. My third-shift dispatcher is burning up the keyboard, probably working on the minutes from our latest briefing.

"Who's on tonight?" I ask.

"T.J."

"Tell him to drop everything and meet me at The Cheetah Lounge."

She looks at me over the top of her glasses. "Chief?"

"The one in New Philly. Tip just came in on our mystery woman. Tell him I'm on my way."

• • •

The parking lot of The Cheetah Lounge was nearly full last time I was here. Tonight—at twenty to midnight—it's jam-packed with vehicles of every shape and size. I circle the lot twice, finally landing a spot in the grass at the rear. Single men and a few couples come and go as I make my way around to the entrance. I'm wearing my uniform and, like the last time I was here, patrons give me a wide berth.

I go through the door and find myself engulfed in an ocean of bodies. A band is set up at the back of the stage, belting out an interesting rendition of Zeppelin's "When the Levee Breaks." Forestage, a young woman wearing nothing more than a patch of sequins at her vee undulates to the beat, her body wrapped around the dance pole. The club is dark interspersed with the flash of strobes. I'm jostled multiple times as I make my way to the bar; all the while I keep my eye out for both Cassidy and the young woman I know only as Angelica.

Every stool is occupied, so I sidle right to where the barkeep is punching buttons on the cash register. He's younger than the previous bartender, busy with his customers, and looks as if he's enjoying himself.

When he glances my way, I have my shield at the ready. "Where can I find Angelica?"

"She do something wrong?"

"I just need to talk to her. Where is she?"

He looks around, feigns confusion. "She was here a moment ago," he tells me.

"Is she working this evening?"

"I think so." Turning, he strides to two men sitting at the bar and pours Patrón into waiting shot glasses.

When he returns to ring up the sale, I ask, "What about Cassidy?"

"Uh . . . she was here earlier, too."

My interest surges. "Where?"

"Been kind of busy," he says. "Can't keep an eye on the girls and do my job at the same time, you know?"

"What's Cassidy's last name?"

He shakes his head. "Everyone calls her Cass."

"Hey, Robbie!" A customer at the end of the bar raises his hand. "We need two beers down here!"

Mouthing "Sorry" to me, the barkeep hustles away.

I'm waiting for him to return, thinking about checking the restroom, when a hand comes down on my shoulder. For an instant, I think T.J. has arrived. I glance left to see the bouncer I met last time I was here.

His hand slides off my shoulder. "You're back," he says.

"I'm looking for your boss," I say, hoping to keep him from throwing me out.

"Isn't everyone?" He laughs, but it's a nasty sound. "He went home for the night."

"What about the manager?"

Frowning, he looks down at the bar in front of me. "Same rules as before, Ms. Chief of Police. No drink. No stay."

I'm aware of the bartender eyeing us as he serves up another trio of drafts. My nod catches his attention. "Coffee," I tell him. "Black."

The bouncer grins nastily. "I gotta get back to work," he tells me. "Don't make me come back."

I stare at him, saying nothing.

Giving the bartender a final look, the bouncer turns away and starts toward the front door.

"Sorry." Sending me a rueful look, the bartender snags a Styrofoam cup from beneath the bar and pours from a glass carafe. "For the record, he's an asshole." He's grinning when he sets the cup in front of me. "It's fresh, by the way."

"Thank you." I reach for my wallet.

He raises his hands. "On the house."

Pirouetting, he hoists two mugs from a freezer beneath the bar and shoves them beneath the tap.

"If you're looking for Angelica, check the break area out back."

I swivel at the sound of a female voice to see a scantily clad server, a tray loaded with drinks upraised to ear level, smiling at me. "She's a smoker," the woman says. "There's a privacy fence out by the dumpster. She's there."

"What about Cassidy?"

Her brows furrow, but she seems to be more focused on her surroundings than me or my questions. "Heard she quit."

"Do you know her last name?"

"No idea."

Before I can ask another question, she spins and melts into the crowd.

Turning back to the bar, I lay down a ten-dollar bill, pick up the coffee, and start toward the door. I sip coffee as I make my way through the crowd and take the exit. Outside, men and women and couples, laughing and drinking, brush past as I take the steps to the sidewalk. I scan the lot for T.J.'s cruiser as I take the walkway to the corner, but there's no sign of him. I round the corner and enter the rear lot. I immediately spot the six-foot-tall privacy fence.

The gate is closed. I go to it, lift the latch. "Angelica?" I say as I push it open. "Cassidy?"

To my surprise, I find Angelica sitting atop a picnic table, smoking a long brown cigarette. Her feet are bare, her toenails painted purple. A pair of high heels sit on the tabletop next to her. She startles upon spotting me. "What the hell are you doing here?"

"I'm looking for Cassidy," I tell her.

She gives me a deer-in-the-headlights look, then shifts her gaze to the back door of the club. "She's not here. And in case you didn't notice, I'm on my break."

I go through the gate and stop a short distance away from her. "Where is she?"

"Do I look like her keeper?" She rolls her eyes. "For God's sake, I can't keep track of everyone."

"You called me," I point out.

She lowers her voice. "Look, I'm worried about her. She was here. I thought you should know. That doesn't mean I want to be seen with you."

I take a drink of coffee, wait. When she doesn't elaborate, I ask, "Where would she go to pick up her check?"

"The office."

"What's her last name?"

"Are you kidding?" she snaps. "Nobody uses last names around here."

She's wearing a button-down shirt over a bikini top. A thong bottom. The tattoo of a dragon on the inside of her right ankle.

"Why not?" I ask.

The exit door at the back of the building swings open. The cacophony of too-loud bass drum and steel guitar pours out. A young woman with strawberry-blond hair peeks out. Her eyes go wide as she takes in my uniform.

Her eyes flick to Angelica. "He's looking for you," she hisses.

Rolling her eyes, Angelica holds her ground. "Tell him I'm on my damn break."

Something about the blond woman snags my attention and holds it. I don't know her; I've never met her. And yet there's something familiar about her.

"Can you come over here and talk to me?" I call out to her.

"No thanks."

"I'm looking for Cassidy," I say. "Do you know where I can find her?"

The two women exchange looks, some silent message I can't decipher passing between them.

"She quit," the strawberry-blond woman says.

Before I can say anything else, she slinks back inside.

Tossing her cigarette to the ground, Angelica slides off the table. "I gotta get back to work. Thanks for ruining my break."

"That young woman," I say. "Who is she?"

"Brandy."

"Is that her real name?"

"Nosy much?"

"That's my job."

"Yeah, well, you ask way too many questions." She bends to slip her feet into the heels. "And there ain't a soul here going to talk to you."

"Why not?"

"Because you're a cop." Straightening, she throws another look at the door. "I'd appreciate it if you didn't bother me again," she says, and leaves the patio area.

I watch her cross to the door and go through. An instant before the door closes, the strawberry blonde sticks her head out and looks at me.

"Check the trailer," she whispers, and then she's gone.

CHAPTER 13

I leave the break area and look out across the rear parking lot. Despite the late hour, the area is congested with vehicles coming and going and revelers walking into and out of the club. I shudder to think how many of these individuals are driving drunk tonight.

Check the trailer.

The woman's words echo in my head as I walk to the edge of the lot. The metal building surrounded by the chain-link fence is to my left. The trailer in question is dead ahead. The porch light is on. There are no vehicles parked nearby, but the windows glow yellow with light. Not for the first time, I wonder why the trailer is there. Does the local township zoning permit it? Is it some kind of extension of the club? An office or break area?

I tilt my head to my radio and hail T.J. "What's your twenty?"

"Just now crossing the interstate," he says, referring to Interstate 77. "Five minutes out."

"I'm here at the club," I say. "Back lot."

"Roger that."

I start across the grass at a brisk pace. I'm midway to the trailer when a bout of lightheadedness descends. I attribute the uncharacteristic sensation to my having missed dinner or maybe I'm dehydrated due to the heat. Brushing it off, I continue on.

Even if I find Cassidy, I'm well aware that she may not be able or willing to help. While Samuel Yutzy may have thought enough of her to keep her photo next to his bed, it's possible they weren't close or even friends. She may have no idea what happened to him or what was going on in his life. At the moment, it's all I've got, so I keep going. I've already decided that if she's not in the trailer, T.J. and I will do one more walk through in the club. If we don't find her there, we'll call it a night and start fresh in the morning.

I'm twenty feet away from the RV. I see insects flying around the globe of the porch light. I'm about to take the metal stairs to the front door when a wave of vertigo assails me with so much power that I miss the first step and stagger right. Startled, I stand there a moment and take a couple of deep breaths. I want to blame the dizziness on the unrelenting heat, too little sleep, or too many hours without food. But I don't think any of those things are the culprit and a tinge of worry lodges in my gut.

Turning, I go back to the stairs, grasp the rail, and start up them. The first step seems to tilt beneath my foot, throwing me off-balance. I stumble back, alarm bells ringing hard in my ears. What the hell is going on? Why can't I make it up those three small steps?

Not trusting my balance, I stand there a moment, baffled and worried. My face burns with heat. My mouth is dry. I press my hands to my cheeks, find the skin hot to the touch and moist with sweat. I'm thinking about going back into the club for water when another wave of dizziness sends me sideways. This time my feet tangle and I go down on my left hip.

"Son of a bitch," I hear myself hiss.

What's wrong with me? The question pounds my brain, but I have no answer. I feel as if I've just stepped off some wild carnival ride and my equilibrium is going haywire.

The knowledge that I'm in trouble lands like a rock in my gut. I mentally retrace everything I've eaten and drunk in the last hours. I think of the coffee I consumed a few minutes ago. The bartender having it ready even before I asked . . .

It takes every bit of strength I possess to get to my feet. The moment I'm upright, another surge of dizziness sends me sideways. I fight it, brace my legs, and manage to stay on my feet. Bending at the hip, I put my hands on my knees and gulp air. I can hear myself breathing hard. Fear, I realize, because I'm pretty damn sure someone slipped something into my drink . . .

The trailer is just a few feet away. The club is farther. *Radio,* I think. T.J. is only a couple of minutes out. Tilting my head, I reach for my shoulder mike, but miss. It's as if my hand weighs fifty pounds. I look down at the mike, reach for it again. My fingers brush the button.

I'm fumbling with the button when in the periphery of my vision, I see movement. I glance left, see a figure moving toward me. Male. Mere feet away. Not T.J. Friend or foe?

"I'm a cop." To my horror, my words slur.

He rushes me. Before I can react, he shoves me with so much force that I reel backward. Arms flailing, I stumble and land on my back hard enough to knock the breath from my lungs.

"Don't touch that motherfuckin' radio," he growls.

I try to sit up, but he puts his foot on my chest and shoves me back. He's standing over me, looking around. His face in the shadows. I don't recognize him. I don't know who he is.

I reach for my .38, but my reflexes are skewed. He drops to his knees beside me. I don't see the blow coming. It lands squarely in the center of my face. Pain zings up my sinuses. My ears begin to ring. I feel the warmth of blood on my lips and chin. In my peripheral vision, I see my attacker yank my .38 from its holster. Quickly, he empties the cylinder, then tosses the bullets and gun.

"I'm a cop." My words slur. I can't speak. My brain is muddled. I can barely conjure a coherent thought.

I lift my legs to kick him, but I'm not fast enough. He leans to me, grasps my arm, and yanks it so that I'm flipped onto my stomach. I've barely gotten my arms beneath me when a hand slams down on the back of my neck. My collar is yanked tight. The next thing I know I'm being dragged by my scruff, facedown, my legs and feet scrabbling.

I twist, grab his wrist, dig in with my fingers. "Let go of me," I choke out.

He doesn't let go, doesn't stop.

I try to get my legs under me so I can get to my feet. But my coordination is wrecked. I get to my knees, end up thrashing uselessly. He continues to drag me, my head and shoulders held off the ground by my collar. The collar digs into my throat, choking me. I reach for it with both hands, try to pull it away from my neck, feel buttons pop.

"Stop!" I shout the word, but it comes out like a kitten's mewl. "Stop . . ."

I bend my knees, flop onto my back, but he keeps dragging me. I lash out with my feet, try to dig in with my heels, but he's too strong.

"Who are you?" I croak. "What do you want?" My brain forms the words but they come out garbled and incoherent.

I stab my nails into his wrist, but he's wearing gloves and doesn't respond. I look around only to realize he's dragged me behind the trailer. It's darker here. No one around.

"Help me!" My voice is a muted cry. "Help!"

Abruptly, he lets go of my collar. The upper part of my body drops to the ground. He rolls me over so that I'm on my back, looking up at him. I try to get my elbows beneath me in the hope I can get to my feet. Before I can move, he comes down on top of me like a ton of bricks.

I punch with both fists, but my position is bad. Somehow, I clout his chin.

"Bitch."

He straddles me, sets both hands around my neck, and squeezes. I wrap my hands around his wrists, try to pry them off, but I'm not strong enough. I buck beneath him, but his balance is good; he's too heavy to dislodge.

"You listen up because I'm only going to say this once," he says. "You get one chance to do the right thing and this is it. You got it?"

The moment is so surreal I almost can't believe it's happening. I stare up at him, try to concentrate on details that will help me identify him later. Ski mask. Black T-shirt. Not enough light to see. Guttural voice. He's large. Strong. Two hundred pounds. Black gloves.

"Back off the Yutzy case. Stay the fuck off it. If you keep coming, I'll come back for you. I'll fuck you up. I'll fuck up your family. I will fuckin' destroy your life and everyone you care about."

I stare up at him, my head swimming. Blood pounding in my ears.

Don't pass out. Don't pass out.

My mouth is open. I can feel my tongue sticking out. My eyes starting to bulge. Undignified sounds squeezing from my throat. Fear crawling up my spine. He's sitting on my abdomen. I raise my legs, slam my knees into his back.

The lights dim. Tunnel vision on his face. Vaguely, I'm aware of my hands falling away from his wrists. No more fight left. *He's going to kill me,* I think, and I can't bear the thought of what that will do to Tomasetti.

You won't get away with this.

The blow is like a boulder slamming into my temple.

A cloak of darkness descends.

The night song that follows is silent and cold.

• • •

"Chief!"

The first thing I become aware of is the sound of voices all around. I'm lying on my back. A jackhammer of pain in my head. I open my eyes to see T.J. kneeling next to me. A young woman holding a longneck beer stands behind him, her hand over her mouth. The first thought that strikes my brain is that I'm not dead.

"How badly are you hurt?" T.J.'s voice comes at me as if from a long distance.

I try to answer, end up groaning.

"Easy does it, Chief," he says. "Just be still, okay?"

T.J. is talking, but the words seem jumbled and running together. He looks worried and out of his depth. I see his mouth moving, but it takes the words a moment to catch up, like a video with the audio askew.

"Can you tell me what happened?" he asks. "Do you know who did this?"

I stare up at him, manage to shake my head. "It's about the case," I croak, and I'm vastly relieved when my words don't slur.

He looks at me as if he's not quite sure my answer can be trusted. "You mean the Yutzy case?"

I nod. "Someone drugged me."

He curses beneath his breath. "Ambulance is on the way. Okay? Just be still."

I take physical inventory as he barks something into his radio mike. My head hurts. My mouth tastes like dirt. No other pain that I can identify. I look around, concentrate on getting my bearings. I'm lying on the ground about twenty feet away from the trailer. I remember the male accosting me. Punching me. Warning me off the case . . .

My temper kicks and I struggle to a sitting position. "Suspect is male," I manage. "Ski mask. Black T-shirt. He jumped me."

T.J. repeats the description into his radio.

"How long was I out?" I ask.

T.J. motions toward a young couple standing a few feet away. "They found you ten minutes ago. Said you were bleeding and out cold."

I look past him, see the young male and female, looking at me. Early twenties. Jean-clad. Concerned expressions.

"Did you see where he went?" T.J. asks.

"No." But my brain cells are starting to spark. "The bartender," I say. "He served me coffee. Go get him."

He hesitates as if uncertain about leaving me, then tilts his head and speaks into his mike. "Where's my damn ambulance?" he snaps.

"Pulling in now," comes Margaret's voice over the airwaves. "Glock, too."

I give T.J. a firm look. "I'm fine. Go get that son of a bitch."

Grinning, he gives me a quick salute. "My pleasure."

• • •

A few years ago, I read an article that outlined the top twenty-five most dangerous jobs in the U.S. I was surprised to find that police officers ranked pretty close to the bottom of the list, just below garbage collectors, farmers, and roofers. I'm thinking about that article tonight as I lie on a gurney in the ER at Pomerene Hospital, trying to recall details about what happened at The Cheetah Lounge.

In the last hour, I've been poked, prodded, injected, scanned, and X-rayed. Much to my relief, nothing is broken. Even so, I know this particular incident is going to stay with me awhile.

I called Tomasetti from the ambulance. Though by then I was able to speak without slurring, he knew immediately that something was terribly wrong. I don't know how much sense I made when I explained what happened. My brain kept misfiring and, of course, Tomasetti kept asking questions I didn't know how to answer. The one thing I do know for certain is that I scared him. I hated doing that to him; John Tomasetti doesn't scare easily and he didn't like it one bit.

I'm trying to decide what approach to take upon his arrival when the curtain surrounding my gurney is ripped aside and he's standing there, looking at me as if I've just stuck a knife in his gut.

"Kate." His face is indecipherable as he starts toward me.

I sit up straighter, tug at my gown, and then he's beside me, his arms going around me, pulling me close, and for the first time in hours I feel safe.

"I'm okay," I tell him.

"Yeah, the blood around your left nostril is a dead giveaway," he mutters, and holds me a little tighter.

I fumble the IV drip as I struggle to get closer to him. I'm not a crier, but I feel the heat of tears behind my eyes. Instinct tells me to crack a joke. Make light of this. Something to reassure both of us that this latest brush with violence is over and we're good to go.

Neither of us says anything.

After a moment, he pulls away, easing me to arm's length, and frowns. "We picked up the bartender. He's in an interview room at the Tuscarawas sheriff's office."

"Did you talk to him?" I ask.

He looks at me a little more closely. "That's a no go."

Belatedly, I realize his being there would have been against policy because we're married. My mind takes me back to the moment the bartender served the coffee. "If I recall," I say slowly, "the bartender who served me went by the name Robbie."

"The guy we picked up is Todd Lewis. He's clean, Kate. No record. There were no drugs found on his person or work area." Tomasetti grimaces. "Look, I talked to the detective. He doesn't think Lewis did it."

"Do they have CCTV cams?"

"None working."

"That's convenient," I snap.

"Our detective says Lewis seems genuinely baffled. And scared. He's claiming there was a small window of time when the cup was sitting on the bar and you were turned away from it, talking to someone. Anyone could have come up and spiked your drink."

I blink at him, trying to remember, to digest what's being thrown at me, not doing a very good job of either. I do recall talking to *someone* . . .

If you're looking for Angelica, check the break area out back.

"The server." I look at Tomasetti. "She's the one who told me I could find Angelica at the break area in the back."

"We'll find her." His mouth tightens. "Did the ER doc do a tox screen?"

I nod. "Blood. Urine. Saliva. He says it's going to be a few days."

"I'll get on it, see if I can light a fire."

But we both know tox screens are usually a slow process. "Thank you."

Tilting his head, he reaches out and lifts my hair out of the way with his fingertips. His face darkens, telling me he's spotted the bruises that are starting to bloom on my neck.

"If I wasn't old enough to know better, I'd punch the goddamn wall," he growls.

My smile feels cockeyed. "There's something to be said for you old guys."

He grins back and I'm so thankful to see it, to be the recipient of it, tears threaten again.

"You want to take me through what happened?" he says.

The last thing I want to do is relive those moments when I was helpless and drugged and at the mercy of someone who wished me harm. I take him through everything I remember, pushing through the tougher details. All the while I'm aware that my knees are shaking beneath the sheet. That my hands have gone cold. And the hair at my nape is wet with sweat.

When I'm finished, he sets his hand against my face. "I'm glad you're okay."

I press my cheek into his palm. "Me, too."

"Any idea how long you were out?"

"I don't know. A few minutes."

"Too damn long." His scowl deepens. "Kate, did he . . ."

"No." I shake my head. "There were a lot of people coming and going. He was more interested in getting his message across." I sigh. "Tomasetti, this was not some random assault. Not even close. It was about the case. Yutzy and Shetler and God only knows what else. This guy threatened me. Tried to intimidate me."

Grimacing, he reaches out and tugs the blanket up over my thighs. "Evidently, the dumb bastard doesn't know you very well, does he?"

"Or you." I choke out a laugh. "Which means he probably hasn't noticed the glowing red bull's-eye on his back."

"When the time is right, he's going to notice," Tomasetti says quietly. "And he's going to have a come-to-Jesus moment with the word Regret. That, you can bet your life on."

CHAPTER 14

It's a hair past eight A.M. and I'm standing at the half podium looking out at my team, trying not to feel self-conscious about my two black eyes and the unsightly bruises at my throat. Someone has set up a floor air-conditioning unit. It's groaning like a zombie, but the room is still as hot as a sauna.

"In case you have any questions about my new look this morning," I begin, "I was at The Cheetah Lounge last night, trying to identify Cassidy, our mystery woman. Someone didn't appreciate my asking questions, spiked my coffee, and assaulted me."

Several of my officers sit up straighter. "Damn," one of them mutters. At the back of the room, Mona makes a sound of dismay.

"I'm fine, as you can see." I hit the highlights of the incident. "But all of you should be aware the situation is heating up."

"Arrest?" Pickles asks.

I shake my head. "The bartender was picked up by the Tuscarawas

County Sheriff's Office for questioning and released without charges this morning."

"What about a suspect?" Glock asks.

"No, but the detectives are all over it." I frown. "That brings me to my first agenda item. From this point forward, all contact with any individual connected to The Cheetah Lounge will be done through BCI, task force personnel, or the Tuscarawas sheriff's office."

Tomasetti is standing next to the door, which is open to let in some air. He hasn't taken his eyes off me all morning. "Sheriff Rasmussen and I will be talking to the bouncer who was on duty last night," he says. "We'll also be talking with the manager, the servers, and the dancers who were on the clock at the time of the incident."

I point at Skid. "Did you find anything on The Cheetah Lounge?"

"Since he's the resident expert," Pickles mutters.

A few chuckles ensue.

Skid clears his throat. "Not much, Chief. They've got a presence on social media. Mostly photos from special events. Promos. Drink specials. Marketing and promotion." He picks up his cell and scrolls. "I did find out that the place was sold four years ago when the previous owner, George Lang, passed away. I couldn't find shit on the new owner. There are several entities involved, including an LLC, which I'm looking into now. The manager, by the way, is one Patrick O'Leary. New Philly resident. No record. No warrants."

I write down the name and look at Tomasetti, raise my brows.

"I'll talk to him," he says.

"Thank you," I say. "I've been getting the runaround."

Tomasetti addresses Skid. "Since BCI has the resources, I'll get legal to get to the bottom of who owns the place. It's been my experience that businesses like that have multiple investors and sometimes the names are buried in a smoke screen of LLCs."

"We're also still trying to get a line on our mystery woman, Cassidy," I say.

Tomasetti is staring at me. "Since I'll be talking to the manager later, I'll get her information for you."

I turn to the enlarged photo of her that's pinned to the board behind me. "If you recall, I found this pic of her during our search of Yutzy's residence. So far, all we know about her is that she was a dancer at The Cheetah Lounge, but recently quit. According to one of the women who worked with her, Cassidy and Yutzy were in a relationship. It's extremely important that we talk to her as soon as possible.

"T.J.," I say. "Run out to the farm store where Shetler worked. Talk to people. Find out who he was close to. See if anyone knows what might've been going on in his life."

He gives me a thumbs-up.

"Glock, I want you to go back out to the property where Shetler's body was found. Look around. Expand our canvass all the way to the highway, which includes four more farms. Check to see if anyone saw a buggy or vehicle they didn't recognize in the area in the last week."

"You got it."

"Mona," I say, "I want you to hit social media. Every platform you can think of. Look at any account that's even remotely connected to The Cheetah Lounge. Employees, including bartenders, bouncers, servers, and dancers."

"On it," she says.

I look at my two remaining officers, Skid and Pickles. I know neither of them has slept, and not for the first time I curse my lack of manpower. "I want you to canvass the area around the nursery again. Hit some of the outlying farms. You've got copies of the nursery's accounting books. Go through the client list. Talk to some of the customers. See if anyone saw or heard anything leading up to Yutzy's murder." I look at Pickles. "Be sure to take enough water with you today."

The old man huffs.

"I'm going to talk to some of the Amish who knew both of these men, including Joseph Stoltzfoos, who was friends with Yutzy and Shetler." I look out at my team. "I think all of us have been around long enough to know that someone always knows something. Sometimes that person is the one we least expect. It's up to us to find them and separate the junk from the jewels."

I bring my hands together. "Let's go."

• • •

Joseph Stoltzfoos lives on Mud Creek Road, a narrow track that runs between Painters Mill and Berlin. Before leaving the station, I ran him through LEADS. I wasn't surprised to find that he has a clean record. No arrests. No warrants. As far as I can tell, he's never been in trouble either civilly or criminally.

I'm thinking about that pristine record as I make the turn in to the gravel lane of his farm. Dust chases me as I head toward the house. I see half a dozen head of Black Angus cattle in the field to my right. A couple of draft horses, one of which has a foal at its side, graze in an adjacent pasture. The roadway curves right, taking me through a copse of pine trees, and then an old farmhouse looms into view. It's a small structure dressed in a fresh coat of paint and sporting a nostalgic wrap-around porch in the front. Beyond, a single barn, a silo, and a chicken house make up the rest of the farm. If memory serves me, the previous owner passed away a couple of years ago and the run-down farm went to auction. By the looks of the fresh paint and scaffolding next to the barn, Joseph Stoltzfoos is bringing the place back to life.

I park in the circular drive in front. I'm on my way to the door when

I notice the wagon loaded with alfalfa bales backed up to the barn. The sliding door is open. In the shadows within I see someone moving around, so I head that way.

I'm midway there when a fat golden retriever slinks out of the barn to greet me. I bend to give her a scratch behind her ear as I go through the man door.

"Watch out for my vicious watchdog."

I glance left to see a tall young man standing in the hay wagon, looking at me. He's dressed plainly in a work shirt, black trousers and suspenders, and a summer straw hat. He's clean-shaven, which means he's not married.

Bending to a bale of alfalfa, he lifts it, hauls it to the rear of the wagon, and tosses it to the floor alongside a dozen others.

"Those bales look nice and heavy," I say as I cross to him.

"Good crop this year." Eyeing the bruises on my face and neck, he jumps down from the wagon. "You look like you might've had a rowdy night."

"You should see the other guy." Smiling, I cross to him and stick out my hand for a shake. "I'd like to talk to you about Samuel Yutzy and Aaron Shetler if you have a minute." I add the "if you have a minute" phrase because it's polite, which is generally a good way to begin an interview.

He gives my hand a solid shake, then picks up one of the bales and stacks it on a waiting pallet. "I knew both of them. Heard about what happened."

"How did you hear?"

"*The Budget* ran a story," he says, referring to a popular Amish newspaper. "To tell you the truth, everybody who's got a tongue is talking about it."

"I understand you were friends."

"I was closer to Sammy." He lifts another bale, stacks it, reaches for another. "We knew each other since we were kids. Went to school together. Went to our first *singeon* together." It's the *Deitsch* word for "singing," which is a social event for Amish teens.

He's sweating from the exertion of his chore, the fabric beneath his arms darkened with moisture. Despite his friendly tone, there's a standoffishness about him. A hardness to his expression. He's got a thin mouth that's more snarl than smile and speaks of harsh judgment.

"The farm's looking good," I tell him.

"Been mine for about a year now. Had my work cut out for me."

He's not wearing gloves and I can just make out the red stripe of a cut on his right hand, between the thumb and forefinger. "How many acres?" I ask conversationally.

"Thirty-one, but the neighbor to the north has another six. Might buy it if I can pull the money together."

"You farm full-time?"

"Naw." He pulls a toothpick from his breast pocket and puts it in his mouth. "I work for Keim Lumber. Been with them almost three years now."

We're dancing around the topic at hand, feeling each other out. To my surprise, he brings it up first. "So what do you want to know about Sammy?"

"When's the last time you saw him?"

"Been a few months."

"Seems like a long time for someone who was a friend."

He shifts the toothpick from one side of his mouth to the other, studies me as if trying to decide if he should answer my question or throw me off his property.

"I kind of backed off, I guess."

"Backed off from your friendship?"

He shrugs. "I didn't like the road he was going down."

I'm still thinking about the cut on his hand. "What road was that?"

"The one to hell, maybe." He doesn't smile.

"Can you be a little more specific?"

He frowns at me. "*Wer lauert an der Wand, Heert sie eegni Schand.*" If you listen through the wall, you'll hear others recite your faults. It's an old Amish saying that basically means people will gossip about you when you're not there. He's talking about Samuel, of course.

"Telling the truth doesn't mean you're disrespecting his memory," I say.

"Fair enough." He picks up another bale of hay. "I got baptized," he says, placing it on the stack. "Sammy didn't. We took different paths. Went our separate ways." He shrugs again. "I'll not stand in judgment of him now, when he's not here to speak for himself."

Over the next minutes, I take him through the same line of questioning as I did with both sets of parents. I try several different approaches, but he doesn't reveal anything I don't already know.

"Joseph, what did you mean when you said Samuel was on the road to hell?" I ask.

He sets another bale on the stack. "Samuel was a good man. But the kind of life he was living wasn't for me, especially after I got baptized." He looks away, appears to study the hay behind him. "I'm getting married in the fall."

"How was Samuel living his life?" I ask.

For the first time he looks uncomfortable, and I realize I'm asking him to breach that Amish wall of silence. "Last few times I saw him, Sammy was partying a lot. Drinking, you know. Smoking dope. Picking up women." He tightens his mouth. "Taking them home. I ain't one to judge, but that wasn't for me."

"Any woman in particular?"

"I wouldn't know."

"Was he into drugs?" I ask. "Dealing?"

He shakes his head. "He was too smart to do that. Sammy was in it for the fun. The women, you know. He liked to have a good time."

"What else?"

Joseph stares at me for a too-long moment, as if wondering if I'm trying to trap him. I see irritation in his eyes; he doesn't want to talk to me. To my relief, he's young enough—inexperienced enough—that he doesn't see a way out of responding.

"I didn't like the company he was keeping," Joseph tells me.

"What company was that?"

He cocks his hip and looks out the door at the house beyond, as if wishing he were there instead of here, talking to me.

"Joseph." I say his name firmly. "This isn't about you or me or anyone disapproving of the way Samuel spent his time. The only thing I care about is finding the person who murdered him. Do you understand?"

He sighs, but he still isn't happy about the intrusion. "That's the thing, Chief Burkholder. Samuel was doing fine." He shakes his head. "Then he started hanging around with them *Englischers.* Running with all them loose women."

"What *Englischers*?" I ask. "I need names."

"I don't know that. A couple of guys. The kind that wear suits and got money, you know?"

"Are these men from Painters Mill?"

"I don't know where they're from."

"What about the women?"

He looks away and I'm surprised by the color climbing up his neck to his face. All that hard-line talk and yet he embarrasses easily.

"All I know is Sammy liked women," he says.

"Amish or English?"

"Both, I reckon."

I pull out the photo of Cassidy. "Do you recognize her?"

He looks at the photo, his expression turning pained. "I met her a time or two."

"What's her name?"

"Cass."

"Last name?"

He shakes his head.

"How did you meet her?"

"There was a big rager a while ago," he says. "She was there."

A "rager" is an Amish party, usually held out of doors, in a field or barn. It draws large numbers of young people, mostly Amish, but sometimes English youth show up, too. Word spreads via social media or word of mouth and it's not unusual for two or three hundred young people to attend. Food trucks are brought in. Bands set up shop. Vendors sell everything from Jell-O shots to T-shirts.

"What rager?"

"The one down to the Campbell farm. Last fall, I think."

I don't recall hearing about a rager at the Campbell farm. Then again, most attendees are pretty tight-lipped. The events are spontaneous. With so many underage youths present and the alcohol and drugs flowing freely, ragers are rife with trouble.

"How did Samuel meet her?" I ask.

"Met her at the rager. Same as me. They hit it off. I didn't see him too much after that."

"Were they involved?"

"Yeah, but . . ." His brows knit. "She was having some problems. Too young to be on her own. It's more like he was trying to save her or something."

"What do you mean by that?"

"She'd just left the Amish. Her parents—"

"She was Amish?" My brain hits the brakes so hard I can practically hear the screech. "Are you sure?"

He looks at me as if that's something I should have already known. "That was her whole problem. Her parents kicked her out of the house. She didn't have any money or a place to stay."

"Cassidy isn't an Amish name," I say.

"I don't think it's her real name."

"Is she from Painters Mill?" I ask.

"Coshocton County, I think."

Which is a different church district and explains why none of the local Amish know her. "Joseph, what do you mean when you say Samuel was trying to save her?"

He lifts a shoulder, lets it drop. "He was always drawn to the women with a lot of drama in their lives. The ones who needed help. Crying and looking all helpless and pretty. The ones in trouble."

I think about that a moment. "Is there anyone I can talk to who might be able to help me locate Cass?"

"I don't know any of the Amish down south." He shakes his head. "All's I know is that Samuel had a weakness for women like that. If they were down on their luck, he rushed in like some fool. Problem is, I'm not sure this woman was worth saving."

"Why not?"

He shrugs. "Just a feeling."

I nod, everything I've learned churning in my brain. "How did you get that cut on your hand?" I ask.

He stares at me, knowing exactly what I'm asking and why. "Cut open a feed bag with my pocketknife. Got in a hurry."

"Where were you Wednesday morning?"

His mouth curves into a smile. "I wasn't at Sammy's nursery if that's what you're asking."

I don't smile. "What about Wednesday evening?"

He frowns. "I had dinner with my fiancée and her parents," he says. "You can check."

"I will," I tell him. "Thanks for your time."

• • •

I'm in the Explorer and nearly to Painters Mill when Tomasetti calls.

"I thought you might want to know the bouncer from The Cheetah Lounge is cooling his heels in an interview room at the Tuscarawas sheriff's office," he tells me.

"There's an image that brightens my day a little."

His laugh is short-lived. "I have a last name on your mystery woman. Cassidy Robinette."

"Thanks, but I think that may be an alias." I recap my conversation with Joseph Stoltzfoos. "She's Amish."

"Didn't have that one on my bingo card."

"He said she was involved with Yutzy. That she was very young and having money problems, didn't have a place to stay. My guess is she used a fake ID to get the job."

"In the state of Ohio, a server has to be nineteen to serve spirits," he tells me. "Twenty-one to be an exotic dancer."

"Sounds like the manager might have some explaining to do."

"He's on his way here now for an interview."

"Nice job, Tomasetti."

"Every now and then I get it right."

I'm still thinking about Cassidy. "I think I'm going to take a drive down to Coshocton County."

"Do you know any of the Amish down there?"

"No, but I just happen to know that the Amish grapevine puts Google to shame."

"As you tap into that particular resource, will you do me a favor?"

"Depends."

"Don't accept anything to drink from anyone."

CHAPTER 15

There are advantages and disadvantages to just about everything in this life, and that includes living in a small town. In Painters Mill, almost everyone knows everyone. That makes it difficult to keep things as private as you'd like, especially if you're part of the Amish community. Take it from me, if you're Amish and looking to break the rules without getting caught, it's not going to go well. When you're a cop, on the other hand, that small-town intimacy can be a gift.

Edna Miller is to grapevine chatter the way the Wright brothers are to flight. She practically invented it. Back when she lived in Painters Mill, Edna was the unofficial gossip authority. Nothing got past her, and once she was in the know you could bet your ass your parents would be told within the hour. I lost track of Edna when she and her husband, Herman, moved away. It was only when Tomasetti and I purchased cabinets when we remodeled our bathroom that I discovered she and her husband moved to Canal Lewisville to open their own cabinetry shop. Lucky for me, Canal Lewisville is just four miles from Coshocton proper. If there's anyone in the area who might be able to fill in the blanks on our mystery woman, Cassidy, it's Edna Miller.

Miller's Cabinet Works is located on the outskirts of a residential neighborhood not far from the Tuscarawas River. It's a good-size place with a showroom in front and a workshop in the rear. A cowbell jingles merrily when I go through the front door.

"You here for some more of those nice maple cabinets?"

I glance right to see Edna sitting on a short stool, stocking a display of wood stain and brushes. She's a large woman wearing a mauve-colored dress with a white *halsduch* and *kapp*.

"That's the thing about living in an old farmhouse," I tell her. "You always need something."

She rises, grunting with the effort, and brushes her hands on her dress. "Those were some nice ones. Made by good Amish hands. Hope you stained them and didn't paint. How's that husband of yours doing?"

"He sends his regards."

"Uh-huh." She gives me a thorough once-over. "Sarah Mullet up to Painters Creek told me you were *ime familye weg.*" The English translation of the phrase is "in the family way," which is how the Amish say "pregnant" because most find the word too crude. "You don't look that way to me."

I clear my throat. "Sarah might be rushing things a little," I tell her.

"Didn't think so." She huffs. "Not with you being police and all. Hope you keep in mind that time has a way of getting past us quicker than we'd like."

I can tell by the excitement in her eyes that she's going to ask me about the murders, so I pull the photo of Cassidy from my pocket. "I'm wondering if you know who this is."

She drags her eyes away from me and focuses on the photo. Her brows pull together and then she frowns. "Haven't seen the likes of that one in a while."

"Who is she?"

She pauses dramatically. "Wilma Ann Borntrager. Last I heard she was on *rumspringa* and told her *mamm* she wouldn't be getting baptized."

"Do you know where I can find her?"

"I wouldn't have the slightest clue. Who can keep up with a girl like that?" She presses her lips together. "Heard she was a bad egg."

"How so?"

"Leaving the fold at eighteen? Is that bad enough for you?"

I wonder if Edna realizes I did the very same thing at the same age. "She's eighteen years old?" I ask.

"That sounds about right. Born the same month as my youngest. July."

"Are her parents around?" I ask. "Do you know where I can find them?"

She tsks. "Her *datt* was killed in a buggy wreck two years ago. It was hard on the family, as you can imagine. Miriam sold the farm and moved to town. Works down to the laundromat there on Second Street. Can't miss it."

• • •

Village Laundromat is like a hundred other laundromats I've driven by on the street and never spared a glance. It's a clean business with ample parking in front, a pleasant storefront, and newish equipment. The smells of detergent and overdried cotton waft over me when I enter. Two ceiling fans circulate hot air. A row of colorful plastic chairs lines the front-facing window to my right. A young woman in denim shorts scrolls through her cell phone, oblivious to the world around her. The

TV is tuned to a local news station. There are restrooms to my right. At the back, an Amish woman stands at a long folding table, one eye on the TV, the other on the clothes she's folding.

I start toward her. "Mrs. Borntrager?"

She's wearing a plain blue dress. Gauzy white *kapp.* Black oxford shoes. Upon hearing her name, she turns to me. I guess her to be in her mid-forties. Mouse-brown hair. Blue eyes. Hers is the face of a woman who works too many hours, spends too much time on her feet, and doesn't have much hope that either of those things is going to change anytime soon.

"*Guder nochmiddawk,*" I say as I approach her. Good afternoon.

"Oh." Her eyes widen as she takes in my uniform. "Is there a problem?"

"No problem at all, ma'am. I'd just like to ask you a few questions if you have a minute."

"I don't see why the police would want to speak to me." She looks past me as if to make sure I don't have a SWAT team in tow.

Nervous, I think, so I move to keep it casual and easy. "My goodness it's a hot one today." I blot my forehead with my sleeve. "Bet those dryers don't help."

"Got the dryers running first thing this morning, so I opened the door to let out the heat. I think I just let more in!" The weather talk seems to relax her a little and she laughs. "Never heard a policeman speak *Deitsch* before."

"I was Amish," I tell her. "A long time ago."

She doesn't have anything to say about my leaving the fold.

I pull out the photo of Wilma Ann Borntrager. "I'm looking for this young woman."

Her eyes land on the photo and she sucks in an involuntary breath. "That's my daughter. Wilma Ann. Is everything okay with her? Is she hurt? Why are you asking me about her?"

"Everything's okay as far as I know," I say. "I just want to talk to her. Do you have any idea where I can find her?"

"Well . . ." She looks everywhere except at me. It's obvious she doesn't want to talk about her daughter. While I may have Amish roots, it's not enough to bridge the cultural gap between Amish and English.

Lucky for me, she's too well-mannered to refuse the question. "Last time I talked to her she was renting a house up to Painters Mill."

"Do you have an address?"

"Only been there once. It's on Lost Creek Road out there by the lake. Hired a driver to take me." She sighs. "It's a trashy old place. Don't know why she wants to live like that."

I'm vaguely familiar with the area; there aren't many homes, so I don't get out that way often. "Mrs. Borntrager, do you have a phone number for her?"

The Amish woman shakes her head. "Seems like that girl gets a new phone every week. Last time I tried to call her I got a recording."

The vast majority of Amish do not have cell phones. That said, most church districts do allow phones inside businesses for business use only.

"Do you have a cell phone?" I ask, hoping Wilma's number is in her contacts or call history.

"I use the one here or down to the phone shanty off of the county road."

I pull out my notebook. "What's your daughter's birth date?"

"July 19. She just turned eighteen."

Eighteen. She's too young not only to be serving liquor, but to be working as an exotic dancer. "Does she live alone?" I ask. "Have a roommate?"

"I don't know. And I sure don't know how she could afford to rent a house, trashy or not, all by herself." She heaves another unhappy sigh. "Some of the Amish turned away from her when she left. Not sure how I feel about that, but there you have it."

I pull out the photos of Samuel Yutzy and Aaron Shetler. I show her the picture of Samuel first. "Do you know this young man?"

"He's the one got killed up there in Painters Mill." She slaps her hand over her mouth, looks at me over the tops of her fingers. For the first time I see distress in her eyes—and fear. "Why are you asking me about a dead man? What does he have to do with my daughter?"

"I'm not sure, but from what I'm hearing, they were involved," I say. "Did you ever meet him? See them together?"

"No, but I don't see her very often." She closes her eyes, her expression the picture of distress. "*Mein Gott.*" My God. "Now you've got me worried."

I show her the photo of Aaron Shetler. "What about him?"

She opens her eyes, studies the photo. "Never seen that one." She turns her eyes to mine. "I always knew nothing good would come of all that running around." She fights tears for a moment. "Chief Burkholder, is my girl in trouble?"

The urge to reassure her is strong. But I learned a long time ago empty promises never help. "All I can tell you is that I'm going to do my best to find her and talk to her."

She nods. "When you do, will you tell her to come see her *mamm*?"

"Of course I will." Reaching out, I set my hand on her shoulder. "Thank you for your time."

• • •

I hail Dispatch as I climb into the Explorer. "Get me everything you can find on Wilma Ann Borntrager." I spell the last name. "White female. Eighteen years old. Last known address Painters Mill. Check for warrants. Run her through LEADS. See if you can come up with any known associates."

"Roger that," comes Lois's voice, and I hear the click of computer keys.

"I'm ten-seventy-six her residence for a welfare check," I say. "She lives out on Lost Creek Road. See if you can come up with a street number. Find out who owns the property."

"Got it."

"Who's on duty?"

"Everyone," she says.

I think about the assignments I doled out this morning. "Tell Mona to drop everything and meet me there."

CHAPTER 16

Lost Creek is a fitting name for the road where Wilma Ann Borntrager resides. It's a twisty stretch of asphalt that snakes through bottomland growth of dense brush and hundred-year-old trees. Only a handful of houses occupy this desolate stretch, half of which are abandoned. I pass by two mobile homes swamped with tall yellow grass. I traverse a bridge with a damaged guardrail and spot the mailbox ahead, the number I'm seeking finger-painted onto the side.

I pick up my radio. "Ten-twenty-three," I say, letting Dispatch know I've arrived on scene.

"Ten-four."

"Mona," I say, "what's your ETA?"

"Coming up behind you, Chief."

Gravel crunches beneath my tires as I make the turn in to the driveway. The house is a circa 1950s cottage with a single-car garage, faded awnings, weatherworn siding, and a crumbling concrete porch. There are no vehicles in the driveway. I can just make out tire tracks in the dust, telling me someone was here not too long ago.

I park several yards back from the house and get out. The sun beats down on me like a hot cast-iron skillet. It's incredibly quiet; not even the birds are singing. I can't help but wonder if it's just too damn hot.

I've just climbed the steps of the front porch when the crunch of tires on gravel sounds. I turn to see Mona pull in and park behind my Explorer.

She gets out and starts toward me. "Doesn't look like anyone's home."

"We'll see." I open the storm door and knock. "Painters Mill Police Department!" I call out. "Wilma Ann Borntrager? Would you come out and talk to me please?"

No one answers.

Mona and I exchange a look.

She shrugs. "Might be napping."

"Or passed out from the heat," I mutter.

I can tell by her expression that, kidding aside, we're pondering the same questions. Is this young woman purposefully avoiding us? Or is she missing?

Using the heel of my hand, I knock again, this time hard enough to rattle the door. "Everyone okay in there?" I call out. "Come out and talk to me!"

Mona sidles left and bends slightly, trying to get a look through the window, but the drapes are drawn tight.

"Check to see if there's a vehicle in the garage," I tell her. "I'm going to go around back."

"Got it." She makes eye contact with me.

I hold her gaze a moment. "Eyes open," I tell her. "Watch the windows."

"Yes, ma'am."

Side by side, we descend the steps. She goes west toward the garage. I proceed east, walk along the side of the house, and round the corner to the back. I keep one eye on the windows as I pass, the other on the trees to my right.

The backyard is a jungle of weeds, brush, and saplings that have been left to proliferate. I trip over a fallen grill, kick it aside, head toward the tiny concrete porch. The iron rail jiggles when I take the steps. The back door is a half lite. Through the glass, I see a small kitchen with an old gas stove. Dark cabinets. Goose-themed wallpaper. A porcelain sink that's pitted with rust. Peeling linoleum on the floor.

Using the heel of my hand, I knock. "Painters Mill Police Department! Ms. Borntrager? Is everything okay in there? Come on out and talk to me please!"

The only response is the incessant whirr of cicadas from the woods.

"Crap." Sweat drips down my right temple as I take the steps down to the yard. I pass by an uncovered window, cup my hands, and peer inside. It's a dining room. Card table. Half-dead fiddle-leaf fig against the window. Scarred wooden floors. No movement. The place looks lived in, but barely.

I continue to the west side of the house to find Mona at the back of the garage. "Is there a vehicle inside?" I ask.

"No windows. The overhead door is locked." She motions toward the gravel. "There are footprints in the dust, though, Chief. Tire tracks. Someone's been here recently."

I tilt my head to my radio. "Lois, were you able to come up with the owner of the property?"

"Still working on it, Chief."

"Anything come back on Borntrager?"

"She's clean. Nothing on known associates."

I join Mona and we continue around to the other side of the garage.

We're on our way to the front when a distinct *thump!* sounds from inside. As if something was dropped onto the concrete floor.

Mona and I freeze, exchange puzzled looks.

"Someone inside?" she silently mouths.

I nod. We stand there a moment, unmoving, listening. A full minute passes without another sound. I start toward the front of the garage. "Painters Mill Police Department!" I call out. "We're here for a welfare check! Can you come out and talk to us?"

I walk past the overhead door and start toward the nearest window of the house. Mona is a few feet behind me, her eyes on the overhead door. Her head is cocked as if she's listening for movement inside.

An engine turns over and revs. I stop, spin. Mona has stopped, too. She's on alert, feet wide, looking at the door.

"Mona!" I scream.

The overhead door explodes.

Pieces of wood fly. Mona swivels to run. She's not fast enough. A vehicle bursts from inside the garage. Wild acceleration. Engine screaming. The front end strikes her hip. Her feet leave the ground. She cartwheels in the air, arms and legs flailing. The vehicle speeds past, motor whining like a jet engine.

Mona hits the ground with a sickening thump and rolls. I charge to her, hit my radio. "Ten-thirty-three!" I scream. Officer in trouble. "Send an ambulance!"

In the periphery of my vision, I see the vehicle fishtail down the driveway. The tires spew gravel and dust. I glance over my shoulder, see the driver go left, take note of the description. Dark sedan. Blue. Midsize. Older.

I drop to my knees beside Mona. "Be still. Don't move."

"I'm . . . okay."

"Where are you hurt?"

Groaning, she rolls onto her back. "Everywhere."

Her face is deathly pale in the bright sunlight. She's squinting. I see sweat on her cheeks. Face screwed up in pain. Vaguely, I'm aware of the vehicle pulling away, engine groaning. Getting away. High rate of speed.

"Hip hurts," she groans.

"Back? Neck?"

She raises her head, gets her elbows beneath her. "I think I'm okay."

"Lie still," I snap.

"To hell with that." She sits up, her eyes zeroing in on the road where the vehicle has already disappeared. "Chief, I'm fine. Go get that son of a bitch."

"Ambulance is on the way."

"I got my radio! Go!"

Then I'm on my feet, sprinting to the Explorer. "Ten-eighty!" I shout. Chase in progress. I rip open the door, slide behind the wheel, jab the ignition button. "Eastbound. Lost Creek Road. Dark sedan. Older. Midsize."

I jam the Explorer into drive. My wheels spew gravel as I fishtail 180 degrees. "High rate of speed."

I hit the gas. The Explorer tears across the yard, bounces through the ditch. The wheels bark when they hit asphalt. I cut the wheel. The engine groans when I stomp the gas. "Ten-seven-eight." Need assistance.

I floor the accelerator. Both hands on the wheel. My every sense is on high alert. I reach for calm, recall my training, search my memory for what I know about this road. No turnoffs coming up, but there are a couple of two-tracks the driver might take to lose me.

I glance down, see that I'm already at eighty-six miles per hour. There's no sign of the vehicle ahead, so I don't back off. Trees flash by as I fly down the road. Vaguely I'm aware of my radio lighting up. Sheriff's office is en route. Two of my own officers.

"What's the ETA on that ambulance?" I snap.

"Four minutes."

"I got an officer down."

The guardrail blurs by as I pass over a bridge. I feel the Explorer go airborne, the steering get squirrely, so I back off the gas. Then I'm past the bridge and I floor it. All the while I'm trying to remember which crossroads are farther ahead. There's a township road. No stop sign.

"Passing Doe Creek Road," I say into my radio, keeping the other cops abreast of my location.

I back off the accelerator to round a curve. Hit the gas in the straightaway. The road curves again. The Explorer takes it like a dream. When the road straightens, I see the flash of taillights ahead.

Gotcha, you son of a bitch.

"Suspect is eastbound on Lost Creek Road," I say into my radio. "Coming up on Township Road 722."

The taillights flicker again. I grip the wheel, my every sense honed on the two red points of light. The vehicle blows past the township road.

"Suspect is past TR 722. Heading toward Burr Oak." I lose sight of my quarry as I maneuver an S curve. "Anyone to intercept?"

Glock's voice cracks over the radio. "I'm southbound on Burr Oak."

"Coming your way," I say.

My speedometer hits eighty-nine miles per hour. I've got tunnel vision on my suspect. I'm gaining, but he's two hundred yards ahead. I'm mapping the road and approaching turnoffs. There's a sharp curve coming. If my suspect doesn't slow down, he won't be able to negotiate—

Thwack! Thwack! Thwack!

My windshield splinters into a thousand white capillaries. Pieces of glass fly at me, pelting my face and neck. "Shit!"

I take my foot off the gas.

Thwack! Thwack! Thwack! Thwack!

Something slams into the headrest inches from my ear. I duck left.

Hit the brake. A quick bark of rubber against asphalt, but the tires hold the road.

"Shots fired!" I shout. "Shots fired!"

My speedometer falls to sixty. I lean left to better see through the windshield. He's less than half a mile ahead now, but I can't see and I'm losing ground.

Thwack! Thwack!

A puff of glass sprays my face and neck. I stomp the brake. Cut the wheel. The windshield collapses, peels in. I'm thinking about punching it out so I can see when the Explorer shudders and goes into a sickening spin.

"Shit!"

The tires hit gravel and lose traction. The front wheels dip into the ditch. The Explorer bottoms out, then bounces violently onto the other side. The front end slams into the wire fence like a tennis ball into a racket. The momentum launches me against my safety belt, the strap cutting into my shoulder like a garrote.

The vehicle stops cold. The engine has died. I reach down. Punch the ignition button. Nothing.

Cursing, I smack my hand down on the steering wheel and snatch up my mike. "I'm out."

CHAPTER 17

It's three P.M. The temperature outside stands at ninety-two degrees in the shade. The humidity isn't much lower. I'm sitting in an interview room—the nice one with a coffeemaker and water cooler—at the Holmes County Sheriff's Office. I've been here for nearly an hour. I've given my statement. Filled out every form known to mankind. And I've participated in at least three interviews. The bad news is I'm tied up here while the person or persons who murdered Samuel Yutzy and Aaron Shetler are still on the loose.

The door swings open. I look up to see Tomasetti enter. He's frowning; I frown back at him. As usual, I can't read his frame of mind. "You doing okay, Chief?" he asks.

"I think the situation is looking up," I tell him.

"Well, there's some balm for a man's soul." The shadow of a smile whispers across his mouth as he pulls out the chair across from me.

"Did you get him?" I ask.

"No." He sinks into the chair. "We put out a BOLO on the description of the vehicle."

"The description I gave matches half the vehicles in Holmes County."

"It's a start. Sheriff's office is out now, looking for CCTV. Game cams."

"Might get lucky, I guess." I sigh. "How's Mona?"

"X-rayed, stitched, and CT scanned," he says. "I think she got a tattoo removed while she was there. ER doc sent her home."

"Good luck with that." I can't help it; I laugh. "No way is she going to sit this out."

"Sounds like someone else I know."

I resist the urge to defend myself.

"We also put out a BOLO for Borntrager," he tells me.

"Did you search the house?"

His eyes flick to the clock on the wall. "Warrant is in the works. We have deputies on scene."

"What happened to exigent circumstances?" I snap.

"It got lost in the if-this-goes-to-court mentality."

He's right. A warrant will not only protect us, but allow for a more thorough search. I sigh again anyway. "Who owns the house?"

"We're digging into that," he says easily.

"Why the hell is everything taking so long?"

He laughs. "That car chase jacked you up a little, didn't it?"

"I don't appreciate some crazy bastard running over one of my officers."

He contemplates me a moment. "Someone went to a lot of trouble to make sure the owner of the property wasn't easy to find."

The words give me pause and I look at him a little more closely. All of the disjointed details I hadn't been able to pull together tighten a notch.

"Something there," I say. "Because that doesn't make a whole lot of sense."

"I agree," he says. "We *did* find the lease."

"Who's the tenant?" I ask.

"Our friend, Cassidy Robinette."

"Who's paying the rent?"

"We're looking at the money trail now." Rising, he goes to the water station, fills two cups, and brings them back to the table.

"Who takes the title of a dumpy little house in a small-town rural area and conceals the name of the title holder in a maze of LLCs?" I ask irritably.

"Homeowners do it for a variety of legitimate reasons," he says. "For example, liability issues with rental properties. Someone breaks a leg and they can't sue you personally and take your assets. On the other hand, some homeowners might set up an LLC and put it on the title to protect their privacy."

"My vote is for the latter," I say.

"Someone has something to hide."

"Like what?" I take one of the cups and sip, my mind running through the gauntlet of possibilities. "Drugs?"

"That particular scourge certainly keeps its share of gnarly company."

It's a reoccurring question. I want to think it fits, but it doesn't. Not completely.

His cell chimes. He glances down at it and frowns. "We got the warrant."

I get to my feet. "Let's go."

• • •

Since my Explorer is out of commission, I ride with Tomasetti and call Glock during the drive to Lost Creek Road. "Any luck with the canvass?" I ask, referring to his search of the ravine where Aaron Shetler's body was found.

"I got nada, Chief. Either they got lucky or they were being extremely careful."

"It was worth a shot." But my disappointment is keen. "Can you come out and canvass the other residences out here on Lost Creek?"

"On my way."

Tomasetti makes the turn in to the driveway of the house and parks in the yard, just outside the crime scene tape. A Holmes County Sheriff's Office cruiser is parked on the shoulder, emergency lights flashing. Mona's vehicle is still where she left it. A BCI crime scene van has been backed up to within twenty or so feet of the garage, its doors open. A technician braves the blazing sun, kneeling to pick up and preserve pieces of the overhead door or vehicle and placing them in bags to be analyzed.

"Your Explorer was towed to the mechanic over on Ohio Street, by the way," Tomasetti tells me as he kills the engine.

"Auggie will be pleased it wasn't totaled," I say.

We exchange a quick smile and get out. Tomasetti walks around to the back of the Tahoe and pulls out shoe covers and gloves. We suit up and make our way to the house. I try not to think of the microscopic slivers of glass from my shattered windshield mixing with the sweat beneath my collar, but I'm itchy and uncomfortable and hope for a shower and change of clothes as soon as we finish.

At the front door, Tomasetti slips on gloves and tries the knob. "Locked," he says, and we go around to the back.

We find the back door unlocked and enter. The first thing I notice is the pong of day-old garbage. We're standing in a small kitchen. It's a run-down space with beat-up cabinets, a built-in desk, and a stained porcelain sink. An ancient-looking hot-water heater peeks out at us from a corner closet. A decade of fingerprints mottles the woodwork.

"Let's clear the place first," Tomasetti says.

"Yep."

My senses hum as we go through the doorway and into the living room. "Painters Mill Police Department!" I call out as we traverse the room and enter the hall. "Search warrant!"

The first door we come to is affixed with a hasp and padlock on the outside. I look at Tomasetti. "That's weird."

"To say the least." He shrugs. "Home office?"

The lock isn't engaged, so I lift it and drop the shackle into the swivel eye, and then I push open the door. "Police department!" I call out as I enter the small bedroom. Dim light filters through a tiny window covered with a blanket that's been nailed to the wall. I go to the bed, kneel, look under it. Tomasetti goes to the closet. No one there.

Then we're back in the hall and on to the next door. It's another bedroom. Another lock on the outside. We clear it quickly.

"BCI!" Moving ahead of me, Tomasetti sidles into a bathroom, shoves aside the shower curtain. "Clear," he calls out.

Back in the living room, we pause, look around.

"This place has an odd vibe," I say.

"A lot of locks."

"Wilma Borntrager wasn't living here alone."

"I think it's safe to say she wasn't driving that vehicle, either."

He starts toward the kitchen. "I'm going to search the desk."

"I got the living room."

It's a cramped space. There's a ragtag sofa against the wall. A bedroom pillow that's not quite clean. A high-end TV that's too large for the room is mounted on the wall. There's a chair with a torn cushion next to the front window. A stuffed animal on the floor. A coffee table piled with mail and advertisements. I page through the mail. A bill from a propane company. An ad from the local grocery store. Everything is addressed to Cassidy Robinette.

Finding nothing of interest, I continue on to the hall, take a right into the first bedroom. The space smells of dirty socks and mildew. There's a full-size bed, unmade, the sheets dull from use. I remove the top blanket, looking for blood or anything out of the ordinary. Nothing but a stained sheet and a pair of wadded-up panties.

A small suitcase lies open on the floor, its top leaning against the wall. I go to it. A pair of women's shorts. Yoga pants. Two T-shirts. Panties. There's a zippered bag. Glad for my gloves, I open it, find a sequin bikini top and bottom inside. The same type of outfit I saw at The Cheetah Lounge.

I move on to the night table. There's a small lamp without a shade. A week's worth of dust. I pull open the top drawer, find a paperback novel, the pages dog-eared from use. A bottle of Tylenol. Lighter. The second drawer contains two boxes of condoms. Personal lubricant.

I go to the third drawer.

Nothing. Nothing. Nothing.

I hear Tomasetti rummaging around in the kitchen. I cross the room, go to the dresser, tug open the top drawer. Surprise ripples through me at the sight of the jewelry. A necklace and earring set by an upmarket designer. There are two turquoise-and-silver rings. I see a thin gold chain with what looks like a diamond pendant affixed. I'm no expert on jewelry, but these items look expensive. How does a single woman with limited finances afford so much nice jewelry?

I go to the second bedroom. This one is slightly more pleasant. A window-unit air conditioner pumps cool air into the room. The drapes are the kind used to darken a room for daytime sleeping. I start with the nightstand. I find a pack of clove cigarettes in the top drawer, two joints tucked in with the smokes. I mark the pot with a small evidence cone and keep moving.

The second drawer contains nothing of interest. I tug open the third drawer and do a double take at the pile of zip tie flex-cuffs. A quick count reveals twelve ties. They are the kind used by law enforcement. Not the kind of thing a single woman keeps in her night table. But if not Wilma Borntrager, then who?

I snap several photos of the zip ties and go to the final drawer. The only item is a neoprene laptop case. I pull the laptop out, set it on the bed, open it. The device begins to hum and prompts me for a password.

I try a couple of generic words. *Pencil. Cassidy. Lost Creek. Robinette. Painters Mill.* All with and without caps. No luck.

"Chief?"

I startle, turn to see Tomasetti standing in the doorway. "Looks like you had more luck than I did," he says.

"Do you think your IT guys can outsmart a password on this laptop?" I ask.

"Is the bishop Amish?" He crosses to me, looks down at the device. "Might take some time, but I've no doubt they can crack it."

I set the laptop on the bed, set another cone on it, and go back to the drawer containing the zip ties. "What do you make of that?"

His brow goes up. "That's a lot of zip ties."

"Bedroom fetish?"

"Odd thing for a female to have." He looks around. "Clothes in the closet belong to a female."

I motion toward the door. "There's a lot of women's jewelry in the other bedroom. Decent stuff."

"Odd combination."

"And it looks like someone was living out of a suitcase."

"Female?"

I nod.

He goes to the closet, peers inside. "This place has something of a transient feel to it."

"People coming and going," I say.

"No one staying too long."

Bending to the laptop, he slides it into the case. "Let's get this sent to the lab and see what this laptop has to tell us."

• • •

Back at the station, I make use of the shower that's in the basement off the jail and rinse the last of the glass from my body. A fresh uniform and I feel human again. I've talked to Tomasetti twice in the last hour. He's still trying to identify and locate the owner of the house on Lost Creek Road. I'm sitting at my desk now, my laptop purring in front of me. Every piece of paper—reports, notes, and crime scene photos—related to the murders of Samuel Yutzy and Aaron Shetler are spread out on the desk. I've looked at all of them so many times the images and information are beginning to run together.

My cell vibrates from its place next to my laptop. Thinking it's Tomasetti, I pick up. "Yep?"

An instant of open air and then the line goes dead. I thumb down to the caller ID. **YODER'S COUNTRY STORE**. It's a grocery and general store next to the Kidron livestock auction. I've been there dozens of times over the years. Wrong number?

I'm in the process of setting down my cell when it vibrates in my hand. **YODER'S COUNTRY STORE**. Perplexed, I hit answer. "This is Kate."

Another silence. I hear breathing on the other end. Shallow. A little too fast.

"I don't know if I should be calling you," comes a young-sounding female whisper. Late teens or early twenties, I guess. Judging from the inflection, she's Amish.

"Can I help you with something?" I say quietly.

A too-long pause. She's on the verge of hanging up, so I add, "I'll listen."

The line goes dead.

I lower the cell, but I don't put it down. I'm thinking about the house on Lost Creek Road. The locks on the bedroom doors. The suitcase. The zip ties. The sense that nothing is as it seems.

"Shit," I mutter, and grab the keys to my rental car.

CHAPTER 18

Acting on a hunch is seldom a wise use of a cop's time. I'm certainly no sucker for a wild-goose chase—probably because I've participated in my fair share. It is a fact that some individuals delight in supplying false information to the police. Usually, the culprit is a young person looking for trouble with too few brain cells, or too much time on their hands. All of that said, experience has taught me to trust my gut. There are times when a reluctant source is more reliable. With two men dead and a young woman missing, I'm obliged to follow through.

That's what I tell myself, anyway, as I make the thirty-five-minute drive from Painters Mill to Kidron. It's after six P.M. when I pull into the parking lot of the livestock auction complex. The grocery store and restaurant occupy the front. During the daytime hours, the parking lot is filled with buggies and trucks and trailers. This evening, there's a single buggy parked in a sliver of shade next to a big Lincoln with an out-of-state plate. The knowledge that I have no idea who I'm looking for hounds me as I start toward the restaurant entrance. I don't know if my mystery caller is an employee or customer or a passerby who's already halfway out of the county. Even if I *do* find someone who matches the loose criteria I've pulled together—young, female, Amish—I may not recognize her voice.

Trip is going to be a bust, Kate . . .

The front door opens to the grocery part of the establishment. I see three checkout counters. Ahead, dozens of rows of shelves jam-packed with everything from fresh meat to birdseed to bulk foods. An Amish woman of about fifty mans the register nearest me. The restaurant occupies the basement, so I amble to the rear where a sign informs me RESTAURANT IN BASEMENT and I take the stairs down.

The restaurant is a charming, old-fashioned diner with subway-tile walls, a handful of booths, and a large counter in the center of the room. An Amish couple sit in the booth against the wall, sharing a plate of fried chicken. My hope that this is going to be an easy in and out sinks when I see the woman of about forty working behind the counter. Probably not my caller, but since she's the only one around I approach her first.

"I'm looking for the young woman who was here earlier," I say, keeping my request purposefully vague.

The woman's wearing a green dress with a white *halsduch* and *kapp*. She looks at me as she stacks cups and saucers on the shelf behind her. She's got bright blue eyes. Bifocals perched on a freckled nose. A pencil tucked behind her ear.

"You mean Naomi?" she asks.

I have no idea, but I nod. "Do you know where I can find her?"

"She's on break, I think." She motions toward the stairs. "Probably eating her sandwich out back." Her eyes take in my uniform and then slide to the wall clock. "She do something wrong?"

"No, ma'am."

She hefts a humorless laugh. "Good, because she's a decent worker and I can't spare her this evening."

She doesn't offer to let me use the exit door at the rear, so I go back up the stairs. Afternoon is waning into dusk when I go through the front doors and make my way around to the rear of the building. The tang of manure from the auction earlier in the day hangs in the air. I see a lighted exit sign above a small concrete landing with a steel rail and stairs, but there's no one there. No one in sight.

"Told you," I mutter.

I'm about to head back to the front when I spot a small object on the concrete step of the landing. I start toward it; I'm ten feet away when I realize it's a sandwich. I take the steps to the landing and try the door; I'm surprised when it opens. An Amish woman standing just inside gasps at the sight of me, her eyes going wide.

Her mouth flaps a couple of times before she manages, "You're not supposed to be back here."

"You left your sandwich," I tell her.

She opens her mouth for a retort, but it doesn't come. Too polite to close the door in my face.

"Are you Naomi?" I ask.

"*Ja.*"

"I'm Kate Burkholder. You called me. Why?"

"I . . . it wasn't me."

"I recognize your voice."

I see her flight instinct kick in. She's thinking about slamming the door and running. To what end, I have no idea. Judging by the way her hands are shaking, I don't think she's thought it through.

"Go away!" she hisses.

"You're not in any trouble," I say. "I just want to know why you called."

"I didn't mean to call you," she says. "I have to get back to work."

"Are you in some kind of trouble?" I set my hand on the door, open it wider, and usher her outside. "Come on out and talk to me."

When she hesitates, I add, "Naomi, we can do this here nice and easy. Or we can do it at the police station. It's your call."

That's not exactly the way it would go down; I've no cause to detain her or take her to the police station. But the implied threat works.

"I don't know what to do." Her breathing is elevated, her eyes flicking left and right. She's spooked, I realize. Frightened. Of me? Or something else?

"Naomi, I'm a police officer," I say gently. "If you're in trouble, I can help."

"I don't need any help." She struggles with the words, then squeezes her eyes closed for a moment. "But I think my friend does."

"Who's your friend?"

"Wilma Borntrager."

The name impacts me like a bare-knuckle punch. "Is she in trouble?"

She's looking at me as if she's about to crawl out of her skin. "She told me not to talk to anyone about this. But I don't think she's thinking straight."

"Do you know where she is?" I ask.

"Are you going to arrest her?"

"I'm going to talk to her," I say firmly. "Where is she?"

She looks down, shakes her head. "Wilma texted me earlier this afternoon. Said she needed some money."

"Is that unusual?"

"She has more money than I do."

"Why does she need money?"

"She said something about running away. To Florida. There's an Amish settlement down there."

"Pinecraft?" I ask.

"*Ja.*"

I nod, not sure what to make of that, but I pull out my notebook and write it down. "Why is she running away?"

"She got in with a bad crowd," she says, lowering her voice to just above a whisper.

"Who?"

"I don't know their names, but it's been going on since she got that . . . dancing job over in New Philly."

"The Cheetah Lounge?"

She nods, her eyes slipping away from mine.

"The people she's running away from," I say. "Are they Amish or English?"

She looks at me as if I'm nuts. "English."

"Why is she afraid of them?"

"She won't say. But I've known Wilma since we were kids. She doesn't scare easily." Her brows come together. "She's in trouble and she won't talk about it."

"Do you think she's in danger?" I ask.

"Maybe."

"Do you know where she is?"

"No."

I'm not sure I believe her, but I don't press. Not yet. "You said she asked for money. Did you give it to her?"

"I told her I didn't have any. That was the truth; I don't. If I did, I'd give it to her just to make her happy again."

"How did she respond?"

"She got mad. Not because she's a bad person, but because she's scared."

We fall silent, tension pulsing around us.

"I know she was involved with Samuel Yutzy," I say.

She opens her mouth as if to dispute the words, but doesn't. Instead, she hangs her head and shakes it. "She knows the police are looking for her."

"Naomi, I think I can help her, but I'm going to need your help."

She raises her eyes to mine. "What kind of help?"

"I want you to text her and ask her to meet you here right now. Tell her you were able to come up with some money and you want to give it to her."

"Oh." Her eyes go wide and she shakes her head. "But that's not true," she says. "I can't lie to her. She'll never forgive me."

"Naomi, two men have already turned up dead," I say. "I want to make sure that doesn't happen to Wilma, too."

Her eyes widen. "You think they'd do that to her?"

"Wilma was involved with Samuel Yutzy," I say. "Look what happened to him."

Lowering her head, she closes her eyes tightly. "I'm afraid for her," she whispers. "Now, you're asking me to betray her. I don't know what to do."

Hoping to gain her trust, I switch to *Deitsch,* recite a well-known Amish adage. "Do the right thing and God will take care of the rest."

She raises her gaze to mine, surprised, her eyes filling. "You're Amish?"

I nod. "I left when I was eighteen." When she doesn't respond, I push a little harder. "I know you don't know me, but I'm going to ask you to trust me." I motion to the pocket of her dress. "Pull out your cell phone. Text her. Ask her to meet you here. I'll take care of the rest."

"She's going to hate me."

"When this is over, she'll understand."

Tears streaming, she reaches for her phone, thumbs in a message, and hits send. An instant later, the cell chimes.

She shows me her phone. I look down at the screen.

I'll meet you in the back. Thank you!

"What does she drive?" I ask.

"I don't know. It's red."

"Any idea when she'll be here?"

"I don't know where she's coming from."

"Go back inside. If she texts you again, don't respond. I'll wait for her out here." I pass the cell back to her. "You did the right thing."

"Or else I'm about to lose the best friend I ever had." Giving me a despondent look, she turns and goes through the door without another word.

• • •

Money is a universally powerful lure, and it doesn't take long for a red Toyota Camry to pull in and idle around the side of the restaurant. It's not terribly unusual for a young Amish male to buy a car and drive during *rumspringa.* Most are self-taught or have a friend show them the ropes. For an eighteen-year-old Amish female to drive is uncommon. I wonder where she got the car and who taught her to drive.

I'm standing just inside the rear exit with the door open enough to give me a decent view of the back lot. Instead of pulling up to the landing, the driver pulls nose-in to the livestock pens of the adjacent auction building, which is out of sight from the street. I watch as a young woman gets out. She's well dressed. Skinny jeans. Midriff T-shirt. Dark hair piled on top of her head. Strappy sandals. Even from fifteen yards away, I can see that her face is made up. She's got her cell phone pressed to her ear, speaking to someone on the other end as she goes up the concrete ramp and ducks into the livestock stalls.

I slip out, descend the steps, and start toward the building. By the time I cross the parking lot and reach the ramp, she's disappeared into the shadows. The auction closed hours ago. There are no animals. No stragglers. Just the twitter of sparrows from a nest in the rafters, the buzz of cicadas, and the intermittent hiss of traffic from the road. The first section of the livestock building contains the pens for goats and sheep. The front is open-air, so my view to the back is relatively clear. There's no movement. No one there.

I continue along the front to the main part of the building and take the concrete steps up to a large overhead door that stands open. Again, I can see to the back and there's no one there. I keep going, passing by half a dozen or so pens. I'm considering going back into the restaurant to see if she went around the other side of the building when movement snags my attention. Someone moving fast, crossing the gravel track that cuts between the two buildings.

I break into an easy jog, keeping an eye on the shadows, watching for movement. Sure enough, I see the silhouette of someone in the back, partially hidden by a column. She's trying to remain unseen, but not doing a very good job of it.

"Wilma Borntrager?" I call out, and identify myself. "Come talk to me."

The woman startles, then takes off running toward the parking lot—and her vehicle. I run parallel to her, keeping her in sight, hoping she'll realize I mean her no harm and stop. No such luck. She throws open a wooden gate, nearly loses her footing, keeps going.

"Shit." I launch myself into a run after her.

She's not a very good runner—the strappy sandals aren't helping—and I easily close the distance between us. "I'm a police officer," I call out to her as I track her across the asphalt. "Hang on a sec."

A quick look over her shoulder and she makes a beeline for her vehicle. I cut her off, raise my hands to let her know I'm not a threat. "I just want to talk to you. That's all."

She pivots, sprints back toward the restaurant landing. I'm a dozen feet behind her. She flies up the steps, reaches for the knob. I take the steps two at a time. She yanks open the door. I set my hand on it, shove it closed.

"Stop," I tell her.

"Get away from me!" she snaps.

She tries to peel my hand off the door, but she's not strong enough. Huffing her aggravation, she slaps her palm against the door and turns to me, her back against the jamb. "Bitch! You can't do this!"

"I just want to talk," I say.

"I don't want to talk to you!"

"If you're as smart as I think you are, you will," I say. "And you'll listen."

"I didn't do anything wrong," she says.

"No one said you did." I pause, not sure if she's going to cooperate or bolt. Not sure what I can do about it if she chooses the latter. "Unless you want to end up like Samuel Yutzy, you'll talk to me."

The words stop her cold. For the span of a full minute, we stand there, breathing hard, two contenders sizing up their opponent. Now that I'm closer, I can see how young she is. Too young. From a distance, the makeup and dyed black hair make her look more mature, but she's just a kid. Part of a tattoo is visible at the neckline of her T-shirt. Both earlobes are pierced too many times to count.

"I'm trying to find out what happened to him," I say quietly. "That's all."

"I don't know!" Her face tries to screw up, but she fights off tears. "All I know is he's dead."

A hundred questions rush my brain, each of them vying for position. But she's badly spooked, so I pull myself back, give her some space.

"Do you have any idea who did that to him?" I ask after a moment.

"I don't know," she whispers.

I nod. "Wilma, Aaron Shetler is dead, too."

"Aaron?" She blinks, and for an instant the tough façade teeters. "I don't believe you."

"It's not a stretch to conclude that you could be in danger, too."

"No one's going to find me," she snaps.

"I did."

She doesn't have anything to say about that.

"Will you come to the station with me to talk?" I ask. "I'll drive you and bring you back to your vehicle when we're finished. Will you do that?"

She looks longingly at her vehicle. "Do I have a choice?"

"You're not under arrest," I tell her. "But I have the authority to detain you for questioning."

"You're a bitch cop, you know that?"

I nod. "Wilma, I think this would be easier for both of us if you just did the right thing and came with me voluntarily."

Cursing me beneath her breath, she shakes her head. "You touch me with cuffs or anything like that and I'll sue you and your stinking little town until you're bankrupt."

"No cuffs," I tell her.

"Then let's get this shitshow over with."

CHAPTER 19

Forty-five minutes later, I'm sitting in the war room of the police station. Wilma Borntrager sits across from me, looking pissed off and ready to throw a punch at the first person who comes through the door. Though the air conditioner is cranking, the room is sweltering and her makeup is beginning to melt.

I called Tomasetti on the drive to Painters Mill. He was waiting for us when we arrived. He left the room two minutes ago under the guise of getting water, but I know he's looking at everything we've uncovered about her so far.

"You've been a tough woman to locate," I begin.

Giving me a withering look, she shakes her head, stares down at her hands, as if she's just made the worst mistake of her life. "Cops aren't exactly my favorite people."

The door swings open. Tomasetti strides in, three water bottles in hand. He's taken on the role of good cop, leaving me to ask the more unpleasant questions, which is probably the best way to play this since the woman sitting across from me seems to have an intense dislike for me.

Tomasetti sets one of the bottles in front of her. As if he's oblivious to the tension in the room—he's not—he pulls out a chair at the head of the table—a neutral position by design—and makes a show of opening his own bottle and checking his cell phone.

"How close were you to Samuel Yutzy?" I ask.

"We were a thing." It's a flippant response, but I didn't miss her involuntary wince when I said his name. She doesn't make eye contact with me, keeping her gaze on the tabletop. Hardened, I think, but the I-don't-give-a-shit suit of armor hasn't quite been perfected.

"Was it serious?" I ask.

"Yeah, I guess you could say that. I mean, he was a decent guy. Really nice. Me?" She gives a head toss. "Not so much."

"How did you meet him?"

"I met him at a rager almost a year ago." For an instant the hardness of her features relaxes into an expression that seems more natural for an eighteen-year-old. "He bought me a beer. We listened to some music. Danced. Got to talking." She shrugs. "He's the last kind of guy I usually like, but we hit it off."

"You started dating?"

She shifts in the chair, frowns at me. "We stayed in touch for a time. I was . . ." She sighs. "Having some problems and he . . . helped me out."

"What kind of problems?"

She looks at me as if I'm dense. "I'm Amish. I'd just left. I didn't have any money. Or anyplace to go. Sammy . . . he helped me out."

"How did he help you?"

"He let me borrow a little money." But she's more thoughtful now. "He had a lot of friends. I mean, he knew everyone. One of his friends said I could stay with her for a while. She took me in."

"What's her name?"

"Shelley."

"Last name?"

"I don't know."

"Where did she live?"

She raises her eyes to mine, insolent and hard. "A little apartment over in New Philly."

"Did you continue to see Samuel?" I ask.

Her expression softens again. This time, her guard is down and it's more apparent. "He kept coming around. We became friends, I guess. He took me out a few times. Went dancing." The hint of a smile on her mouth. "He was kind. And he was a lot of fun."

"Did you have to pay Shelley rent?" I ask.

Her smile falls. Her features go hard again. "I didn't have any money. I mean, not one cent. Shelley let me stay, but it was temporary."

"What did you do?"

She tightens her mouth. "Sammy said he knew a guy who owned a restaurant. He said they were looking for servers. No experience necessary. He said he could get me on there if I wanted."

"Where?" I ask.

She shakes her head. "The Blue Lake Tap in Millersburg."

Across from us, Tomasetti sits up straighter.

"How long did you work there?" I ask.

"A few months."

"You were still seeing Samuel?"

She nods. "We were . . . pretty close by then. He was like . . . the best thing in my life at that point. I mean, everything else had pretty much gone to shit."

I nod, let the words settle, keep moving. "Do you know Carter Brooks?"

"I met him a few times."

"How well?"

Her eyes latch on to mine. "Well enough to know the guy's a creep."

"How so?"

"He got into it with Sammy over some frickin' trees or something." She tightens her mouth. "Brooks knew I was with Sammy, and he started treating me like shit."

The landscaping contract dispute, I think. "How serious was the disagreement between Samuel and Brooks?"

"Early on they got along just fine. But after Sammy did that job and Brooks's basement flooded, Brooks turned into a real asshole."

"In what way?"

"Sammy and I were at the brewery one night. We were having a good time, had a couple of beers. Then out comes Brooks, all foaming at the mouth and looking for a fight. He accused Sammy of ripping him off. After a few minutes, Brooks came unglued and punched Sammy in the mouth."

"Cops get called?" I ask.

She looks at me as if I'm a dimwit. "No one called the cops."

"Did Brooks threaten Samuel?" Tomasetti asks.

She looks at him, her eyes flicking to the wall clock above him. "Threatened to sue."

"How long ago did this happen?" I ask.

"Three months or so."

"Did you continue to work there?"

"I quit," she tells me. "Sammy said he had another job for me. A better one where I could make more money. So, I took it."

"Where?" I ask.

"A club," she says. "Don't remember the name of it."

Tomasetti sighs. "We know you were employed at The Cheetah Lounge."

She sneers at him. "Look, I give zero fucks about whether or not you approve."

I say her name firmly. "We're not here to approve or disapprove."

"Whatever." She shakes her head. "I don't expect you to understand how frickin' impossible it is to leave the Amish. I had nothing. No money. No place to stay. No vehicle. I needed a job so I took it. You can take your judgment and shove it."

"No one's judging you," I say.

"Right." She flicks hair out of her face. "I made damn good money. I bought a car. Clothes. I was able to pay my rent."

I think about what happened to me at The Cheetah Lounge. "Who did Samuel know at The Cheetah Lounge?"

"He didn't say."

She's starting to shut down, so I give her a moment before shifting gears. "Wilma, did Samuel have any enemies you know of?"

She shakes her head. "The only person he had a beef with was Brooks. Most everyone liked Sammy."

"Someone didn't," Tomasetti points out.

She raises her eyes to him, then to the wall clock behind him. "I guess not."

"How well do you know Aaron Shetler?" I ask.

"I met him a few times." She shrugs. "Aaron and Sammy were tight. They worked together sometimes. Hung out together. Partied together."

"What kind of partying?"

"Drinking, mostly."

"Drugs?"

She looks down at the tabletop again. "Look, they weren't druggies or anything like that, but they got high."

"Did they sell drugs?" I ask.

"No."

"Did Aaron have any disputes or arguments with anyone?" I ask.

"Not that I know of." Her eyes slip to the clock again.

"You got somewhere else to be?" I ask.

She hands me a disdainful look. "I just want to get this crap over with."

I remind myself that my opinion of this young woman doesn't matter. My job is to find out what she knows, if anything. But I don't like what I see. I don't trust her. I'm not sure if she's credible.

"How long did you work at The Cheetah Lounge?" I ask.

"A few months."

"Where did you get the fake ID?" I ask.

The shadow of a smile crosses her mouth. "I don't remember."

She nearly jumps out of her chair when a brisk knock sounds on the door. Simultaneously, my cell phone goes off. Frowning, Tomasetti rises and goes to the door. I stand, reach for my cell to see that it's Jodie at reception.

"There's an attorney on his way back, Chief," she says. "I couldn't stop him."

Tomasetti opens the door. A burst of adrenaline hits my gut when I see his hand hover above the holster beneath his jacket. I stride toward him when I hear the voice of a male coming from the hall outside the door.

"I'm Brett Adamson with the Adamson and Schneider law firm out of Cleveland," says the voice. "I'm here for my client."

I come up behind Tomasetti, look over his shoulder. The man is very well dressed. Custom suit. Hermès tie. Wing-tip oxfords. He's about forty years old with a neat man bun at his nape. A diamond winks from his left earlobe. He's craning his neck, trying to see past Tomasetti to get a look at Wilma Borntrager.

Tomasetti isn't cooperating. "How about you show me some ID?"

The lawyer's mouth curves as he unfolds his wallet. "You've got my client in your interview room. If she's not under arrest or being detained, she'll be coming with me."

Tomasetti sighs.

The other man laughs, makes eye contact with me. "Is Ms. Borntrager under arrest? Is she being detained?"

"No." I move closer to the door. "We're conducting an interview."

He tsks. "Without her attorney being present."

"Evidently," Tomasetti mutters.

"The interview is over." The lawyer ducks his head, turning his attention to Borntrager. "Hi, Wilma. Grab your bag. We're leaving."

Behind me, I hear Wilma gathering her things. I wait for her to look at me. "You don't have to go with him if you don't want to," I tell her.

"Go fuck yourself," she says, and brushes past.

• • •

"Might be a stretch, but I don't think she learned to talk like that at the Amish school." Tomasetti is sitting in the visitor chair adjacent to my desk.

"She's a scared, dumb kid." I'm at my desk, trying in vain not to fret about a situation I wish I'd handled differently. "We should have detained her."

"She didn't commit a crime."

"I think she's in danger."

He shrugs. "You did your best."

"Not good enough." I slap my hand down on the desk. "Damn it."

Behind me, the window unit pumps more hot air than cool; my shirt is sticking to my back like a wet towel and I resist the urge to spin around and punch it.

"She knows more than she's letting on," he says.

I recall the way she kept looking at the clock. "She knew the lawyer was coming."

"Speaking of . . . he didn't look cheap. Didn't care for the man bun."

"Be interesting to know who's paying him."

"Someone who doesn't want her talking to the cops."

We stare at each other a moment, our minds whirring.

After a moment, Tomasetti leans back in his chair and crosses his ankle over his knee. "In all fairness, she *did* give us a few things to unpack."

"She worked for Brooks," I say.

"When you talked to him, he didn't mention he punched out Yutzy."

"He doesn't have an alibi."

"All of that makes him worth talking to again."

His cell phone buzzes. His frown deepens as he reaches for it and scrolls. After reading, he shoves it back into its case at his belt and smiles at me. "That was my legal guy," he says. "We might have a lead on IDing the title holder of the house. He stayed late for this. I'm going to run up to Richfield and meet him."

"I'll see you at the farm later?"

"You bet." Rising, he crosses to me and bends to press his mouth to mine. "Don't be too late."

"Same goes," I say.

And then he's gone.

• • •

Even in the midst of a double homicide investigation, the police station is quiet this time of night. I try to take advantage of the lull, use it to digest and absorb and drill myself on the myriad what-if questions I don't have time to entertain during the day when everything around me is on fire.

My desk is buried beneath reams of paper. There are photos, sketches, handwritten notes, reports, and interview transcriptions. I've been through all of it a dozen times in the last two hours. I've dissected every word, looked at every scrap of information from multiple angles. Despite my efforts, nothing new has emerged. Or else I'm too damn tired to see it.

There simply comes a time when the brain needs to rest and the body must recharge. I know that no matter how hard I look at the information in front of me, how desperately I want to find that earth-shattering breakthrough, it's simply not going to happen when I'm bleary-eyed and exhausted.

Time to call it a day, Kate.

I've just closed my laptop when my cell jangles. I glance at the display and smile when Tomasetti's name pops up. "I just got to the farm," he tells me. "I wish I could tell you I'm surprised you're not here."

"I'm shutting down now," I say, curbing a little rise of guilt. "Any news from legal?"

"The rental house is owned by the LLC Genesis Property Solutions out of Cincinnati."

"Is there a name to go along with that?"

"He should have that for us tomorrow." He clears his throat. "Some people actually have lives outside of their job."

"You're not sending me a strongly worded hint, are you?"

I hear clinking on the other end and I picture him in the kitchen of our farmhouse. Taking off his jacket. Pouring a drink. Winding down. I miss him, I realize, and suddenly I can't wait to get home.

"You just about got things tied up there?" he asks.

"You're not missing me, are you?"

"While that is a very real possibility, I'm also wondering if I should go ahead and open this bottle of Chilean Carménère or put a couple of IPAs in the freezer since it's still eighty degrees out there."

"Let's go with the IPA," I tell him.

"See you in a few."

• • •

I've just backed out of my parking slot when the call comes over my Bluetooth. "Hey, Margaret," I say.

"Chief, I know you're trying to get home, but I just took a call from Buster McGary right there off of Lost Creek Road. He claims someone just pulled into the driveway of the residence where that incident with Mona happened."

"That's interesting."

"I thought so."

"I'm ten minutes away," I tell her. "Who's on duty tonight?"

"Pickles."

"Tell him to meet me there. No lights."

"Roger that."

CHAPTER 20

It's eleven P.M. when I make the turn onto Lost Creek Road. I punch off the headlights and creep slowly along the road, stopping when I reach the rental house. There are no lights on inside or out. No vehicles in sight. The only light comes from a sliver of moon overhead. It's so dark I can barely make out the silhouette of the roof.

I speak into my lapel mike. "Ten-twenty-three," I say, letting Dispatch know I arrived on scene. "Pickles, what's your ETA?"

"I'm ten minutes out, Chief."

"Roger that."

Headlights off, I pull into the driveway and shut down the engine. I sit there a moment, looking around, but there's no movement. The only sound comes from the chorus of crickets and the flip-flap of the scrap of crime scene tape left over from earlier in the day. Risking the dome light, I get out. I'm on my way to the front door when I hear the horse blow. It's a common sound, one I've heard a thousand times, telling me there's someone in the backyard.

Pulling out my mini Maglite, but not turning it on, I walk along the side of the house and look around the corner. Sure enough, a horse and buggy are stopped in the center of the yard. Someone is standing next to the buggy. A second person is on the back porch. I flick on the flashlight as I leave the cover of the shadows, and shine the light on the person next to the buggy.

"Police department!" I call out. "Do not move. I'm coming over to talk to you."

As I close the distance between us, I realize there are two people standing next to the buggy. One female. And a child.

I'm midway to them when the male standing on the porch bolts. He takes all four steps in a single leap, then hits the ground running with the speed of an Olympian sprinter. Arms pumping. Feet pounding. Heading toward the woods.

Shit.

I launch myself into a run. "Stop!" I shout.

The runner doesn't acknowledge me. Doesn't slow down.

He's running at an angle to me, so I veer left and cut him off. "*Shtobba!*" I shout in *Deitsch.* Stop!

My flashlight beam plays crazily over the ground as I sprint toward him. The runner is male. Not much bigger than me, but fast. Faster than me, in fact, but I have a shorter distance to cover, which gains me some ground. We're midway to the woods when I reach him. I make a wild grab for his arm, latch on tight, use the momentum to swing him around.

"*Shtobba!*" I say. "I just want to talk to you."

He stumbles backward, raises his hands, looks around as if he's thinking about bolting again. "Okay! Okay!"

I grip his arm, get my flashlight beam on him. There's no weapon I can see. "Keep your hands where I can see them," I snap.

"Okay! Fine! What do you want?"

I guess him to be about sixteen years old. Blond hair. Blue eyes. Straw hat. Blue work shirt and suspenders. He's looking at me as if I'm the Grim Reaper about to cut out his soul with my scythe, so I release him.

"What are you doing here?" I ask.

"Nothing."

"Why are you running from the police?"

"You . . . scared me. That's all."

I jab my thumb toward the house. "Who's with you?" I pose the question even as I swing my beam toward the house.

"M-my s-sister and little b-brother," he tells me.

A young Amish woman wearing a lavender dress, an apron, and plain sneakers stands next to the buggy, her hands up as if she's being accosted by muggers. Beside her, a little boy of about ten gapes at me, eyes wide, his hands stretched far above his head.

"We didn't do anything!" he squeals.

What the hell?

It's an odd combination of individuals to be visiting a recent crime scene this time of night. I turn my attention back to the young man and motion toward the buggy. "Let's walk over to the buggy," I say. "Nice and slow."

Shaking his head with the theater of a ten-year-old being remanded to bed without dinner, he starts toward the buggy.

"We weren't doing anything wrong," he mutters.

"It's called trespassing." I fall in behind him. "You can put down your hands now."

He does.

"What's your name?" I ask.

He tightens his mouth as if he's thinking about not answering, but he reads the seriousness of the situation in my eyes and changes his mind. "Noah."

"Noah what?" I snap.

"Yoder," he mumbles.

"How old are you?"

"Fifteen."

We reach the buggy and I get my first good look at the other two. The young woman is about twenty. The boy looks to be about ten. They're scared. As if they've been caught doing something they know they shouldn't be doing.

"Is there anyone else with you?" I ask.

"No," says the young woman. "Just us."

I make eye contact with her. She's tall and slender with a face pretty enough to be on the cover of a magazine. She stares back at me with huge green eyes fringed with sooty lashes. She's got blond hair. Her complexion is like porcelain except for the scattering of freckles on her nose.

"What's your name?" I ask.

"I'm Rose." She looks at the boy next to her. "That's my little brother, Mervin. He's eleven."

"All of you are siblings?" I ask.

"*Ja,*" she replies.

"Rose, how old are you?"

"Almost twenty-one."

I study their faces a moment. Noah stares down at the ground. Mervin busies himself running the toe of his sneaker through dirt. Rose is the only one who holds my gaze.

"What are you doing here?" I ask.

She looks away. I see her brain scrambling. Looking for an answer that's more acceptable than the truth, whatever that is. After a moment, she sighs. "Getting my things."

"What things?"

"My . . . clock," she says. "The singing bird clock. It belonged to my *grohs-mammi.*" Grandmother. "I wanted it back."

"Were you living here?" I ask.

Her eyes slide right and then left as if seeking a lie, but she can't conceive one. "No, but . . . I was. I mean, I moved out. A few months ago. I . . . left some of my things behind."

"Why did you wait until now to pick up your things?" I ask.

"I . . ." Again, she struggles to find the words, stumbles over her answer. "I didn't want to come back."

"Why not?"

Her expression turns pained. "I didn't want to run into anyone. I didn't want to see them or talk to them. After what happened today, I didn't think anyone would be here."

"How did you find out what happened today?" I ask.

"Brick Solly down to the feed store told me," Noah interjects.

"They weren't very nice people," Mervin mutters.

"*Beheef dich!*" Rose says sharply. Behave yourself.

I study the three young people, trying to figure out the dynamics of the situation. "Who are you talking about exactly?" I ask. "Who didn't you want to see?"

The little boy's eyes hit the ground.

I turn my attention to Rose to see her expression flatten. *Shutting down,* I think, and I realize I'm not getting the whole story.

"Wilma Borntrager?" I ask.

She gives a reluctant nod. "Wilma doesn't like me much."

"Does she live here?"

She nods.

"Does anyone else live here?" I ask.

"Sometimes."

"Who?"

"I don't know their names," she says. "Just . . . different girls. Sometimes a man."

I've no doubt there's a lot more going on than meets the eye. Or perhaps more than she can say in front of her younger siblings. "This is an odd hour for you to be picking up your things," I say. "Especially with your little brothers in tow."

Noah puffs out his chest. "No one's going to bother her with me around."

I look at him. "Who would bother her?"

He tightens his mouth, looks away.

I look at Mervin. The younger boy blinks and swallows hard. "I just came because I woke up."

I turn my attention to Rose. "Where are you living now?" I ask.

"Home," she tells me. "With my parents."

"She's going to get baptized," Mervin asserts.

Rose elbows him, rolls her eyes.

"Who are your parents?" I ask.

"Clarence and Esther Yoder," she says.

I know of the family. They're Swartzentruber Amish with half a dozen kids and live on a hog farm a few miles to the south. "Where are your parents this evening?" I ask.

"They went to a wedding," she tells me. "In Geauga County."

"They're spending the night," Mervin adds.

"Do they know you're here?" I ask.

The young woman turns her attention to the ground, studies the beaten-down grass as if it's the most interesting thing she's ever encountered. I look at Noah and his eyes skate away. Same with the little guy.

"Chief?

I turn at the sound of Pickles's voice and see the yellow glow of his flashlight beam as he comes around the corner of the house.

"Everything okay here?" He reaches us, suspicious old man's eyes flicking from me to the young Amish people.

"Everything's fine," I tell him. "Miss Yoder and her brothers stopped by to pick up a few of her things."

Pickles wasn't born yesterday; his eyes narrow on mine. "Uh-huh."

"I'll escort her inside so she can get what she needs." I motion to the boys. "Pickles, these are Clarence and Esther Yoder's kids. Would you mind escorting them home?"

"Happy to, Chief." He whistles at the boys. "Climb into the buggy, boys, and I'll follow you home."

• • •

Rose and I hold our ground in the yard and watch as the buggy and Pickles's cruiser roll toward the front of the house.

"Your brothers are protective of you," I say when they're out of sight.

"I didn't want either of them to come," she tells me. "Noah wouldn't let me go alone. And we couldn't leave Mervin by himself."

I motion toward the house. "The doors are locked. How did you plan to get inside exactly?"

"I still have my key," she says simply.

"Of course you do."

We cross the yard and ascend the steps to the porch. I wait while she fishes the key from her apron pocket and we go inside. She flicks on the kitchen light and we both squint as our eyes adjust.

"The clock is in the living room." She starts that way.

I follow. "How long did you live here?"

She crosses to the sofa. Sure enough, an old-fashioned singing bird clock is mounted on the wall above it. "Six months or so."

"Were you friends with Wilma Borntrager?" I ask.

"I barely knew her." She glances at me over her shoulder. "She wasn't a very good roommate."

"Why not?"

"She was . . . mouthy and wild and drank too much. She wasn't always a nice person."

She toes off her shoes and steps up onto the sofa. Biting her lip, she stands on her tiptoes and reaches for the clock.

"Did you know Samuel Yutzy?" I ask.

Her shoulders stiffen as she sets her hands on the clock. "I knew Samuel." She lifts the clock from its hook. "I heard what happened to him."

"Did you have a relationship with him?"

"No." Huffing at the personal nature of the question, she steps down from the sofa. "Samuel was with Wilma."

"So how did you know him?" I ask.

"He was just . . . around. Helped me get a job once."

I recall Wilma telling me the very same thing. "Where at?"

She shoots me an annoyed look. "Why does it matter?" she snaps. "I don't work there anymore."

"Where?"

"A stupid club in New Philly."

"The Cheetah Lounge?"

Her eyes widen, color spreading to her cheeks. She wasn't expecting me to know, I realize, and she's ashamed.

"I didn't work there very long," she says quickly.

"How long?"

She looks away as she slips her feet back into her shoes. "A couple months."

"Did you quit?"

"Of course I quit." Without looking at me she carries the clock to the kitchen, sets it on the table, and runs her finger over its face.

"It's beautiful," I say.

"It's an old thing," she murmurs. "Grohs-mammi loved it. Gave it to me before she died. She knew I'd take care of it. I couldn't bear the thought of it being left in this house."

"So, you left the Amish for a while?" I ask.

"I was a silly teenager. On *rumspringa,* you know." The laugh that follows embodies the regret of a woman long past her teenage years. "It was a mistake."

I'm still thinking about Yutzy. "How did you meet Samuel?"

She continues to stare at the clock, wipes at a smudge with her fingers. "I met him at a rager."

Same as Wilma Borntrager . . .

"Did you know Aaron Shetler?" I ask.

"I don't know who that is."

"Rose, did Samuel have any enemies that you know of?" I ask.

"I don't know." Picking up the clock, she strides to the door only to realize she can't open it because she's holding the clock.

"When's the last time you saw Samuel?"

"I don't want to talk about this anymore." Muttering beneath her breath, she kicks the door with the toe of her sneaker.

"I've got it." I'm reaching past her to push open the door when I notice the tattoo peeking out of the space between her collar and *kapp* at her nape. I only catch a glimpse, but it looks like someone's initials printed in an Old English font.

I open the door. "That's an interesting tattoo," I say. "Where'd you get it?"

She goes through the door without answering.

I follow her down the steps and into the backyard. "Rose, can you tell me what was going on in this house?"

"There was nothing going on."

"Why are there locks on the outside of the bedroom doors?" I ask.

Staring down at the ground, she doesn't respond.

"Was someone being kept against their will?" I ask.

She hugs the clock more tightly against her. "I have to go."

I wait, but she doesn't respond. "Rose, I don't know if this matters to you, but I used to be Amish." I switch to *Deitsch.* "I know what it feels like to walk away from your life. I know it's not easy."

She tosses me an angry, defiant look. "You didn't become a dancer, though, did you?"

"I became a cop." I offer a smile. "Some people might think that's worse."

"I don't want to talk about it," she whispers. "I just want to go home."

CHAPTER 21

"We interviewed the bartender and two of the bouncers, all of whom were working the night your coffee got spiked."

Sheriff Mike Rasmussen is sprawled in the chair next to the air conditioner. Judging by the circles beneath his eyes and the five-o'clock shadow on his usually clean-shaven face, he didn't make it to bed last night.

"They weren't very cooperative when I talked to them," I say.

"A trip to the sheriff's office must have adjusted their attitudes." His smile looks more like he's got a hamstring cramp. "The only employee with a criminal record is the maintenance guy. He wasn't there the night it happened."

"You guys get a search warrant for the place?" I ask.

"We executed it during non-business hours." He shrugs. "Our culprit had plenty of time to flush whatever they had on hand. We didn't find shit."

I didn't expect them to discover who spiked my drink. Still, I'm disappointed.

I look at Tomasetti. "Lab results come back?"

He scowls. "Gamma-hydroxybutyric acid. It's a Schedule I controlled substance. The prescription form is called sodium oxybate. It's sold on the street as a party drug. Also known as Georgia home boy, G, goop, grievous bodily harm, and liquid ecstasy."

"Lovely," I mutter.

It's seven thirty in the morning and I'm in the war room with Tomasetti and Rasmussen. Despite the hour and the rattle of the air conditioner in the corner, it's hot and stuffy and none of us are in the mood for any of it.

Rasmussen picks up his coffee and gulps twice. "Heard you had trespassers last night at the house on Lost Creek."

I recap my conversation with Rose Yoder. "It's no coincidence that two of the young women living at that house knew Samuel Yutzy and were employed at The Cheetah Lounge."

"So, we have a few interesting connections," Rasmussen says.

"Borntrager and Yoder met Yutzy at an Amish rager," I begin. "According to those two young women, Yutzy later got them jobs, either at the brewery in Millersburg or The Cheetah Lounge."

Tomasetti takes it from there. "That's a pattern. But to what end?"

Rasmussen shakes his head. "So, we have a pattern. And there may very well be other individuals involved that we don't know about yet. But I gotta be honest here. I don't see how Yutzy getting these women jobs at a topless club plays into the murders."

"That's the sixty-four-thousand-dollar question," Tomasetti mutters.

"One of the things that links all of these young people," I say, "is that they're Amish—Yutzy, Shetler, Borntrager, and Yoder. Most of these kids have led protected lives. They're not savvy or street-smart. They don't have the life experience to deal with that kind of freedom—"

"Or someone who would take advantage of that," Tomasetti puts in.

I nod. "They make bad decisions. They go overboard. Get in over their heads. That makes them vulnerable."

"And while a business establishment like The Cheetah Lounge has its inherent fair share of shade," Tomasetti says, "the larger question here is whether the club or the people connected to it had a motive to murder Yutzy and Shetler."

Rasmussen puts out the obvious question. "What's Yutzy's connection to the club?"

"Who did he piss off?" Tomasetti adds.

"He had to have been tight with someone who does the hiring," I say.

"Who owns the strip club?" Rasmussen asks.

"That's where the plot thickens." Tomasetti's frown deepens. "Normally, we could simply contact the Ohio Secretary of State at which time BCI would be supplied with the names. The LLC that holds the title to The Cheetah Lounge is based in New Mexico."

"New Mexico?" Rasmussen makes a face. "That's weird."

Tomasetti's mouth curves into a humorless facsimile of a smile. "It just so happens that if you're a privacy-minded individual and want to form an anonymous limited liability company, New Mexico is the shining star in terms of confidentiality."

"Makes sense." Rasmussen sighs. "If someone doesn't want their name floating around in connection with a strip joint."

"Odd that both the house and strip club are owned by LLCs," I put in.

"We're waiting to hear back from both states." Tomasetti growls low in his throat. "We're going to do our best to light a fire today."

I'm still considering the local angle. "Do we know who at The Cheetah Lounge does the hiring?" I ask.

Tomasetti flips a page. "Carl Monaghans. Get this: He's on vacation in Cancún."

"That's convenient as hell," Rasmussen mutters.

"We'll pull him in the day he gets back," Tomasetti says.

I've just glanced at the clock when my cell erupts. I look down to see Glock's name pop up on the screen. Simultaneously, Rasmussen's cell goes off. Pounding sounds on the door.

It swings open. "Chief?" Margaret looks at me wide-eyed. "Just took a call from Glock. Amish boys out on Township Road 122 found a body."

I get to my feet, my mind revving. "What's the address?"

"The boy who called said it's right there on the south side of the cutoff with County Road 407. Says there's a lady on the ground just past the ditch in the trees."

"I'm on my way."

• • •

It takes me six minutes to reach the scene. Glock's cruiser is parked at the mouth of Township Road 122, blocking the road in both directions. The emergency lights on his vehicle are flashing, but Glock is nowhere in sight. He's set out flares and cones to block the northbound lane of CR 407. An Amish boy is leaning against the front fender, looking shaken up and out of place.

"Ten-twenty-three," I say, letting Dispatch know I arrived on scene.

I park behind Glock's cruiser, grab a bottle of water, and get out. Heat and humidity slap me in the face like a wet palm. A chorus of cicadas and birds sound from the woods.

I speak into my shoulder mike. "Glock," I say, "what's your twenty?"

"I'm about ten yards into the woods, Chief. I think you need to see this."

"Be right there." I start toward the boy. "*Guder mariye.*" Good morning.

I guess him to be about fourteen years of age. Skinny and blond with a summer straw hat and a work shirt that's torn at the sleeve.

He gives me a nod, his expression grim and scared.

I hand him the water bottle. "You okay?"

"*Ja.*" He jabs a thumb toward the woods behind him. "That girl . . . she ain't okay."

"What's your name?"

"Levi Miller."

"What are you doing out here?"

He ducks his head. "My friend and I were out in the woods, trying out my new BB gun."

"What happened?"

"We found a girl. At first, I thought it was a . . . I don't know, one of them store mannequins. Then I saw all that blood . . ." He shudders. "I think she's dead."

"Where's your friend?"

"He went to call you guys. Ain't back yet."

"He on his bike?"

"*Ja.*"

"Okay." I look toward the woods. "You stay right here for me, okay? I'm going to take a look and I'll be right back. If your friend shows up, tell him to stay with you, okay?"

"Yeah."

The woods are thick with old and new growth and tangled with bramble. Resigning myself to poison ivy and bug bites, I leave the road's shoulder, cross through the ditch, and fight my way through.

"Glock?" A dozen feet in and I call out.

"Over here."

I glance left, spot the blue of his uniform through the brush, and I head that way. I find him standing next to an ancient black walnut tree. At his feet, the body of a young woman is sprawled in the weeds. She's wearing blue jeans and a white T-shirt that's stained with blood. She's lying in a prone position with her head turned to one side.

"Oh no," I hear myself murmur.

"Looks like a gunshot wound there in her back," Glock says quietly.

I lean closer. "Too much blood to tell if it's an exit or entrance wound."

He nods, his eyes meeting mine. "She looks young."

"Yeah."

I'm aware of my heart beating too fast. Sweat dribbling down between my shoulder blades. I think about the Amish kid leaning against the car and I hate it that he had to see this.

"Did you look around?" I ask.

"A little. Not much to see." He motions in the general direction of the road. "A couple of broken twigs when I was coming in." He sighs. "Brush is frickin' thick as peanut butter."

He's right. There's no path and too much overgrowth for anyone to get in or out easily.

"You think someone shot her and dumped her?" he asks.

Dumped her.

It's such an indecent, offensive word. The kind of action that applies to a piece of garbage or some object no one cares about. *Someone cared about this young woman,* I think.

"I didn't notice any drag marks," I say.

"Could have carried her."

Now that some of my shock has settled down, I look a little more closely at the body. "She may have gotten out of a vehicle. Tried to get away. Ran into the woods. Someone followed. Shot her down."

"Or shot her in the back as she was running away." He shakes his head. "Chief, what the hell is the world coming to?"

"I don't know." At the moment, it feels as if the world is on a collision course with doom. "We should probably clear out."

Neither of us moves.

He looks down at the body, his expression going hard. "Any idea who she is?"

The last thing we should be doing at this point is trampling the scene or touching the body. There's always a risk of contaminating evidence and it's a rookie mistake. But we're here, and I'm reminded that if this young woman is local, her parents are probably wondering where she is. That there's a good chance I know them.

Careful where I step, I sidle closer to the body. I'm about two feet away from where she lies, so close I can make out several abrasions, on her elbow, the heel of her hand, her cheekbone . . .

Her head is turned to one side, facing away from me. I take another step. I see blood at her temple, the hair soaked and matted. A thin red line where it dripped down her cheek and onto the forest floor. I take another step and recognition mule-kicks me in the gut. I hear my own intake of breath, feel the quick punch of disbelief.

"That's Wilma Borntrager," I hear myself say.

Glock cuts me a sharp look. "Holy shit."

I take an involuntary step back. "We need to clear out. Get the road blocked. A grid search set up for the entire area." I glance behind me. Through the trees I see another set of flashing lights, telling me Rasmussen and Tomasetti have arrived on scene.

Using the same path that brought us here, Glock and I back out of the scene.

• • •

An hour later, I'm leaning against the door of my rental car, trying in vain to make sense of the death of yet another Amish young person on my watch. To protect the scene, all LEO vehicles have been moved out of the designated perimeter, which is quite large. Permitted personnel include the coroner and his technician, Tomasetti, and a second BCI agent who specializes in crime scene investigation.

"Kate."

I look toward the yellow tape that's strung along the perimeter of the scene to see Tomasetti duck beneath it and approach. "Anything?" I ask.

"Not much," he growls. "The whole area's a damn jungle."

The image of the dead woman lying facedown in the weeds has been branded into my brain with such power that I can't get it out of my head. "It looks like she was shot in the back," I say.

"Looks like a gunshot wound at her temple, too," he says.

"Did you see any indication that someone else was there?" I ask.

"We marked a few areas. There are a couple of broken branches. What *might* be a shoe impression."

"She's not wearing shoes," I say quickly. "She ran into those woods barefoot. If there's a footwear impression, it wasn't hers."

The muscles in his jaws flex and he looks away. "Okay." I can tell by his demeanor he's feeling the same thing I am. That we failed her.

"Tomasetti, we *had* her," I whisper. "We fucking had her."

"I know."

"Now we have *three* dead young people. They were . . ." I don't know how to finish the sentence; I'm too emotional and keenly aware that it's not a good look. "Maybe we should have—"

He cuts me off. "Should have what, Kate?" He asks the question sharply, his eyes fixing on mine. "What could we have done differently?"

"Had we taken a harder line, she might still be alive, damn it."

"This wasn't your fault," he snaps. "And it wasn't mine. We did what we could. We knew she was holding out on us."

The logical side of my brain knows he's right. The emotional side of my brain rages against the odious reality of what happened to her.

"What about the lawyer?" I ask. "At what point last night did he part ways with her?"

"I'm on my way to see him as soon as I leave here," he tells me.

I want to go with him; I want to look into that smug son of a bitch's eyes and ask him when he last saw her. Where she was going. Who she was with. I want to know who's paying him and why. Of course, I can't because we're stretched thin and as soon as I finish up here, I'm going to speak with Carter Brooks.

"I think the bigger question," Tomasetti says, thinking aloud, "is what did she know that got her killed?"

"She'd been a topless dancer," I say. "She rubbed shoulders with a lot of the wrong kind of people. She lived a high-risk lifestyle."

"Could be drug related." He shrugs. "Maybe the wrong person found out she'd been picked up by law enforcement. They were afraid she might turn over on them. And they eliminated her."

The issue of drugs has come up a dozen times in the course of the investigation, and yet we've not found evidence indicating any are being sold. "Could be an illicit-relationship kind of thing," I say. "Maybe she got into a relationship with a client. Maybe he was married or a high-profile individual who didn't want his reputation sullied. Or his marriage ruined."

"Or you could take that angle a step farther," he says. "What if she engaged in some illicit affair or relationship and tried to cash in?"

"Blackmail?"

He shrugs. "Any of those situations are powerful motives to do away with someone."

We fall silent, our brains grinding through all the broken pieces of information.

"Tomasetti, everything about this case is . . . off-kilter," I say. "There are a lot of connections, but none of them seem to actually connect. It's like there's something there, hiding in plain sight, and the harder we look the more elusive it becomes."

Scowling, he scrubs a hand over his jaw, looks at me over his fingertips. "Look, Doc is getting ready to move her. He says we can go in. He'll give us what he can."

The last thing I want to do is wade through that snarl of bramble to see the dead body of a young woman I spoke with less than twenty-four hours ago. But as is usually the case with any homicide investigation, information takes precedence over petty human comforts.

Tomasetti walks over to the crime scene tape, lifts it, and waits. My feet feel as if they're encased in concrete as I duck beneath it. We fight through stickers and thorns and find Doc Coblentz kneeling next to the corpse. He's wearing a Tyvek suit, his head, feet, and hands covered. He looks up when we approach and I notice the redness suffusing his cheeks, see the dribble of sweat on his temple.

"Hi, Chief." He nods. "Tomasetti."

The body of Wilma Borntrager lies supine on a plastic sheet that's been placed beside the body bag that's unzipped and waiting. Her face is pale and slack with the vague hint of blue veins beneath the skin. Both eyes are open and covered with the cloudy film of death. Someone has placed paper bags over both hands and secured them with rubber bands.

"Anything you can share?" Tomasetti asks.

"I think it's safe to assume this is a homicide," Doc says.

"We saw the gunshot wound." I'm looking at him, but I'm hyper-aware of the body. The cloudy eyes. The incessant drone of flies all around. The vaguely unpleasant smell of blood and bodily secretions.

"As both of you are well aware," Doc begins, "any information I relay to you at this juncture is subject to change once we perform the autopsy."

"Of course," I hear myself say.

He looks down at the body. "From what I can tell, there are actually *two* penetrating wounds, presumably gunshot wounds." Using a long, cotton-tipped swab, Doc indicates the gunshot wound on the victim's abdomen. "This is likely an exit wound," he says. "Don't quote me on that."

"They shot her in the back," I murmur.

Nodding, Doc shifts the swab to a red-black hole above and in front of the victim's ear. "This was likely the fatal wound. You missed it initially because there was less bleeding. And her hair was covering it."

"Once she was down," Tomasetti says, "she was shot execution-style."

"That's a solid theory at this point," Doc says.

"They shot her a second time just to be sure." The words come off my tongue like acid. "Just like Yutzy."

The coroner nods grimly. "The second gunshot wound likely killed her instantly."

Not instantly, I think. And I can't help but wonder how long she'd lain there waiting for the killing shot.

"Sexual assault?" I ask.

"There's no indication that I can see," Doc says. "She's clothed, of course. No blood or bruising or semen that's visible. Of course, I won't be able to answer that definitively until we get her on the table."

"Any other wounds?" Tomasetti asks.

"There's blood on the fabric at both knees," Doc tells us. "Some scratches, likely from the stickers and brush. Some bruising, but no other penetrating wounds that I can discern at this time."

"She got away from them," I say. "She ran. The killer came after her and shot her in the back. She was still moving so the son of a bitch finished her off with a shot to the head."

"I won't be able to answer the medical aspect of that definitively until post-autopsy," Doc Coblentz says. "But yes."

I try not to think of the horrors this young woman must have endured during the final minutes of her life. With that torturous thought in mind, I turn and start back toward my vehicle.

CHAPTER 22

I call Mona on my way to Millersburg. "Anything else come back on Brooks?"

"Plenty." A flurry of keyboard clicks and then, "On the weapons charge, he took a plea deal. Felony was dropped. He pleaded guilty to the misdemeanor of possessing criminal tools. He paid court fines of five hundred dollars. Jail time was suspended. He was ordered to perform thirty hours of community service."

"Did the court return the firearm?"

"He forfeited the Beretta."

"Judge must have been in a good mood," I mutter.

"Or Mr. Brooks had a very good attorney."

The statement stops me cold, my mind looping back to Wilma Borntrager. "Who was his attorney?"

More tapping of keys. "Brett Adamson with Adamson and Schneider out of Cleveland."

Bingo, I think. "I'm ten-seventy-six the brewery."

"Roger that."

• • •

A blazing sun boils like molten steel on the western horizon as I pull into the parking lot of the Blue Lake Tap and Brewery. The place is busy and it takes me several minutes to find a parking place. I'm sweating by the time I go through the front doors.

I see the same bartender as last time I was here and veer left to avoid him. I want to catch Brooks off guard this time and see how he reacts to the news of Wilma Borntrager's murder.

I weave through a smattering of tables, sidle past the opposite end of the bar, and push through the swinging doors. No one notices me as I stride past the kitchen and enter the hall at the rear of the building. Brooks's office door stands open about a foot, a slant of light spilling into the hall. I go to the door, peer inside, see Brooks bent over a laptop, pounding the keys as if he's in the midst of a speed test.

I rap on the jamb. "Mr. Brooks?"

His head jerks up, his eyes narrowing. "Chief Burkholder." He stands, looking past me as if expecting someone else. "What are you doing here?"

"There's been a new development in the Samuel Yutzy case," I tell him. "Do you have a few minutes?"

His mouth goes flat. "To tell you the truth, it's a busy night." He closes the laptop. "Tomorrow morning would be better."

"I won't take up too much of your time."

The desktop phone on his desk beeps three times as I enter. He glances at the display and frowns. "Hang on."

I take the visitor chair across from him while he talks to the person on the other end of the line about a late delivery and refrigeration problems.

It's a slightly heated exchange and he sets down the phone with a little too much force.

His face is taut when he turns his attention to me. "What can I do for you?"

"I understand you have a former employee by the name of Wilma Borntrager."

He gives me a how-would-I-remember-something-so-mundane stare. "I have a lot of employees. I don't recognize that name."

I pull a photo of her from my pocket and slide it across the desk so that he can see it. "Wilma Borntrager. She just turned eighteen."

"I don't hire anyone under the age of nineteen here at the brewery," he tells me. "I know Ohio employment laws."

"So you don't recognize her?" I ask.

Sighing in annoyance, he looks down at the photo. "Well, she is kind of familiar." His brows knit. "I don't think that's her correct name, though."

"She used the alias of Cassidy Robinette."

"That's it." He snaps his fingers. "Now I remember. She worked here for a short time and then just stopped showing up."

I nod. "Did she have any problems with any of her fellow employees while she worked for you? Any problems with customers?"

He gives a not-so-covert glance at his watch. "Not that I recall."

"Mr. Brooks, Wilma Borntrager was found dead this morning."

He starts to get to his feet, but my words seem to stop him. He opens his mouth to say something, but then sinks back into the chair without comment. "Wow. She's dead? That's awful. What the hell happened to her?"

"We're looking into it." I hedge, keeping it vague. "We believe there was foul play involved."

"She was murdered?"

"We're waiting to hear back from the coroner," I tell him. "Right now, I'm gathering as much information about her as possible."

"Sure." Another quick glance at his watch.

"You forgot to mention the altercation between you and Samuel Yutzy here at the brewery."

"I don't recall any such thing," he tells me.

"Let me refresh your memory. Yutzy and Borntrager were together that night. Here at the brewery. I have a witness who saw you punch Yutzy in the face."

He stares at me, his expression flat, nostrils flaring. Color climbs up his throat and spreads to his cheeks. *Temper,* I think. Because he got caught in a lie? Or because he has something to hide?

The phone on his desk rings again; he ignores it this time. "That's bullshit," he says. "I didn't punch Yutzy."

I hold his gaze. "You think the witness is mistaken?"

"I think someone is feeding you lies and, evidently, you're swallowing them hook, line, and sinker."

I nod, unperturbed. "How did you meet Wilma Borntrager?"

He shrugs, but his shoulders are so tight he can barely manage. "Most of the people we hire here fill out an application online. If we're interested in hiring them, we call or email or text and ask them to come in for an interview."

"Did you interview her?"

"Either I interviewed her or my lead server did. I honestly don't recall."

"Did Samuel Yutzy recommend her for a job?" I ask.

"I suppose it's possible." He shrugs. "Maybe he mentioned her in the course of a conversation and I pulled her application out of the pile as a favor to him. I don't recall."

"Could you take a look at her personnel file maybe?"

Impatience flares in his eyes. "I use a payroll service. I can give them a call in the morning."

"Thank you," I say agreeably. "The sooner we can get to the bottom of all this, the better."

He sends another pointed glance to his watch. "Anything else, Chief Burkholder? I've got a sick server to cover for and a party of sixteen arriving in ten minutes."

"One more quick question." I smile. "Are you aware that Wilma Borntrager and Samuel Yutzy were involved?"

He blinks at me. "How would I know that?"

"That's quite a coincidence, don't you think?"

"I don't know what you're getting at and my patience is running thin."

"They both worked for you and now both of them are dead," I say. "What are the odds?"

He stares at me, the flush at his throat deepening. "Are you accusing me of something, Chief Burkholder?"

"I'm trying to put a few connections together."

His face goes taut. "Well, I don't like it. I sure as fuck don't appreciate you coming in here and making a bunch of vague accusations when I'm trying to run my damn business."

"Is it true that you initially inquired about Samuel Yutzy at the country club?"

"I think so," he snaps. "I asked about the landscaping work and the manager gave me his name. I told you all of that."

"Are you a member of the club?"

He rolls his eyes. "Yes."

"Who was it who gave you Samuel's name?"

"I told you," he says irritably. "The manager."

"Lance Wingate?"

"I believe that's his name."

"Are you friends?"

"I'd say we're more acquaintances."

He stares at me, unmoving, for the span of several heartbeats, then gets to his feet. "Look, I'm not trying to be rude or evasive, but I've invested enough time in this interview. If you have any additional questions, I suggest you call and make an appointment with my attorney."

"Who is your attorney, by the way?" I ask.

"Brett Adamson," he says. "He's in the book."

Taking my time, I get to my feet. "It's interesting that you and Wilma Borntrager have the same attorney," I say. "What are the odds?"

"This conversation is over." He points to the door. "Out."

I smile, but it feels nasty on my face. "If you think of anything else that you'd like to share, give me a call."

Brooks rounds his desk, brushes past me, and pulls open the door. "Have a good day."

I leave without thanking him.

• • •

"We're going to have to do something about that fucking cop," said the burly man as he picked up the crystal tumbler and swirled the amber liquid inside.

The words echoed uneasily between the two men. Like a declaration of war, or a call for surrender when no one wanted either.

It was nearly last call and, around them, the bar was hushed. They'd chosen a booth at the rear where the lighting was dim and there were no tables close enough for curious ears to eavesdrop.

The man in the sport coat picked up his beer and sipped. "The situation is too hot for anything rash."

"I'm not suggesting anything rash." The burly man wore blue jeans and a white shirt with the sleeves rolled up. A gold chain peeked out from the collar at his throat. Expensive watch was strapped to his wrist. "But she's got to be dealt with. Now. Before things get too complicated."

"I'm loath to point this out, but we wouldn't be in this situation if your people hadn't screwed things up in the first place."

"There's nothing I can do about that now." Thoughtful and unperturbed, the burly man picked up his whiskey and sipped. "Listen to me. If we don't stop her, she's going to keep coming. Sooner or later, she's going to find something and do some damage."

"So we do a little housekeeping—"

"Too late for that."

"What do you suggest?"

"We've tried warning her." The burly man shrugged. "It didn't work. I say we take it to the next level."

The man in the sport coat stared at him. "And what level is that?"

"We make her disappear."

He scoffed. "And the attorney general's goon? Do you think he's just going to go away?"

"We ride out the storm," the burly man said. "If things get dicey, we go to plan B."

"I don't like it. Any of it."

"Neither do I." The burly man took another drink of whiskey, grimaced against the burn, swallowed hard. "This isn't going to resolve itself. We've got too much invested, too much to lose, to let some two-bit cop fuck things up."

The man in the sport coat leaned against the booth back, thinking. "I'm assuming you have a plan."

"Let's just say I know the right people." He picked up the glass, knocked the last of the whiskey back. "These guys are pros. They know how to get things done. And they won't leave so much as a trace."

"Do you have a timeline in mind?"

"I'll get things rolling now. As soon as the opportunity presents itself, I'll get it done."

The man in the sport coat stared down at his beer. "You screw this up and I will not go down with the ship. Do you understand?"

"This is the only way," the burly man said. "We eliminate her from the equation. There's nothing left. Nothing to trace back to us. End of story."

But when he set the empty tumbler on the table, he was already wishing for another drink.

CHAPTER 23

It's half past two A.M. and I'm sitting at the kitchen table at home, my laptop open and humming. The table is piled with reams of paper—official reports and photographs, handwritten notes and sketches. The Yutzy, Shetler, and Borntrager homicide files are stacked to my right. I'm on my second cup of coffee, which isn't exactly smart since at some point I'm going to have to sleep. The ghosts of the dead haunt me in earnest tonight.

Around me, the farmhouse is silent. Tomasetti was already in bed when I arrived home at midnight. I was too wired, too troubled, to sleep, so I made coffee and set up shop in the kitchen, and so far I've accomplished exactly zero.

"I have two dead men," I say aloud, not bothering to acknowledge the exhaustion and frustration in my voice. "One dead woman. They were young. Amish."

I flip through the Yutzy file until I come to a paper-clipped stack of my notes. I read aloud: "The murder and dismemberment were done at the tree nursery. The remains were buried in the woods a quarter mile away. That means the killer or killers transported the remains, likely with garbage bags."

I turn the page and come to the official report from the BCI crime scene unit agent. "No fingerprints. No footwear imprints. No foreign DNA. No fibers. No tire-tread impressions."

I sigh, thinking about ghosts . . .

"Want some company?"

I startle at the sound of Tomasetti's voice and look up to see him come through the kitchen door. He's wearing a Cleveland Division of Police T-shirt and boxer shorts. His hair is tousled, his left cheek is creased from the sheets, and he's holding a gray tabby cat in his arms.

"I didn't mean to wake you," I say, embarrassed.

"I needed to get up in a couple of hours, anyway."

"It's two thirty in the morning and I'm talking to myself."

"No judgment." Setting the cat on the counter, he goes to the coffeemaker and pours. "I'm meeting legal at seven in Columbus. We're going to interview Brett Adamson."

"I thought you already talked to him."

"He stonewalled me. I'll have legal with me this time." Tomasetti scowls. "Adamson is a slick son of a bitch."

It's a step in the direction of progress, but I can't quite muster the appropriate level of enthusiasm. "Be nice to know who's paying him."

"I'll do my best to find out."

The cat sits, lifts its paw, and begins licking. "You know there's a cat on the counter," I say.

"I saw that."

"We don't have a cat."

"We do now." He brings the carafe to the table and tops off my cup. "He adopted me this afternoon."

"I never had you pegged as a cat guy."

"I've got a few secrets up my sleeve."

I nod, look a little more closely at the cat. "He doesn't have a tail."

"He's either a Manx or had an unfortunate encounter with a coyote." He replaces the carafe, picks up the cat, and sets the animal on the floor. "Might help us with the mouse population in the barn."

"I like him already."

He grabs his smartphone off the counter where it's charging and settles into the chair across from me. "Kate, you look tired."

"Can't sleep."

"Ghosts?"

I nod because I know it's an existence both of us are intimately acquainted with.

"Tomasetti, whoever murdered these three young people . . . they left absolutely nothing behind."

He sips coffee, looks at me over the rim of his mug. "I know."

"Yutzy's murder and dismemberment must have taken quite a bit of time. We're talking a chain saw and knives, and moving a dismembered body a quarter of a mile through wooded terrain. And yet there was no foreign DNA. Not a single hair. We have at least one of the garbage bags and the chain saw that was used, and yet there were no fingerprints. No footprints. No glove or casings or cigarette butt. Same with Shetler. Same with Borntrager."

"They've done this before," he says slowly.

"We're not dealing with amateurs or some crime-of-passion scenario."

"They aren't local."

I nod, find myself thinking about patterns. "Yutzy helped Borntrager get a job. First at the brewery in Millersburg. Then at The Cheetah Lounge in New Philly. He helped Rose Yoder get a job at The Cheetah Lounge. That's a pattern."

"What's his connection to The Cheetah Lounge?"

"I don't know."

"He could be a customer. A regular who became friendly with the staff, the dancers, the bartender or bouncer."

My brain is already off and running, and I find myself recalling my conversation with Joseph Stoltzfoos. Something about Samuel having a weakness for a certain kind of woman . . .

I reach for my notebook, dig through until I find what I'm looking for. I look at Tomasetti. "When I asked Joseph Stoltzfoos about Yutzy's relationship with Wilma Borntrager he said something interesting, so I wrote it down, and I quote: 'He was always drawn to the women with a lot of drama in their lives. The ones who needed help. The ones in trouble.'"

"Was Borntrager in trouble?"

"She'd left the Amish. She didn't have a place to go. Or a place to stay. No money. No friends. Her family wouldn't speak to her, let her visit, or even take meals with her."

"What about Rose Yoder?"

"She'd left the Amish, too." I think about that a moment. "When you leave like that, you basically walk away from everything you've ever known, including your friends and family. Any ties you've ever had. You have no money. No place to stay. No support system. If someone dangles something you need in front of you, something like friendship or security or support—"

"Or a job—" he interjects.

"You're going to go for it."

"Whatever Yutzy's motivations, good or bad or somewhere in between, he wasn't exactly doing these women a favor."

"Short term, they would have money and some semblance of security."

"Long term . . . jobs like that can lead to exploitation and worse."

Tomasetti's eyes sharpen on mine. "These women, Yoder and Borntrager, were young and attractive."

I nod. "For Amish women, they were outgoing. Independent minded. They had some attitude and yet they were naïve."

"Vulnerable."

The word teeters, refuses to settle, and I find myself thinking about predators. Not coyotes, but the human variety.

"Let's look at Brooks," Tomasetti says. "How does he play into all of this?"

"Wilma Borntrager worked for him. Samuel Yutzy did some contract work for him. The landscaping. Now, both of them are dead. That's a tangible connection. Gotta be something there." Hearing the exasperation in my voice, I lean back in the chair and sigh. "This is why I was talking to myself earlier."

His phone chimes. Frowning, he glances at the screen and taps a key. "Looks like my IT guy worked late," he murmurs.

"Some solid information would be nice about now," I mutter.

"How about a window into the laptop from the rental house?"

I sit up straighter. "That'll do."

"First things first." He swipes the screen. "The serial number traces back to Wilma Borntrager."

"She purchased it."

"Doesn't mean it's hers." He nods, keeps scrolling. "Looks like we've got some email to take a look at. There are photos. Videos. IT guy thinks he got some chat-room logs. The browsing history, too. He's still looking at that."

"Can you send me the data?" I ask.

"I can send you what I have so far." He lowers his cell and frowns. "Do me a favor?"

"Just ask."

"Before you jump into all that data, will you grab a couple hours' sleep?"

"First you bring home a stray cat and now you're being sweet to me." I say the words teasingly, but I mean them.

"I like to think of it as charming."

"That works."

"I'd appreciate if you didn't start any rumors." His smile is followed by a sigh. "Look, I've got to hit the shower and get going."

"Want some company?" I ask.

Grinning, he reaches over and closes my laptop.

• • •

No matter the crime—whether it's a homicide or robbery or an assault—a large chunk of an investigator's time is invariably spent on the mundane. Things like paperwork and the filling out of official forms, and untold hours combing through random information that may or may not be helpful or even related to the case.

Somehow, another day has blown by. It's nearly eight P.M. and I'm in my office at the police station, staring at my computer monitor and wishing I had chosen the reading glasses with the higher magnification. Before leaving for his meeting with the lawyer in Columbus this morning, Tomasetti forwarded several zipped data files, which I downloaded from a secure cloud storage website. I spent much of the day skimming through hundreds of emails, flagging anything that might be relevant to the case. The laptop was being used by multiple individuals. I don't recognize most of the names. Some could be pseudonyms, but Tomasetti is working on pulling IP addresses. Unfortunately, it's going to take some time.

The majority of the correspondence appears to be benign, everything from résumés to hookup messages, to breakup messages, to dinner-and-drinks plans.

Despite being formerly Amish, Wilma Borntrager was well versed in all forms of electronic communication. She'd been seeing several men simultaneously, though her relationship with Samuel Yutzy seemed to be the most serious. In spite of her financial woes early on, she always seemed to have enough money to go out on the town, either alone or with friends.

Not only was Wilma involved in multiple relationships with varying degrees of intimacy, she flirted excessively. Initially, I assumed that because of her financial situation and displacement after leaving the Amish, she was looking not only for companionship but for a man willing to help her out financially. The more I see, the more I realize that's not the case. Wilma Borntrager was hooking up with multiple available men; some of them were giving her cash and gifts. To what end I can only guess.

Finding little of interest in the emails, I go to the file that contains several chat-room logs. Most are written almost solely with emojis, abbreviations, and pseudo acronyms.

I'm NIFOC.

LMIRL

WTTP?

CU46?

WTGP?

It's almost as if the exchanges are written in code. Curious, I go to my laptop, pull up my search engine, and plug in a few of the acronyms.

NIFOC: I'm naked in front of the computer.

LMIRL: Let's meet in real life.

WTTP: Want to trade photos.

WTGP: Want to go private.

Even more disturbing are the emojis.

In some circles, a growing heart emoji indicates a minor person is available for sex.

A cherry or cherry blossom emoji indicates a person who is a virgin is looking for sex.

"What the hell were you into?" I murmur as I read on.

The phrase that follows stops me cold.

Sex traffickers use emojis to advertise their services, coordinate operations, and evade detection by law enforcement. Emojis can be used as a coded language to communicate.

I consider everything I know about Samuel Yutzy and Wilma Borntrager. I think about all of the connections that don't quite connect. The patterns of behavior that aren't quite patterns. And for the first time, it begins to make sense.

Is it possible Wilma Borntrager was being trafficked for sex? Was she helping to traffic other women? I recall reading that some trafficking victims don't initially even realize they're being trafficked. Is it possible Wilma didn't realize what was happening to her?

The second zip file contains dozens of JPEG files, most of which are photographs of people I don't recognize. Midway through, I come upon a slew of odd-looking close-ups. At first, I'm not even sure what I'm looking at, but I quickly discern the blue-green tint of tattoo ink on pale flesh. Why would someone photograph a tattoo? I focus on the tattoos. One is of a crown. Another image is that of a red heart affixed to a chain.

I see a barcode that's been tattooed onto what looks like someone's nape. Another of initials done in an Old English font. I make a mental note to research more in depth and keep going.

The next file contains what looks like screenshots of social media posts. I recognize Wilma Borntrager in some of them. Outwardly, the images look like something a twenty-year-old woman might post on her Instagram account or Facebook page to share with her circle of friends. But the deeper I go, the more obvious it becomes that these photos are not all fun and games. I can't put my finger on it, but there's something off. The photos look posed. They look forced. The smiles a little too bright . . .

I skim through some of the screenshots' captions:

Check out my new dress. Got it for a steal. Squeal!

Picnic this afternoon with my guy. Rose or sauvignon blanc (or both)?

A photo of three young women, one of whom is Wilma Borntrager, all three raising margarita glasses. *Out on the town and on the hunt for 53X!*

Another photo of Borntrager. This one taken out of doors. She's topless and wearing bikini bottoms, her head thrown back as if she doesn't have a care in the world. The caption reads: *All turnt up and lookin' for Smash!*

I've just opened another file when my cell chimes. I glance down, see Tomasetti's name, and snatch it up.

"I'm halfway through the zip files," I tell him.

"Of course you are."

"Tomasetti, is it possible we're dealing with some form of sex trafficking?"

A heavy beat of silence. "That would explain a lot."

I tell him about the photos, the emails, the chat-room logs, and some of the code being used. "I looked up the acronyms and emojis. They're talking in code."

"Emojis are tougher to search for and track."

"What about the tattoos?" I ask.

"Those are brands," he tells me. "They're used to show ownership of someone who's being trafficked."

A waxy sense of nausea rises into my throat. "Human trafficking?"

"It's no longer just a big-city problem."

I force the information into my brain, try to process it, make it make sense. It's like trying to shove a square peg into a round hole. "So, you knew."

"Not until I saw those files," he says. "I'm barely into the first."

I sense our thoughts zinging and he poses the question both of us are asking. "How does Samuel Yutzy fit into all of this?"

Images from the files fly at me. I think of everything I know about the investigation so far. The relationships and connections and all of the things that don't add up.

"Yutzy met Borntrager at the rager here in Painters Mill." I'm thinking aloud, giving my brain free rein. "She was in trouble. Needed money. A place to stay."

"She appealed to him," he says. "She needed help."

"He got her the job at the brewery," I add. "When that went south, he got her the job at The Cheetah Lounge."

"Samuel Yutzy brought her in," he says slowly. "He recruited her."

The words hit me like quick, hard punches. Such a terrible word, the meaning of which is not lost on me. "At some point, they became involved."

"Was it serious?"

"And unexpected." My mind spins through the implications of that. "Yutzy's parents told me in the last few weeks he'd come back to them."

A beat of silence and then he says, "His relationship with Borntrager may have changed things."

"He realized what he was doing was wrong. That he was hurting people. And he stopped."

"But he was already in too deep."

"All of them were. Yutzy. Shetler. And Borntrager. They knew too much about the wrong people and they became threats."

"Shit."

I hear voices in the background and realize he's still in his office in Columbus. "Kate, look, I'm about to jump back into this meeting. I think we're on track. Keep at it. I'll try to keep up with you, but I've got another meeting. In the interim . . . I called to let you know . . . Carter Brooks paid for Borntrager's attorney."

"They weren't exactly on friendly terms. Borntrager quit without giving notice. Why would he pay for her attorney?"

"I don't know, but there's more. We heard back from the New Mexico Secretary of State's office. Get this: Brooks is also part owner of The Cheetah Lounge."

The information lands another blow against my brain. "The missing link," I say. "Any word on the owner of the house on Lost Creek Road?"

"Still cutting through red tape."

I'm still thinking about Brooks. "Brooks is in this up to his eyeballs."

"We don't know how," he says. "Or who else is involved."

"The brewery. The Cheetah Lounge. Those types of businesses appeal to and employ attractive young women."

"They used the businesses as a recruiting mechanism," he says, thinking aloud. "Yutzy, maybe even Shetler, brought in the women. Brooks hired them. Earned their trust. Groomed them. Add the trafficking angle and some of these weird connections start to make sense."

My mind races with possibilities. "Where's the lawyer?"

"We had to cut him loose."

"He give you anything?"

"Nothing."

"What do you have on Brooks?" I ask.

"Not enough," he growls. "We're looking at IP addresses now. If we can get that, we can contact the providers with warrants and conceivably get physical addresses and names."

"How long will that take?"

"Too damn long."

"At least now we know what we're looking at."

"I've got to run," he says. "Keep on doing what you're doing. I should be out of here in twenty minutes and then I'll head your way. I got a briefing lined up with Rasmussen. Can you meet us there?"

"Wouldn't miss it," I say.

"See you in a couple of hours."

And then he's gone.

CHAPTER 24

I spend another hour combing through data files. I'm energized by the new information from Tomasetti, and for the first time since the start of the investigation, I feel as if we're on the right track and making headway.

That something so insidious has found its way to Painters Mill makes me feel sick inside. At least two Amish females were targeted and, apparently, became victims. I know small towns aren't immune. Still, I'm shocked and it hurts.

At nine P.M. I grab coffee and dig into the third zip file. I've come up with a good system now, flagging any exchange or photo that could be related to trafficking and rearranging them so that I can sort by flag type. Some of the photos are risqué, but not pornographic. Most seem like young women doing fun things: partying with friends at a pool or bar or restaurant. I've come across several photos of Amish women clad in traditional garb, which is surprising since for religious reasons most Amish do not allow their picture to be taken. Occasionally, an unthinking tourist will snap a photo, and if the person being photographed is aware, they'll avert their face. Not the case here and I can't help but wonder if that's by design.

I'm paging down, hitting keys with my index finger, going too fast, when one of the photos stops me cold. I go back to the image, use my mouse to full-screen it. The photo is of Wilma Borntrager, Samuel Yutzy, and a fiftysomething male I don't recognize. They're at a bistro table with a swimming pool in the background. Yutzy is holding up a beer cheers-style and grinning at the camera. The other man's eyes are fastened to Borntrager with unconcealed male appreciation. She's wearing a sky-blue golf shirt with a black miniskirt, an outfit that's vaguely familiar.

I'm in the process of flagging the photo when something else gives me pause. The pool area, I realize. I've seen it before. I've *been* there. Leaning closer to the monitor, I use my mouse to enlarge the image. One of the table umbrellas looms into view and I spot the logo.

"The Club at Paint Creek." Even as I murmur the words, I recall that's why I recognized the outfit, too. The servers wear sky-blue golf shirts with black miniskirts. Did Wilma work at The Club at Paint Creek, too?

I'm not exactly sure what the information means in terms of the case, but it's another connection that wasn't there before. One that brings Lance Wingate back into the equation.

Quickly, I print a black-and-white version of the image. A glance at the time on my computer tells me I still have an hour before meeting Rasmussen and Tomasetti at the sheriff's office in Millersburg.

I call out to Margaret, my dispatcher. "How late is the country club open?"

Footsteps and then she appears in the doorway of my office, her expression curious. "Nine, I think."

"Who's on tonight?"

"Mona."

"Call her and tell her to meet me there."

"Anything I need to know about, Chief?"

"I just have a couple of quick questions for the director," I tell her.

"Roger that."

"Margaret?"

She turns to me, raises her brows.

"Use the phone, not the radio."

• • •

The Club at Paint Creek is as elegant and stately after hours as it is during the day. The trees along the driveway are lit up with novelty lights. I take the same route Tomasetti and I did when we were here before. The parking lot is nearly vacant with only three vehicles and a pickup truck hitched to a cargo trailer, a lawn service logo emblazoned on the side.

I park next to the truck and call Mona. "I'm ten-twenty-three," I say. "What's your ETA?"

"Twelve minutes, Chief."

"I'll meet you in the lobby."

"Roger that."

I don't expect some earth-shattering revelation to come from this impromptu meeting this evening. Service employees, particularly food servers, bounce from job to job. It's entirely possible Wilma Borntrager worked here before her stints at the brewery and The Cheetah Lounge. Then again, Yutzy was in the photo with her; the other man didn't look like some innocent bystander.

I formulate my line of questioning as I take the sidewalk to the front of the building. To my relief, the front doors are still open. I enter the lobby to chilly air and the aromas of eucalyptus and lavender. It's so quiet I can hear my feet against the floor as I make my way to the front desk. Through the windows to my right, I can see the pool area and deck. Even from this distance, I discern the Club at Paint Creek logo emblazoned on the umbrellas. The front desk is vacant. There's no perfunctory bell to ring, so I walk to the hall that will take me to Wingate's office.

Warm yellow light slants out through the open door of his office at the end of the hall. Midway there, the sound of his voice reaches me. Talking on the phone. Something about membership and a long-running promotion.

I knock, peering inside. "Hello?"

Wingate sits behind his desk, the only light coming from the Tiffany lamp to his left. I don't miss the quicksilver flash of annoyance on his face an instant before he beams a smile at me.

"Call you back," he says to whoever's on the other end of the line, and sets the phone in its base. "Chief Burkholder. What a surprise."

"I hope I'm not catching you at a bad time," I say as I enter his office.

"End of the workday is always a good time." He motions me into one of the visitor chairs. "Have a seat. What can I do for you?"

"Just a couple of quick questions," I say as I settle into the chair.

He scoots closer to his desk, sets his elbows on the blotter. "Do you guys have any leads on what happened to Samuel Yutzy?" he asks.

"We've got a few things in the works," I say, keeping it vague. "Still following up."

A shadow of a smile crosses his features. "Everyone's going to rest a hell of a lot easier when you make an arrest."

"That's a true statement." A beat of silence and then I get to the point. "Mr. Wingate, was Samuel Yutzy a member of the club?"

He looks at me as if I've asked a silly question. "No."

"While he was working on the landscaping contract, did he have access to your facilities or interact with any of the employees or members?"

"He usually ate lunch in his truck." His brows pull together as if he's trying to remember. "I may have given him a complimentary lunch or two. To show my thanks, you know. I appreciate a hard worker. Why do you ask?"

"I'm trying to get the dynamics straight in my head." I smile agreeably. I'm in the process of fishing my phone out of my pocket when a *tap-tap-tap* sounds on the door.

"Mr. Wingate?"

At the sound of the female voice, I look over my shoulder. A pretty young woman, a tray holding a bottle of sparkling water and a glass in her hands, enters the office. She's wearing a shimmering sequin tank top and a black satin skirt that falls to mid-thigh. She's blond haired with eyes as green as a cat's. She's decked out in gold jewelry, full makeup, and an artistic manicure that must have taken hours to paint.

A quick smile and then she sidles past and strides to his desk. "I didn't realize you were in a meeting." She slants an uncertain smile in my direction. "Or I would have brought two glasses."

"Thank you, but I can't stay," I say amicably.

Bending slightly, she sets the tray on the desk. She's pouring water over ice when her hair shifts and the tattoo at her nape comes into view. I only catch a glimpse before her hair falls over it again, but a spark of recognition stings my brain. A crown in blue ink. I've seen a similar tattoo recently, but where?

"Thanks, Lucy. That'll be all." Wingate clears his throat. "You can call it a day if you'd like."

"Of course." Her smile is toothy, but only adds to her charm. "Don't work too late."

He clears his throat again.

"'Night." The young woman smiles at me as she starts toward the door.

As I make eye contact with her, a dozen details strike my brain at once. She's too young to be working here. Trying too hard to look older and impress in a way that's not quite appropriate.

Having recognized her accent, I smile back at her. "You're Amish," I say enthusiastically.

She stops and looks down at me, her eyes widening as if I've noticed something I shouldn't have noticed. "How do you know that?"

"I can tell by your accent," I say. "I used to be Amish."

"Oh. Um." Looking uncomfortable, she glances at Wingate and back to me. "Well, I'm not Amish anymore."

Keenly aware that Wingate is watching the exchange, that he's impatient for her to leave and wishing I'd shut the hell up, I lean back in my chair and try to keep it light.

"Which church district are you from?" I ask.

"Lucy is from the Pittsburgh area." Wingate looks at his watch.

I'm still thinking about that tattoo and I remember where I saw it before: Angelica at The Cheetah Lounge. And suddenly I know it's relevant and important.

I move to keep her talking. "How long ago did you leave the fold?"

The young woman swallows hard, her eyes flicking to Wingate again, then back to me. She's growing increasingly nervous. As if she's talking about something she's not supposed to talk about. "A few months."

"I know it's not easy to do." I send a hapless smile to Wingate. "She's very brave."

"Well . . ." Her eyes flick from me to Wingate and back to me.

Holding on to my smile, I turn my attention back to the young woman and switch to *Deitsch.* "If you're in trouble, I can help you."

"I don't know what you're talking about." But she responds in *Deitsch.*

"I know what that tattoo means," I tell her, still in *Deitsch.*

Subconsciously, her hand goes to her nape and she fingers the tattoo. "I have to go," she whispers in English.

Spinning, she strides to the door and then she's gone.

I grin at Wingate. "I hope I didn't embarrass her too much."

"She's a new hire." He doesn't return the smile. "An intern, actually. Still learning the ropes, I guess."

A beat of silence and then his cell chimes. "Sorry," he mutters. Frowning, he taps the screen a couple of times and then sets it on the blotter. "What did you want to talk to me about, Chief Burkholder?"

I pull out my cell, scroll until I find the photo I'm looking for. "I'm wondering if you can identify the woman in this photo." Keeping my voice neutral, I lean forward and turn my phone so that he can see the screen.

Wingate slips on his reading glasses and leans forward, his brows knitting. "Well, there's Samuel Yutzy. Hmmm . . . I don't recognize the woman."

"She's wearing a uniform like the servers here at the club." I indicate the photo with my index finger. "You can just make out the logo on that umbrella."

"Lots of servers wear uniforms like that." He shrugs. "Maybe the two of them had lunch here or something. I wouldn't know." He makes eye contact with me. "Who is she?"

"Her name is Wilma Borntrager," I tell him. "She was Samuel Yutzy's girlfriend. She was murdered two nights ago."

He feigns shock, presses his hand against his chest. "Holy shit. That's awful."

"Mr. Wingate, that uniform she's wearing is the same uniform I saw your servers wearing the other day when Tomasetti and I were here."

He scoffs. "You're mistaken."

His eyes flick to the door behind me. I hear the shuffle of shoes against the floor. I turn to see Lucy enter. She's carrying a bottle of sparkling water and a glass. Her smile lands on me. "Here you go, Chief Burkholder."

I turn slightly, take the bottle and glass. "Thank you."

I've just turned back to Wingate when I feel her hand thump down on my shoulder. Something pricks my skin, like a bee sting. An instant of pressure.

Twisting, I jump to my feet, knock her hand away. "What the hell are you doing?"

The girl stumbles back.

A wave of horror descends when I spot the syringe in her hand. "What is that?"

"I'm sorry," she cries.

I lunge at her, grasp her wrist, stare down at the hypodermic needle. A hundred thoughts hit my brain at once. It's an intramuscular injection. The barrel is half empty. "What did you do?"

She gasps when I squeeze. Her hand opens. The syringe falls to the floor at our feet.

I draw back, clock the left side of her face with my fist, and shove her away. Raising her hands, she flies backward.

I spin back to Wingate. He's rounded the desk. Two feet away. Coming at me fast. Lips peeled back. Right arm cocked. I reach for my .38. "Stop!" I scream. "*Stop!*"

I yank my weapon from its holster. Finger inside the guard. Bring up the muzzle. Wingate lunges at me. The blow lands on my left cheekbone. Pain zings from temple to jaw. My head snaps back. My vision blurs.

I clutch the gun, bring it up, swing it toward him. "Back off!" I pull off a shot, but I know it's a miss.

I don't see the second blow coming. Pain explodes as something comes down on the back of my head. A lightning storm in my brain. Vaguely, I'm aware of my knees hitting the floor. The world going topsy-turvy.

I pitch forward and then I'm not aware of anything at all.

CHAPTER 25

Mona had lived in Painters Mill her entire life and not once had she been to The Club at Paint Creek. It was the kind of place for the affluent few. The kind of place she drove past and thought: *Maybe someday.* Generally speaking, she wasn't easily bedazzled, but as she drove her cruiser down the tree-lined driveway, she was duly impressed.

"Damn," she muttered as she pulled up to the front of the main building. Admiring the novelty lights and stonework, she picked up her radio. "Ten-twenty-three," she said, letting Dispatch know she'd arrived on scene.

The place was closed now, but lights blazed inside. Not seeing the chief's rental car parked in front, she idled past the entrance and cruised into the parking lot. There were three vehicles, but none of them belonged to the chief. She picked up her radio again. "Chief, what's your twenty?"

Air hissed for the span of several seconds and then Margaret's voice came back to her. "She ten-twenty-three'd seventeen minutes ago."

"Huh." Mona looked around. "Let me see if there's a back lot."

Putting the cruiser in gear, she drove around to the back of the building, but there was no parking, just a dumpster area for the garbage truck.

Remembering that the chief had asked for radio silence, she picked up her cell and dialed the chief's number. She listened to it ring half a dozen times and go to voicemail.

"That's weird," she murmured, and tried the radio again. But there was no response.

She dialed Dispatch. "Margaret, I'm at the country club and the chief isn't here."

"Are you sure? That's not like the chief."

"No, it's not." Mona looked toward the double glass doors, but there was no movement inside the building. "I'm going to go inside and ask around."

A short pause and then, "You worried?"

"Getting there."

• • •

The first thing I become aware of is vibration against my cheek. I'm lying on my side with my knees drawn up. The air around me is still and hot and I'm soaked with sweat. I open my eyes to complete darkness. Confusion and disorientation tangle inside my head. I don't know where I am or how I got here. The only thing I know for certain is that I'm in trouble.

I try to straighten my legs, but there's not enough room. I shift to free my arms only to realize they're bound behind my back.

What in the name of God happened?

Alarm spreads through me like fire on gasoline. Heart pounding, I raise my head and look around. I can hear the low hum of an engine and the whirr of tires against asphalt. I'm locked in the trunk of a vehicle, I realize, and a creeping fear wraps around my chest and squeezes . . .

The incident at the club descends like a nightmare. My encounter with Lance Wingate. The woman injecting me with some unknown drug. I glance down at my duty belt. A greasy layer of helplessness grips me when I see that my weapon and radio are gone. My cell phone is gone.

"Shit," I whisper. "*Shit.*"

I can hear myself breathing hard, feel my body shaking, and I realize I'm an inch away from panic. Squeezing my eyes shut, I take a breath, reach for calm, remind myself that Dispatch knows I was at the club. Mona was on her way to meet me. My rental car is parked in the front lot; she'll find it. It's only a matter of time before someone comes looking for me.

I try to focus, to map out my options and find a way out of this. But my thoughts are sluggish and disjointed, my physical reflexes slow. The drug, I realize. The sense of doom that follows is crushing.

Bringing up both knees I slam my boots against the side of the trunk. I test the bindings at my wrists only to realize I'm bound with my own cuffs. "Son of a bitch." I kick the side of the trunk again and again, but it's a waste of energy.

I have no idea where I'm being taken, or by whom. I don't know what they have planned for me. I think about Wingate and wonder what he could possibly hope to accomplish; surely, he knows he can't get away with something so brazen and foolish. I think about Samuel Yutzy and Aaron Shetler and can't help but wonder if a similar fate awaits me.

Knowing that most vehicles are equipped with an emergency trunk release, I use my legs to maneuver myself around so that my back—and hands—are against the taillights and latch. Once in position, I feel around with my fingers. Sweat drips down the side of my face as I try to locate the release. Most latches are a simple plastic handle attached with a cord. Some are inlaid. A few have buttons.

I struggle for several minutes before realizing someone has probably cut the cord or removed the handle. Breathing heavily, I feel around for anything I can rip out or break—wire or plastic or even a flap of carpet. If I can disable a brake light, I might be able to get this driver pulled over by a traffic cop. But my efforts are futile. Finding nothing vulnerable, I inch my way around and use my feet to kick at the plastic.

On the sixth kick, plastic cracks beneath the heel of my boot. Hope jumps in my chest and I redouble my efforts, feel something shatter. Abruptly, the vehicle bumps and then judders, rocking me. The cadence of the tires changes, crunching over what sounds like gravel. The driver is either pulling over or we've reached our destination.

"Come on," I pant. "Come on."

I kick harder, using my heels. Once. Twice. Breaths hissing, I scooch around so that my hands are against the broken plastic. I feel around, my fingers seeking wire, anything exposed. The vehicle stops hard enough to roll me. Choking back fear and frustration, I wriggle back to the rear of the trunk, hook a finger in wire, and pull, snapping it.

The trunk swings open. I look up, see the silhouettes of two males an instant before the flashlight beam blinds me.

"Someone's been busy," one of them says.

"I'm a cop," I say. "You can't do this. Let me go."

"Get her out of there," comes a vaguely familiar voice.

Strong hands fall upon my shoulder and arm, fingers clamping like vises. "Help me!" I wrench free, swivel on my back, bring up my knees, lash out with my feet. "Help! *Help!*"

"Shut her up," he snarls.

Recognition pings my brain. Carter Brooks, I realize. "What the hell do you think you're doing?" I ask.

"Something I wanted no part of," he clamors. "Thanks to you, here we are."

The second man leans in. I can just make out his face in the periphery of the flashlight beam, but I recognize him. The bouncer from The Cheetah Lounge.

He makes eye contact with me. A smile touches the corners of his mouth as he pulls a roll of duct tape from his pocket and tears a length of it off with his teeth. "Hold still."

I try to jerk away, but I've nowhere to go. The bouncer is ready and slaps the tape over my mouth, hard enough to cut my lip.

"Pull her out," Brooks growls. "We don't have all damn night."

The bouncer hauls me from the trunk. My feet hit the ground. I try to shake off his grip, but his fingers dig into my biceps hard enough to bruise.

"You give us any trouble and we'll inject you," Brooks says. "You got that?"

I look at him over my shoulder. His face is stark in the glare of the flashlight beam, his forehead slicked with sweat. I see stress in his features. His eyes are furious as they climb over me. "You dumb bitch. Do you have any idea what you've done? What you've put into motion?"

The bouncer seems more relaxed. Shifting his hand to the back of my neck, he squeezes so hard my spine tingles. I'm pushed into a walk. We're in a gravel parking lot, approaching a tall chain-link fence topped with three strands of barbed wire. Keys jangle as Brooks punches numbers into the gate combination lock. Beyond, I see a large metal building, a light burning above the man door.

The bouncer pushes me through the gate. I hear my breaths rushing in and out. My nose is running onto the tape covering my mouth. I'm aware of Brooks locking the gate behind us and the sense of being trapped nearly overwhelms me. As we cross to the building, I look around to get my bearings, take in as many details as I can. A black wall of trees on the horizon to my left. I hear the low drum of music in the distance. I glance right. At the sight of the RV, I realize we're in the back lot of The Cheetah Lounge. For the life of me, I don't know if that's good or bad.

Brooks unlocks the door and the bouncer forces me inside. Overhead lights spill down from industrial-type lighting, illuminating a large interior that's part living room, part office space. To my left is a grouping of furniture—a sectional sofa, coffee table, and large-screen TV. There's a small kitchen, replete with a table and chairs, a stove, and a refrigerator. To my right is a glassed-in office containing a desk, file cabinet, and high-back chair. Beyond, I see a narrow hall with three doors, each affixed with a sleek keypad for locking from the outside. In the far corner, there's some type of stage with overhead spotlights and a fireman's pole. An antique-looking chaise lounge is parked against the wall.

Brooks goes directly to the kitchen without speaking or looking at me. The bouncer wraps his hand around my arm and muscles me over to the sofa.

"Sit." He tries to force me onto it, but I brace my legs and manage to stay on my feet.

"Have it your way." Grasping the cuffs at my wrists, he pushes them up toward my shoulder blades. Pain streaks across my shoulders. I bend forward, hear myself cry out beneath the tape. He swings me around and shoves me onto the sofa.

Grinning, he points at me. "Good girl."

He strides to the kitchen and pulls a beer from the fridge. Brooks is standing at the counter, looking at me, his expression agitated. I don't see a weapon on him, but his shirt is untucked and he could have a pistol tucked in the waistband of his slacks. He pours two fingers of whiskey into a glass, slams it back, and pours again. Finally, he picks up the tumbler and starts toward me.

"Do you have any idea the problems you've caused?" he says.

I can't speak, so I simply stare at him.

"You should have backed off when you had the chance." Leaning closer, he rips the tape from my mouth. "Now we've reached the point of no return."

"You son of a bitch," I say.

"Yeah, I know." Sighing, he plucks a tissue from a box on the end table and wipes my nose and mouth.

"My dispatcher knows where I am," I tell him.

"No one knows where you are."

"She knows I was at the country club. There are CCTV cams there. My vehicle is parked in the front lot."

"Hate to break this to you, Chief, but the security cams aren't working this evening." He raises the tumbler and sips, looks at me over the rim. "And your vehicle is *not* parked in the front lot." He looks at his watch and frowns. "In fact, it's probably on its way to the chop shop as we speak."

"Where's Wingate?"

He doesn't answer.

I glance at the bouncer. He's sitting on a barstool, watching the exchange, nursing a beer, and looking amused.

"You're crazy if you think you can get away with this," I say.

Brooks takes another sip, gives me the whiskey grimace. "We'll see."

"It's not too late to stop this," I say. "Take these cuffs off me."

He laughs, but the sound is fraught with tension. "Those cuffs are the least of your worries." He wipes his mouth with his sleeve.

I'm keenly aware of the bouncer's eyes on us. He might be enjoying the situation, but Brooks seems as if he's under extreme stress. Because he knows this is a no-win situation? Or is there something else going on?

"What are you going to do with me?" I ask.

Giving me a contemptuous look, he tosses back the remainder of the whiskey, rises abruptly, and goes to the kitchen for another.

I scan the room, looking for a back door or window, or anything I might be able to use as a weapon. There's a lamp on the end table. A floor lamp behind the sofa. Are there knives in the kitchen drawer? I look toward the office, seeking a landline phone or computer, but neither is visible from where I'm sitting. I think about the cuff key in my duty belt, wonder if I can get to it without either man noticing.

A knock sounds. Brooks nearly jumps out of his skin. Smirking, the bouncer takes his beer with him and answers. He speaks in a low voice to someone unseen. A moment later, Lance Wingate strides into the room. The young woman who was with him at the club—the one who injected me—is on his arm.

Wingate looks at me and smiles. "I wish I could say I'm pleased you could join us this evening, Chief Burkholder. Since you're here, can I get you a drink? I'm betting you're craving something strong by now."

I give him the best go-to-hell look I can muster, but his smile only widens. He turns to the young woman at his side. "You know the rules."

Eyes defiant, she unbuttons her blouse and removes it. She's not wearing a bra, but her nakedness doesn't seem to bother her. It's not until I see her walk toward the kitchen area that I realize she's not quite steady on her feet.

"Get me a whiskey," Wingate says to her and then looks at me. "Get the chief one, too. She and I are going to have a quick chat."

Wingate crosses to where I'm sitting and takes the chair across from me. "I suspect you're regretting your decision to pursue this case so doggedly about now."

"The only thing I regret is that I couldn't get to my thirty-eight fast enough to put a bullet in your forehead."

He grins. "That's good, Chief Burkholder. You hold on to all that bad attitude. You're going to need it."

"There's still time for you to stop this," I tell him. "Release me. Turn yourself in."

"And why would I do that?"

"Because we both know there's no way in hell you or any of your dipshit pals are going to get away with whatever you have planned."

"Perhaps we'll wait and see how this plays out then."

"I'm a cop," I remind him. "You kill a cop in the state of Ohio and you're looking at the death penalty."

"Not if there's no body."

"My department, BCI, and the sheriff's office are looking for me right now," I tell him. "They won't stop until they find me."

The young woman approaches us, two tumblers of whiskey in her hands. Wingate takes one without looking at her, without thanking her. She offers one of the glasses to me. Her eyes are glazed. A false smile painted on her mouth.

I address her in *Deitsch.* "They're going to kill me. They're going to kill you, too, because you've seen my face. If you want to live, call 911. Now."

She raises the tumbler to her lips and knocks back half of the whiskey, but not before I see the flash of uncertainty in her eyes.

"Shut up," Wingate snaps at me, then glowers at the woman. "Get lost."

Giving him a disdainful look, the woman turns and strides back to the kitchen.

Wingate rests his left arm across the chair back and gives me his full attention. "You speak to her again and I'll tape your fucking mouth shut. You got that?"

"How old is she?" I ask.

"Old enough to know how she wants to spend her time and who she wants to spend it with."

"What did you give her? Heroin? Fentanyl?"

"Her choice, not mine."

"You're a sex trafficker," I say. "A self-aggrandizing piece-of-shit pimp."

"Such harsh judgment." But the feigned good humor falls away. "Every individual is in charge of his or her own destiny." When I don't respond he continues. "If a young, unencumbered woman wants to take a walk on the wild side, who am I to stop her?"

"You're a predator."

"I'm an entrepreneur."

I hold his gaze, the fingertips of my right hand brushing the handcuff keeper on my belt.

He motions toward the young woman. She's sitting on a barstool next to the bouncer. "Does she look preyed upon?" He waves his hand dismissively. "She's free to go anytime she wishes."

"She has no idea what she's gotten herself into," I say. "She's young. Naïve."

"And Amish." He sips whiskey, thoughtful, then looks at me over the rim of the glass. "Those are exactly the traits that make her so special. She knows that. And she's compensated handsomely." He empties his glass, raises it, clinking the ice cubes inside, and calls out to her. "Lucy, tell us how your new life here with us compares to your old Amish life?"

The young woman crosses to him and takes his glass. "It beats washing dishes and shoveling chicken shit all day."

Wingate throws his head back and laughs. "See?"

I speak to her in *Deitsch.* "They're going to kill you."

Tossing me a contemptuous stare, she returns to the island and refills his glass.

Wingate has the gall to look amused. "You see, Chief Burkholder, the moral dilemma doesn't lie with those who supply the product. It lies with those who utilize it."

I stare at him, apprehensive because I don't think I can unseat the keep snap of the cuff compartment on my belt without him hearing it. "What product is that?" I ask.

"Innocence."

"There's nothing innocent about any of this."

"Oh, that's where you're wrong. In fact, innocence abounds here." He sits up straighter, leans closer, his expression intensifying. "That is the theme of everything we do. You see, Chief Burkholder, there exists a certain faction of men who will pay an exorbitant amount of money for innocence and the opportunity to sully it."

I scoot forward as if trying to better hear him, and I use that moment to cover the noise when I thumb off the snap. "You're a monster."

"Wrong again, I'm afraid." He motions toward the young woman. "Take Lucy, for example. She's young and free and having the time of her life."

I stare at him, my heart pounding as I slide my fingertips into the keep. "You don't believe that. Neither does she."

"Three months ago, she was a virgin. She'd never been touched by a man. Do you know how rare a find that is?"

Revulsion wells inside me, but I swallow it and jab my index and middle fingers into the keep. But my angle is bad. My shoulders are cockeyed. I'm an inch away from giving myself away. *Come on . . .*

"A doctor from Toronto paid ten thousand dollars to spend a few hours with her. It's called lust. It's been part of humanity for centuries and there's an endless supply to this day. I simply connect lust to satisfaction. Believe me, it's a booming market. Everyone wins."

I keep my eyes on Wingate and feel the key slide between my index and middle fingers. I'm aware of Brooks and the woman walking into one of the rooms down the hall. The bouncer talking on his cell, his voice low. Wingate stares at me, unhurried, as if he's waiting for something.

Keep him engaged.

"How do Yutzy and Shetler fit into this?" I ask.

"Samuel was a very interesting young man. He was Amish, of course, but he loved the fast lane. He loved women. Booze. Drugs. He understood the power of lust because he himself was a victim. He was valuable to me because he had all the right connections."

"I don't believe you."

"Now who's being naïve?" Smiling, he shakes his head, a parent disappointed by a slow-witted child. "Samuel recruited dozens of young Amish women for us. Beautiful, pure young women. He knew which girls were coming of age. What do you call it? *Rumspringa?*"

He mispronounces the word, but I don't correct him. Instead, I concentrate on easing the key from its nest.

"Once the girls came to us, we simply added a little polish, purged some of those old-fashioned inhibitions, and my clientele . . . let's just say they couldn't get enough."

I bank a rise of disgust, steer the conversation back to Yutzy. "If Samuel was so valuable, why did you do away with him?" I shift as I ask the question, wincing as if the cuffs are bothering me, and I use that motion to free the key from the keep.

Wingate is so immersed in telling the story that he doesn't notice. "Unfortunately for Sam, he got involved with the wrong woman. A woman he himself recruited and farmed out to the highest bidder."

"Wilma Borntrager."

"All of that Amish morality." He shrugs. "Irony is a bitter pill, isn't it?"

I nod, shifting again to conceal my efforts to insert the pin into the keyhole. "What about Aaron Shetler?"

"Once Samuel was gone, I knew Aaron would become a problem." He shrugs. "There was loyalty there and I couldn't have that, now could I?"

"It was incredibly reckless of you to do away with the bodies right here in Painters Mill."

"I wasn't involved with that." He cocks his head, looks at me a little more closely. For an instant I think he's noticed what I'm doing. Or suspects me of wearing a wire. But he's only enjoying the moment, the cruelty of it. "They won't make the same mistake with you."

The threat isn't lost. My hands are shaking so violently, it takes me two tries to get the pin into the keyhole. All the while my brain chants, *Keep him engaged. Buy some time. No one is coming to help . . .*

Turning slightly, Wingate looks at the bouncer. "Go get the van. Let's get her out of here before things get hot."

Ending his call, the bouncer walks to the door and leaves us.

Wingate finishes his whiskey and sets the glass on the coffee table. I push the key into the hole and twist. An instant of resistance as the key flag strikes the lock bar, and then the single strand of the cuff snicks open.

"What happens next?" I ask.

He gives me an appropriately grim look. "One of our members has a yacht docked on the lake in Cleveland. My bouncer is going to drive you up there. The rest . . ." He shrugs. "If I were you, I wouldn't think too hard about it."

The cuff slips from my left wrist, the right cuff still attached. I stare at Wingate, my heart pounding, adrenaline burning like fire in my veins. He's larger than me. Stronger. My initial attack is going to have to be effective. If I can use the cuffs as brass knuckles, break his nose, the pain might disable him long enough for me to reach the door.

The door in the hall where Brooks and the Amish woman disappeared opens. Wingate turns to look. The woman comes out wearing only panties and heels, squinting in the light.

"Where's Brooks?" Wingate asks her.

"Sleeping," she says.

"Tell him to get the hell up." He snaps the words as he turns back to me. "It's time to roll."

Vaguely, I'm aware of the woman coming toward us. Something in her hand. In that instant, it occurs to me she didn't obey Wingate's orders to wake Brooks.

Keep him talking.

Heart pumping nitro, I look at Wingate. "It's not too late to stop this."

"Not going to happen," he says.

"There's still time for you to run," I say. "Brooks, too."

"Shut up or I'll tape your mouth," he snarls.

The woman reaches us. I don't look at her. I don't know if she's friend or foe. The one thing I'm pretty sure of is that she's about to distract Wingate, which will give me the opportunity I need.

"You can lock me in the back room," I tell him. "That'll give you time to—"

"I'm not going to let you kill us," the woman hisses.

Wingate swivels to her, glowering as if he wants to rip her apart with his bare hands. "You dumb little bitch, I told you to—"

A scream tears from her throat. "I didn't bargain for this!" Raising her hand, she comes at him with the syringe.

I lunge at Wingate, land on top of him. The force of my weight shoves him against the seatback. I draw back, punch him square in the face with the makeshift brass knuckles. His nose shatters on impact. Blood spatters his shirt and face. Roaring, he twists, tries to buck me off, reaches for the pistol in his waistband. I draw back a second time, land a second punch atop the first, feel what's left of his nose cave in. He lets out an animal bellow, brings up his hands to protect himself.

I clamber off him, jump to my feet. Wingate grapples for his pistol, face contorted, blood streaming from his nose. In the periphery of my vision, I see the woman stumble back. The syringe falls to the floor. Wingate's eyes on me. His hand on the pistol. I bring up my right foot, catch the side of his face with the toe of my boot. He drops the pistol. I kick it under the sofa.

"Call 911!" I scream to the woman.

"No cell!" she cries.

I glance toward the hall, expecting Brooks to emerge, but the door is closed.

Clutching his face, Wingate lurches from the sofa, staggers toward me, blood gushing. Murderous eyes land on me. "You bitch!" he roars.

I look at the woman. "*Shpringa!*" Run!

And we sprint to the door.

CHAPTER 26

I slap the bolt lock open with my hand and we go through the door as a single unit.

"Hurry!" Kicking off her heels, Lucy runs down the walkway to the chain-link fence. She snaps up the lock. Her fingers tremble violently as she punches in the code. "They're coming!" she hisses.

I watch the door behind us, expecting Wingate or Brooks to come through any second, pistol in hand. "Where's Brooks?"

"I locked him in the back room."

But I know that will only slow them down a few seconds. Wingate is likely already unlocking the door . . .

The padlock snicks open. She tosses the lock to the ground. I throw the latch and then we're through the gate.

"Run to the club!" I tell her as we start across the parking lot at a dead run.

She looks at me as if to argue, but obeys.

We're midway to the rear door of The Cheetah Lounge when I hear the clang of the gate behind us. I glance over my shoulder to see Wingate and Brooks charge through. I can tell by Wingate's silhouette that he's on the phone. Calling someone inside the club. Brooks's hand is low and by his side. *Pistol.*

I reach the rear of the building with Lucy close behind me. To my left are the privacy fence and picnic table. I try the back door, but it's locked.

"Shit."

"I got it." Choking back sobs, she slaps both hands against the door and pounds with her fists. "Let me in!" she screams, panic resonating in her voice. "Hurry!"

To my left, across the parking lot and through the trees, I can just make out the lights of a service station. A hundred yards away. I'm thinking about abandoning the club and making a run for it when the door swings open.

"Come on." Angelica, one of the women I met before, hesitates an instant before stepping aside. "They're looking for you," she says to Lucy.

Lucy pushes past her. "He's going to kill us!"

Angelica tries to close the door on me before I can enter, but I shove it open and muscle through. "Give me your phone." I slam the door behind me and lock it. "Now."

An instant of indecision plays across her features. "We're not allowed to have phones," she whispers.

"There's one in the dressing room," Lucy hisses. "They don't know about it."

"Take me," I say. "Hurry."

I'm not sure if I can trust either of these women; they could be setting me up for an ambush. Knowing I don't have a choice, I follow. As we make our way through the storage area, I hear pounding on the exterior door behind us, telling me the men saw us enter the building. No doubt they'll go around to the front and be on us in less than a minute. I have seconds to get to the phone and call for help.

"He's going to kill us!" Lucy whispers.

"No he's not," I snap. "Stay with me."

We enter a narrow hall. The music pours over us, too loud to hear anything else. To my left is the bar. Beyond, I see the stage lights. The silhouettes of patrons drinking and dancing. A few eyes turn our way as we walk along the back of the room and I'm keenly aware that Lucy is wearing nothing more than panties.

We enter an alcove. Ahead, I see another door, marked PRIVATE.

I come up beside Angelica. "Is anyone here armed?" I ask.

She barely spares me a glance. "They're always armed," she whispers. She reaches the door, pounds with the heel of her hand. "Open up!"

A young woman wearing a robe, her hair piled on top of her head, opens the door. Her eyes widen when she notices my uniform. "Why are the cops here?" she asks.

I brush past her. "Give me the phone." I motion to Lucy. "Get her a shirt. Lock the door. Quick." I look at Angelica. "Is there another way out of here?"

"There's a window," she says. "In the bathroom."

We're standing in the foyer of a dressing room. There's a mirrored vanity against the wall to my right. A changing area with a bench and privacy curtain. Six lockers against the wall. Farther, a narrow door opens to a restroom.

Lucy darts to one of the lockers and jerks it open. She drops to her knees, yanks out a platform high-heeled shoe, and reaches into the toe. Turning to me, she hands me a flip phone.

"If anyone asks, it's not mine," she whispers.

I snatch it out of her hand, punch in Tomasetti's number.

He answers on the first ring, his voice harried and curt.

"I'm at The Cheetah Lounge," I say quickly. "In trouble. I'm with three women in the dressing room in the back. Brooks and Wingate are armed. Bouncers, too."

He starts to say something else, but pounding rattles the door. "Open the fucking door!"

I disconnect, drop the phone in my pocket. I look around, spot the vanity. "Help me drag that vanity to the door. Barricade it."

In tandem, the three women join me. Grunts and the shuffle of shoes sound as we shove it against the door. When it's in place, I sprint to the bathroom. It's a small space that smells of urine and drugstore perfume. "The cops are on the way."

"You're leaving us?" Lucy's face crumples.

"It's me they're after," I tell her. "You'll be safer if I'm not here."

"But—"

"Don't let anyone in," I say, cutting her off. "If they get through that door, tell them I left."

I turn to the window. It's tiny with frosted glass. Barely enough room for me to get through. I slap open the lock, throw it open. Stepping onto the commode, I brace my legs and shove my shoulders through.

"I got you."

I glance down, see Angelica standing below me. "Go! I'll hold your legs."

I work my shoulders through, my hips, reach out to break the pending fall. "Okay!"

She releases me and I plummet. My shoulder hits the ground, so I roll, get to my feet, look around. I'm at the side of the building. The rear lot is to my left. The trees and, farther, the service station just beyond. I've no flashlight. No idea if anyone is back here, looking for me. No time to waste. I take off at a jog, keeping my eyes on the parking lot to my left. The front of the building to my right. People walking around in the front lot.

I pull the cell from my pocket as I run, hit the redial.

"Where are you?"

"Service station behind the club."

"Got it." I hear stress in his voice. The hum of a vehicle and I know he's on his way. "I'm four minutes out. Skid's on his way."

"Hurry."

I disconnect as I enter the copse of trees. Glad for the cover. I drop the cell into my pocket as I go over a tumbledown wire fence. Another twenty yards and I'm through the trees. I cross a narrow grassy area. The lights of the service station seem unnaturally bright. The pumps are to my right. Two vehicles filling up. Dumpster to my left. Convenience store dead ahead, another vehicle parked in front.

I'm midway to the store when headlights flash to my right. A vehicle turns in to the station off the street, moving fast. At first, I think the driver is pulling in to get gas. But the engine revs and the vehicle comes straight at me.

I've no cover. Nowhere to run. I launch myself into a sprint, head for the building. Nearly to the sidewalk, I swing left, toward the back. I'm keenly aware of the vehicle bearing down. The headlights playing over me. I glance right, see the grille. Ten feet away. Closing fast. I know he's going to get me . . .

I pivot, do a quick switchback, and change direction. The vehicle jigs left. The grille tracking me. Engine screaming. The left fender slams against my right hip. The impact launches me into the air, pain zinging hip to ankle. I tumble, sound and light spinning. The ground crashes into me. I'm facedown. Hurting. Dazed, I get to my hands and knees, try to get my feet under me. All I can think is I'm not dead as I scramble to my feet.

"Don't fucking move!"

I glance left, see Carter Brooks striding toward me, right arm extended, a pistol leveled at me. His face is contorted with rage. Out of control, I think, and I brace for a bullet.

I put my hands up. "Don't," I say, but my voice is shaking and weak. "Don't do it."

"You fucking bitch."

A flash of headlights to my right. I see the blur of a vehicle. The high-pitched hum of an engine. I stumble back, try to get out of the way. Brooks doesn't see it coming. The impact propels him with such force that he cartwheels twice, crashes to the ground, and skids six feet. His pistol skitters past me.

Tires bark against the asphalt as the vehicle jerks to a halt. The driver's door flies open.

"Kate!"

Tomasetti.

Choking back a sob of relief, I stagger toward him, reaching. His arms close around me. "I got you," he says. His hands skim down my arms, barely touching, as if he's afraid if he touches too hard, I might disintegrate.

"Are you hurt?" he asks.

"I have no idea."

Vaguely, I'm aware of a second vehicle pulling up next to the Tahoe. Skid, I realize, and for the first time in hours, I feel safe.

A few feet away from me, Brooks moves. He sits up, looking around as if he has no idea where he is or how he got there. Skid goes to him, kneels, and snaps handcuffs into place.

"Can you walk?"

I turn my attention back to Tomasetti, see the depth of concern in his eyes. "I think so," I tell him.

"How about if we get you checked out anyway?" he says.

"Probably a good idea."

"Ambulance is on the way."

"I'm not going anywhere without you."

His eyes flick in the direction of The Cheetah Lounge. "Everyone else okay?"

"The three women," I say. "They're in the dressing room."

"We'll take care of them." Putting his arm around me, he helps me to the passenger side of the Tahoe, but I stop him.

"Wingate?" I ask.

"In custody."

I nod, not sure why the news feels so hollow. "They murdered Samuel Yutzy and Aaron Shetler," I tell him. "Wilma Borntrager, too."

"Trafficking?"

I think of the senselessness of all of it and feel the heat of tears in my eyes. "Yutzy wasn't exactly innocent," I say. "He was a player." I think about that a moment. "But he fell in love with Wilma Borntrager. Had a change of heart. Tried to get her out. Got himself out, and they killed him for it."

Tomasetti grimaces as he helps me onto the seat. "The bouncer's involved?"

"Two of them." I lean against the backrest. "Tomasetti, I think there were a lot of people involved. I think what we've uncovered is just the tip of the iceberg."

"We'll get it figured out." He motions toward the club with his eyes. "Sheriff's office is locking down the club now. Task force guys will be interviewing people all night. They'll likely get a search warrant, too."

"The women," I say. "Lucy and Angelica and the girl in the dressing room. They risked everything, including their own safety, to help me. They gave me the cell phone. Helped me get out that window."

"Skid and Mona went in to get them. They'll be interviewed, too. We'll provide food and housing for however long it takes for them to get back on their feet. We've got a trafficking counselor on the way. She's good."

The torrent of exhaustion that follows presses down on me like a lead weight, makes my knees go weak and suddenly I feel every bruise and cut on my body. "I want to talk to them."

"You'll get your chance. Going to have to wait until morning." Arching a brow, Tomasetti looks at me a little closer. "In case you didn't notice, you took one hell of a hit."

"I noticed." I turn to him, set my hand against his face, let it slide across his cheek, and I brush my thumb over his mouth. "Did anyone ever tell you that you have excellent timing?"

"All the time," he says. "What do you say we forgo the ambulance and I'll take you to the ER myself?"

"I think I can live with that," I tell him.

And he closes the door.

CHAPTER 27

There is a kind of psychological zen that descends after surviving a life-threatening situation. A physical and emotional repose that comes with the ebb of adrenaline and the knowledge that you get to live another day. That you'll get to see your loved ones again.

After the turn of events at The Cheetah Lounge, Tomasetti drove me directly to the Pomerene Hospital ER, where I was checked out by the on-call physician. Despite rumors to the contrary, Dr. McGill and I are not on a first-name basis, though I have been a patient of hers enough times to know that she got married six months ago, that she's taking cooking lessons in Millersburg, her mom passed away last spring, and she and her husband are expecting their first child in March. I like to think it's a small-town kind of thing. That's what I tell myself, anyway.

I'm concussion free—thanks to my thick skull, according to Tomasetti. I have no broken bones or penetrating wounds. I did, however, sustain numerous bruises and abrasions, all of which required nothing more than a quick cleaning, a dab of ointment, and a bandage. My most serious injury is the Grade 2 sprain of my right wrist, which likely occurred when I clocked Lance Wingate with my makeshift brass knuckles. The doc supplied me with a splint, instructions to ice for the next twenty-four hours, Tylenol for pain, and a lighthearted suggestion that I consider a career change at some point in the next few years.

It's well past midnight now. I'm sitting at my desk in my office, said Tylenol and caffeine streaming through my system, a cup of coffee cooling in front of me. Tomasetti is in one of two visitor chairs across from me. He hasn't let me out of his sight since he pulled into the service station and found Carter Brooks an inch away from putting a bullet in me. Not for the first time this evening, I'm thankful to be alive. On a deeper level, I'm thankful to have him in my life; God only knows what I did to deserve him. I think I'll keep him around awhile.

Sheriff Rasmussen is sprawled in the chair next to Tomasetti, talking to his chief deputy on his cell. With the exception of Mona, who's on patrol this evening, my officers—most of whom haven't slept since the start of this case—were sent home.

Rasmussen ends his call and clears his throat. "Carter Brooks and Lance Wingate have been booked into the Holmes County jail. Our prosecutor is working on charges now. He'll be filing first thing in the morning."

"What about the bouncers?" Tomasetti asks.

"Deputies took both men into custody. They're being interviewed by detectives now. Formal charges pending." The sheriff pages through the notebook in front of him. "Needless to say, they won't be going home tonight."

"Any other arrests?" I ask.

"Probably not tonight," he says. "In the coming days? If this trafficking ring is as far-reaching as we suspect, I have no doubt there will be multiple arrests in the coming days and weeks."

It's the three former Amish women who dominate my thoughts this evening. All of the girls and women who were sucked into the trafficking nightmare and subjected to such utter inhumanity.

"What about the women?" I ask.

Tomasetti looks at me, holds my gaze. "Trafficking counselor interviewed them at the sheriff's office in Millersburg. Afterward, transported them to a nearby hotel for the night. We took their contact information. We made sure they were given meals. They'll likely be interviewed again first thing in the morning."

He turns his attention to the sheriff. "Just so all of us are on the same page," he says. "I talked to the attorney general earlier. Wingate and Brooks will likely be implicated in and charged with sex trafficking."

"Nasty business," Rasmussen says.

"And a growing problem." Tomasetti turns his attention back to me. "Interestingly, the AG had just instituted a human trafficking initiative. This is exactly the kind of situation we've been training for. Thanks to you, and those women who spoke up and did the right thing, we got some bad guys off the street."

I nod, but this success carries with it a hollow resonance. There were too many young lives lost. Samuel Yutzy. Aaron Shetler. Wilma Borntrager. I think about the shattered families left behind. I think about the three women lying awake in their hotel room beds tonight, wondering what will happen next, and it hits me all over again that for some, the pain will linger for a very long time.

As if reading my thoughts, Rasmussen grimaces. "I read your statement," he says. "It seems to me that Samuel Yutzy was just too damn young and inexperienced and shortsighted to fully understand the repercussions of what he was doing and how it affected the women he brought in."

"When you're twenty-one and drunk on life, you don't think about the long-term stuff," Tomasetti says.

"Or think at all for that matter," Rasmussen mutters.

The last thing I want to do is malign the victim of a homicide, especially when his family is grieving, and there's no one left to defend him. But while Samuel Yutzy and Aaron Shetler were victims themselves, they were not innocent and the truth will make for a harsh judge.

"I don't believe any of us will ever figure out all of the ins and outs—or the rights and wrongs—of this case," I say. "All I can tell you is that according to Wingate, Samuel Yutzy was recruiting young Amish women for him. Most of these women were teenagers."

I feel the weight of my own troubled teen years and try not to think too hard about parallels. "Knowing what I do about the Amish, I suspect these women were naïve. They were probably on *rumspringa* and experiencing their first taste of freedom, rebelling against the rules, making a lot of bad choices."

Tomasetti nods. "Was Shetler recruiting, too?"

"I don't know," I tell him.

"How exactly did Yutzy recruit them?" Rasmussen asks.

"Drawing from everything I've been told and what I've been able to piece together," I reply, "I believe Yutzy approached these women at parties or, in this case, a local 'Amish rager.' He talked to them, got to know them, and if they fit the profile—a woman in need of money or security or a place to stay—he offered them a job, telling them they could make a lot of money in a short period of time."

"The Cheetah Lounge?" Rasmussen asks.

"I believe there was a sort of job hierarchy involved," I say. "Depending on the personality of the woman and how the initial interview went, she either went to work at the brewery as a server or The Cheetah Lounge as a server or dancer. They were evaluated during their employment and a few of the women were eventually introduced to Wingate and invited to work at The Club at Paint Creek."

"You mean for sex?" Rasmussen says. "With members?"

"Their employment might've begun with being a server or even a caddie. Later . . ." I shrug. "The more outgoing girls likely engaged in sex with members."

Tomasetti grimaces. "I talked to the trafficking counselor earlier. While she was getting the women fed and checked in to the hotel, one of them told her about a so-called 'poker room' located in the basement of the country club. There was a pool table. A bar. Expensive art. An adjoining private suite with a shower and bedroom." His jaw flexes. "The room wasn't used for poker."

The ugliness of that goes through me like a knife. "This is not a small operation," I say.

Tomasetti sends me a pointed look. "Deputy director of the task force agrees."

"How big are we talking?" This from Rasmussen.

He shrugs. "We're talking yachts. Hotels. Private residences."

"You have your work cut out for you," I say.

He nods, and the smile that follows is a few degrees above freezing.

The sheriff leans back in his chair and crosses his ankle over his knee. "So, if Yutzy was recruiting women, he would have been pretty valuable. How did he end up dead?"

I recall my conversation with Wilma Borntrager and feel an unexpected quiver of grief in my chest. "After Borntrager was recruited, she and Yutzy became romantically involved. When things turned serious between them, I suspect Yutzy realized what he was doing to these women and he had a change of heart."

Rasmussen grimaces. "So, while his judgment was in the toilet, his conscience was still intact."

"When he tried to walk away," Tomasetti says, "they killed him."

I nod. "Wingate was afraid Yutzy would either go to the police or talk to the wrong person. He was a loose end, so they sent hired guns to the nursery to murder him."

"Seems like Wingate would have known a body would draw a lot of unwanted attention," Rasmussen says.

"The killer or killers were supposed to do away with the body in Lake Erie. But they got lazy and buried it, not realizing the local coyote population would unearth it."

"What about Shetler?" the sheriff asks.

"And Borntrager?" Tomasetti adds.

"Wingate knew Shetler was loyal to Yutzy, so they wanted him gone, too," I say. "Once that happened, Wilma Borntrager freaked out and went on the run, thinking she could escape to Florida. They caught her, of course, and because she knew too much, they did away with her, too."

"Jesus." Rasmussen scrubs a hand over his mouth. "All of that and not one of these young people said a word. None of these sons of bitches were on our radar."

"That's why this case was so difficult to figure out." I shrug. "Yutzy and Shetler were Amish; they're not going to come forward. Neither Wingate nor Brooks had records. The women were afraid—and ashamed—so they didn't say a word."

"Until you showed up," Tomasetti points out.

"If it hadn't been for those three women," I say, "I wouldn't be sitting here this evening."

The silence that follows has a hard, uneasy edge.

"Speaking of past records," Tomasetti says. "We just started looking at the club Wingate managed a few years ago in Cincinnati. Interestingly, Brooks worked there at the same time."

"That's how they knew each other," Rasmussen says.

Tomasetti nods. "Get this: Three years ago, the owner of the club in

Cincy was arrested for sex trafficking. Wingate and Brooks had already left the company by then and were never implicated."

"They'd had a taste of it." Rasmussen's voice is bitter. "Evidently, they liked it. Decided they'd try their hand here in Holmes County."

"I'm glad we were able to show them that we don't oblige criminals here in Painters Mill," I say.

"Thanks in part to the victims themselves," Tomasetti puts in.

And the hollow feeling that had previously stolen any semblance of gratification transforms into something a little closer to justice.

CHAPTER 28

Even when you're young and Amish and ensconced in the protective web of your community, innocence can be a precarious thing. The three young women who were there the night Lance Wingate and Carter Brooks tried to kill me are a case in point. Taking my own history into consideration, it occurs to me that I'm a case in point, too.

Two weeks have passed since the incident at The Cheetah Lounge. Life in Painters Mill has recommenced full bore. Summer with its unrelenting heat is little more than a glimmer in the rearview mirror. The Amish are harvesting corn, early due to the drought. Alas, the first frost is right around the corner. My small department has resumed taking the usual calls: loose livestock, Jim McCormick's son driving his Mustang too fast, and some as-of-yet-unknown individual egging the high school cafeteria windows. The older I get, the more I've come to realize that the mundane is underrated.

The Yutzy, Shetler, and Borntrager cases may be closed, but I've spent a lot of time in the last couple of weeks thinking about them. I spent more time thinking about the women who were caught up in the trafficking ring. They are the survivors. Damaged and forever changed, but alive and with futures. Each of them has a long journey ahead. A journey that likely won't be easy. I've reminisced about my own formative years, too, my troubled teens, and the trauma of that fateful summer when I was fourteen. Parallels, I think, and I make it a point not to examine any of them too closely.

Lance Wingate, Carter Brooks, and the bouncer, Gene Rossi, were formally charged with aggravated murder, murder, engaging in a pattern of corrupt activity, compelling prostitution, felonious assault, and trafficking a fentanyl-related compound. The other bouncer, who's since been identified as Jake Hopkins, turned state's evidence and to date has only been charged with two of the lesser crimes. It's a far cry from fair, but such is the nature of the justice system. On a personal level, I find some comfort in knowing there's a higher court that waits for all of them and their true day of reckoning will come.

The dinner hour is in full swing when I pull into the dusty gravel lot of The Sweet Maple Kitchen. The diner is located in a low-slung cinderblock building on County Road 407 between Painters Mill and Charm. There are only two vehicles parked outside the front door. I park next to the vintage pickup truck and head inside.

The aromas of coffee, toasted bread, and seared meat greet me when I enter. A row of four booths, two of which are occupied, line the wall to my right. A smattering of tables to my left. I'm not here to eat, so I go to the counter and claim a stool.

There's a serving window between the counter and the kitchen. Through the opening, I see a young man in a white apron and hairnet hovering over a grill, his face shiny with perspiration. The double doors leading to the kitchen swing open. I glance over and see Angelica Kuhns come through, a stack of restaurant-style cups and saucers in her hands. She's wearing a light blue waitress dress that falls to just below her knees, a white apron with pockets, off-brand sneakers on her feet. Her hair is pulled into an unruly bun at her nape. She's not wearing a *kapp.*

She spots me immediately. I don't miss the falter in her stride, the uncertainty in her expression as she carries the dishes to the counter.

"*Guder nochmiddawk,*" I say.

"We're getting ready to close," she mutters as she sets the cups and saucers on the counter.

"I can't stay long." I upend the cup in front of me. "I hear you guys have good coffee."

She chokes out a laugh. "We don't."

"I'll take my chances." I slide the cup and saucer toward her.

Taking her time, she pours from a carafe and then places a tiny bowl of creamer and sugar packets in front of me. "How did you find me?"

Now it's my turn to laugh. "Painters Mill is a small town and I am the chief of police. It wasn't too hard."

"And of course the Amish are gossips."

"That, too."

She looks away, concentrating on arranging the cups and saucers just so on the counter.

"How are you doing?" I ask.

She sets the final cup on the saucer. When she runs out of things to do, she comes back to where I'm sitting. "I found an apartment," she says a little too brightly. "In Charm. It's small, but furnished and clean."

"That's great." I sip coffee. "And the job?"

"The tips aren't great, but Mrs. Anderson lets me work overtime. Pays me extra for cleaning."

"Sounds like a good start."

"I guess." Bending, she pulls out a canister of sugar and starts to fill the countertop dispenser. "I heard about Lucy."

She's referring to Lucy Yoder, the young Amish woman who was also there that night at The Cheetah Lounge. She was slated not only to testify against the traffickers when the case goes to court, but to name some of the clientele who patronized the business. Unfortunately for everyone involved, Lucy flew the coop a week ago and no one has seen her since.

"Do you have any idea where she is?" I ask.

"No." She shakes her head. "Her *mamm*'s worried."

"I don't blame her." I wait a beat, then ask, "Do you know why she took off?"

"I only talked to her once. She didn't know how to deal with . . ." She struggles to find the word. "The coming back, I guess."

I know the Amish well enough to read between the lines. While they will welcome one of their own back to the fold with open arms, there are always a few individuals who don't make it easy. The Amish may be obedient to God, but they're also human beings and fall to gossip and small cruelties just like the rest of us.

"If you hear from Lucy," I say, "will you ask her to call me?"

"I don't think I'll be talking to her again."

Leaving the counter, she goes to one of the booths to refill the cups for the couple. She exchanges a few words and returns to the counter. The silence that follows isn't quite comfortable.

"I don't know how to fit back in," she whispers in a low voice. "I tried, but . . . it didn't feel right. I don't think I can do it. I don't know what's wrong with me."

She looks incredibly young without all the makeup. Sky-blue eyes. Freckles on her nose. Pale mouth pulled into what seems like a perpetual frown born not of disapproval, but of genuine unhappiness.

"Be patient with yourself," I say easily. "Give yourself some time."

"I . . . went to worship," she blurts. "With Mamm and Datt."

"How was it?"

"*Shlimm.*" Awful. For an instant, I think she's going to cry. To her credit, she doesn't. "The Amish girls whispered about me," she says.

"There's nothing you can do about that," I tell her.

"They thought I didn't see it, but I did."

"They'll come around."

Huffing in doubt, she looks away. "I want to go back, but I can't. I miss my *mamm* and *datt.* My brothers and sisters. My Amish friends. I want it to be like it used to be. But . . . nothing is the same. I'm afraid it won't ever be the same."

"I know it seems impossible right now, but you'll find your way back if it's meant to be. You'll find a new place for yourself. You'll grow and learn and find a whole new you. I think you'll find peace, too."

"I can't stop thinking about what happened." She speaks the words so quietly I have to lean closer to hear her. "The things I saw. The things I did. I want to forget, but I can't."

"You may not be able to forget, but I do believe you'll find a way to put this behind you and move on."

"You make it sound like it's an easy thing," she snaps. "It's not."

"I can't presume to know what you went through," I tell her. "The one thing I can tell you is that I understand."

She stares at me, her face a mosaic of pain, of misery and skepticism and the utter certainty that no one could possibly comprehend. I don't blame her; that lack of scope is a frailty of youth.

"Did you know I used to be Amish?" I ask.

She frowns. "It's not the same," she says dismissively.

"I was your age when I left. I know what it's like to not fit in. To be lost and have nowhere to go."

A glimmer of genuine curiosity peeks out at me from behind the mask of despair. "What did you do?"

"I survived," I tell her. "Just like you. And I found a way to move on."

"I don't know if I can be Amish again," she whispers. "I mean, after what happened. I don't know if it's the right path."

"There is no right or wrong resolution," I tell her.

She looks away.

"Angelica—"

"It's Angie."

I repeat the name, liking it. "You know that what happened isn't your fault, right?"

Her face crumples, a war between grief and shame and a hundred other emotions she can't contain. "Who else is there to blame?"

"Lance Wingate for starters," I say firmly. "Carter Brooks."

"They were bad men, yes. But I did what I did. I was stupid and—"

"You were courageous, too," I cut in. "If you hadn't stepped in when you did that night, they would have killed me. Think about that the next time you're beating yourself up."

She closes her eyes, tears squeezing through her lashes. "I'm so ashamed, I can't bear it."

That is the insidious nature of trafficking. The piece of the equation that devours the heart, destroys lives, and steals every last scrap of innocence. "You're barely twenty years old," I tell her. "Wingate and Brooks are twice your age. They took advantage of you. Your youth. Your inexperience. They preyed on that."

We fall silent and for the span of a full minute the only sound comes from the clinking of dishes from the kitchen. The murmur of conversation from the couple in the booth.

After a moment, I set my hand on hers and squeeze. "My *mamm* had a saying for those of us with troubled hearts."

"Amish *mamms* always have sayings." She mutters the words with affection.

I switch to *Deitsch.* "'When the caterpillar thought her world was ending, she became a butterfly,'" I quote.

She stares at me, tears glistening on her cheeks, her mouth trembling. "My parents want me to be baptized. In the spring. After communion. They want me to start *die Gemee nooch geh* this fall."

Die Gemee nooch geh is a momentous occasion for a young Amish person and a lifetime commitment they will honor until death.

"That's a big step," I say. "A big decision."

"I don't know what to do."

"You have some time to think about it."

"I love my parents. I don't want to lose my family."

In that instant, her pain pierces my heart. The ache that follows is so intense, I flinch. "I got my family back," I tell her. "It wasn't easy and it's sure not a perfect situation. But I got them back."

The bell on the door jingles, announcing the arrival of another customer. We both look, see an Amish family enter, husband and wife and four children.

Bringing her fingertips to her face, she quickly swipes at the tears. "I have to get back to work." Turning away, she starts toward the family, already pulling out her order pad.

"Angie?" I say.

She stops, hesitates, then looks at me over her shoulder.

"You're going to be all right," I tell her.

Giving me the shadow of a smile, she turns and walks away.

• • •

It's dusk when I pull into the gravel lane that will take me to the farm I share with Tomasetti. I park behind his Tahoe and start toward the back door only to hear someone pounding on something in the barn. After setting my laptop on the step, I turn and head that way.

Whack! Whack!

I find him just inside the door, splitting wood with an ax. His back is to me and I take a moment simply to enjoy the view. "I thought you were going to buy that log splitter we talked about," I say.

He swings the ax a final time, scoring a perfect split, then turns to me. His hair is mussed. There's a sheen of sweat on his forehead. He's a little annoyed because he's been at it awhile and I'm sure his fortysomething muscles are feeling it. I resist the urge to go to him and wrap myself around him.

"If I recall," he says, "someone thought we weren't going to use enough firewood to warrant the cost of the log splitter."

"In all honesty, that someone probably doesn't have to get her butt out here and chop wood."

Cocking his leg, he sets the ax against the wood siding and crosses his arms. "That's a likely scenario."

"If it's any consolation, Tomasetti, I like the way you swing that ax."

"That helps. A little."

I bend to pick up the newly split logs and toss them into the bed of the pickup with the rest of the wood he's chopped.

"Something on your mind, Chief?" he asks.

"Log splitter aside?" I straighten, turn to him. "I just talked to Angie Kuhns."

He sobers. "How is she?"

"Feeling guilty. Beating herself up. Trying to adjust back to Amish life."

"Can't be easy after what she's been through."

I nod. "She asked about Lucy Yoder."

He nods, all too aware of who that is. "There's still a chance she'll come around," he says. "It's only been a week."

"Too long."

"You worried?"

"Not yet."

"If Lucy's going to get in touch with anyone, it'll be you. You left that door wide open."

I watch as he goes to the pickup, turns, and heaves himself onto the tailgate. Picking up a water bottle, he downs half of it. "Weather guy says this winter is going to be a snowy one," he says. "I thought it might be a good idea to cut some extra wood for the fireplace."

Trying to shake off the remnants of my worry about the wayward Amish girl, I go to him. "Maybe we should reconsider that log splitter."

"You think?"

"I do." I slide between his knees and put my arms around his neck. Smiling, he pulls me close and sets his mouth against mine. He smells of fresh-cut wood, this morning's aftershave, and his own unique scent. For the span of a full minute, the rest of the world falls away and I'm reminded that these small, seemingly mundane slices of time are priceless.

"I've got a six-year-old bottle of Petite Sirah sitting on the counter," he murmurs. "A couple of steaks in the fridge."

"Baked potatoes?"

"Scrubbed and ready to go."

I'm about to pull away when the cat vaults onto the tailgate and proceeds to brush against us, first in one direction, then the other.

"I think he likes it here," I whisper.

"I don't blame him," he says. "I kind of like it here, too."

It's a small thing, but it makes me laugh. It makes me happy.

Taking my hand, he slides off the tailgate, and with the cat in tow, we start toward the house.

ACKNOWLEDGMENTS

I owe a mountain of gratitude to my publishing family at Minotaur Books. I'd like to thank my editor and friend, Charles Spicer. You are the best of the best and you always make this writer's heart happy. I'd also like to extend a huge thank-you to my agent extraordinaire, Nancy Yost, for being there in so many ways—agent, friend, and purveyor of smiles. Last but not least, a heartfelt volley of thank-yous to everyone at Minotaur Books: Jennifer Enderlin. Andrew Martin. Sally Richardson. Sarah Melnyk. Hannah Pierdolla. Kerry Nordling. Paul Hochman. Allison Ziegler. Kelley Ragland. David Baldeosingh Rotstein. Marta Flemming. Martin Quinn. Joseph Brosnan. Lisa Davis. Mac Nicholas.

ABOUT THE AUTHOR

Pam Lary

Linda Castillo is the author of the *New York Times* and *USA Today* bestselling Kate Burkholder mystery series, set in the world of the Amish. The first book, *Sworn to Silence,* was adapted into a Lifetime original movie titled *An Amish Murder,* starring Neve Campbell as Kate Burkholder. Critically acclaimed as "the master of the genre" (*People* magazine), Castillo is the recipient of numerous industry awards including an Edgar Award, the Sue Grafton Memorial Award, a nomination by the International Thriller Writers for Best Hardcover, a nomination for an Audie Award for best mystery audiobook, and an appearance on the *Boston Globe*'s short list for best crime novel. Her books have sold over 4.5 million copies worldwide.

In addition to writing, Castillo's other passion is horses. She lives in Texas with her husband and a menagerie of animals, and is currently at work on her next book.